HELLHOUND SUMMONERS

HELLHOUND
SUMMONERS

K.D. LOVELACE

Hellhound Summoners

RawRiot Publishing

Fort Worth, Texas

Cover by: Book Designs by Shae

Editing: Jessica Hughes& Shae Coon

Formatting and Typesetting: Shae Coon

TRIGGER WARNING

Written by someone who knows exactly what you're getting into.

This book contains violence, explicit, spicy scenes, blood, death, monsters, hellhounds like me, emotional compromises with humans, questionable leadership, bad decisions made under stress, and consequences no one listens to ahead of time.

There will be fear. There will be pain. There will be feelings you aren't prepared for. If that bothers you, you may want to stop now.

If it doesn't? Good.

Keep reading. I'll be watching.

DEDICATION

To the untamed spirits who walk between worlds. To the fierce hearts that beat in time with ancient rhythms. And to the unwavering courage that faces the encroaching darkness with a defiant roar. May your shadows be as powerful as your light, and may your bonds be forged in the fires of destiny. This story is a testament to the wild magic that resides within us all. A reminder that even on the deepest night, there is always a hellhound waiting to answer your call.

To my family, whose unwavering support is my personal fortress against the mundane, and to the muses who whisper tales of magic and mayhem in the quiet hours. Thank you for breathing life into these pages and for understanding when the scent of ozone and ancient magic is more present in my life than the aroma of coffee.

You are my pack, my sanctuary, and my greatest inspiration. May the amethyst flames of your own inner fire burn bright and guide you through every challenge. This is for you, my fierce, brave readers, who dare to delve into the heart of darkness and find the light within. Embrace your inner summoner.

CONTENTS

PROLOGUE

Around the fireplace, Mara was in her chair, and the small children and I were sitting on the floor, listening to her tell the story. They came without warning. Not from the skies in blazing ships, nor from the earth in trembling fury, but from the darkness between shadows, from the places we never thought to fear black silhouettes with no faces, and only the faint shimmer of malice where eyes should have been. We called them Wraths, because no other name felt big enough for the hunger they carried.

At first, they stalked the edges of our world, street corners at midnight, abandoned warehouses, the spaces under bridges where even light seemed nervous to enter. But within a year, they no longer waited for darkness. Daylight fractured under their presence. Skyscrapers fell silent, whispers and screams replaced the hum of cities, and the modern world crumbled in on itself.

Towns became ruins. The great cities, once iron and glass, monuments to human triumph, became hollow bones picked clean by shadows. Electricity faded, machines rusted, and humanity staggered back into the olden days.

We lived in scattered villages, huddled around firelight,

as if flame alone could keep the Wraths from our doors.

But there is one force they feared.

The Hellhound Summoners. Legend said the first of them were born in chaos, men and women chosen by something older and darker than the Wraths themselves. They called forth beasts ten feet tall, with bodies of iron sinew and eyes like molten fire, glowing in a colour no mortal tongue can name. Their paws struck the ground like thunder, their breath smoldered, and their growl could drive a Wrath back into the shadows it came from. Summoners did not choose their hounds. The hounds chose their summoners. And the choice is everything.

If the bond was made, Summoner and Hellhound shared their life, strength, and a piece of the same soul. But if the bond failed, death claimed both the Summoner and the Hellhound. Within minutes, nothing but empty shells remained.

Wraths were growing bolder.

Villages were falling faster than they could rebuild. And somewhere beyond the reach of firelight, the shadow was calling more of its kind.

Even our Highland village, small and wind-worn against the cliffs, was no longer beyond their reach.

And that was when the mark appeared.

I woke before dawn to the sound of the wind clawing at the last of the shutters. For one terrible heartbeat, I thought the Wraths had come.

The Highlands were restless in the dark, mist rolled low over the hills, and the sea beyond the cliffs thrashed against black rock. Our cottage stood at the edge of the village, its stone walls veined with cracks, mortar crumbling grain by grain with time. Grandfather had always said the house had good bones.

Lately, even bones felt fragile.

Loki had been curled against my hip, warm and steady. I might have drifted back to sleep if not for the heat that bloomed beneath my skin.

It started on my left wrist.

A slow burn. Then sharper. Then unbearable.

I bit down on my blanket to stop from crying out. The pain tunneled deep and merciless, as if something ancient were carving its claim into me. My pulse thundered in my ears.

Not now. Please, not now.

Not after Grandma.

The burning crested white and blinding and then vanished as suddenly as it had come.

Shaking, I pushed myself upright and pulled back my sleeve.

A crescent moon curved along the inside of my wrist. Not ink. Not a scar.

It shimmered faintly, like embers trapped beneath my skin.

Outside, beyond the sagging rooftops and leaning chimneys of the village, the tent fields stretched toward the moors. The tents made out of torn sails and old cloaks snapped in the wind. Families who had fled when the Wraths devoured their towns now live in those tents. Every month, the sea of tents crept closer. Every month, another village fell.

Summoners were rare.

Most had not survived the bond or the trials.

And those who had survived never stayed.

The crescent pulsed.

Not pain.

A pull.

Like a thread tied somewhere deep in my chest, tugging east toward the ridgeline where ruined watch towers stood against the sky.

“Elara?”

Grandpa’s voice drifted from the next room, thin and uncertain. I hurried to him. He was sitting upright in bed; blankets twisted around his legs. Dawn painted the hills pale gold beyond the window. His once broad shoulders seemed smaller each morning, his memory faltering like a candle fighting the wind.

For a fleeting breath, recognition filled his eyes.

“There you are,” he murmured. “Your grandmother was just here.”

It's only been the three of us.

Mara had already taken in two children from the tent fields. She had been as strong as the old oak that clung to the cliffs. If anyone could have kept Grandpa safe, it would be her, as I have to leave the village.

The crescent pulsed again, this time stronger. A flash split through my mind: fire racing across the moor. Tents collapsing. Shadows spilling through our doorway.

The Wraths hunted power.

And now power lived beneath my skin.

If I stayed, I would have been a beacon.

Grandpa reached for my hand. His fingers brushed the mark. The crescent moon flared at the touch. For one heartbeat, his eyes cleared.

"You must go," he said.

The words shattered me. Outside, beyond the mist and heather, a howl rolled across the highlands.

Deep.

Ancient.

Waiting.

And the mark answered.

CHAPTER I

WOLF MARK

ELARA

Glass breaking, not the sharp tinkle of a dropped bottle, but something deeper, heavier, as if the air itself had shattered. I'm crossing the village square when the torches flicker. Shadows twist along the ground, stretch thin, then peel free, like solid smoke.

"Wraths!" The panic shreds the quiet. Chaos erupts. The first glides forward through the square like heat over stone. No face. No mouth. Only twin slits of white light in a head that isn't there.

More pours from every corner like spilled ink. The air fills with ash and rot.

My chest locks, heart slamming against my ribs. Screams rip through the square.

Market stalls collapse as villagers run, clutching children, dropping baskets, food spills across the stones in blind panic.

I try to move, but my legs refuse. A Wrath turns toward me, gliding, frost blooming in the dust beneath its path.

The ground splits.

A low, ancient sound rolls through the square. Fire bursts through the cracks. The night is full of orange and blue flames of knocked-over torches. Something steps through the blaze, massive shoulders blotting out the stars.

A Hellhound. Ten feet tall at the shoulder, all muscle and shadow, veins stitching red hot through its body. Its eyes burn molten. When they catch onto mine, heat blooms in my chest, not mine, but theirs.

Stories whisper that if it comes for you, it won't be here for anyone else. Invisible threads between us, pulling, demanding. Behind it, the Wraths shrink back.

Before the bond can seal, the hound's molten gaze shifts toward my grandmother.

Her black braid streaked with silver; hunter's jacket scorched from other battles. I have never seen her eyes widen like that. The hellhound steps toward her, each paw falling like a war drum. Wraths squirm at the fire's edge.

"You," my grandmother whispers, staring down the Hellhound, not an ounce of fear on her face.

The hound lowers its head, molten eyes meeting hers. Heat shimmers between them. My grandmother doesn't flinch. Not even when the hound's furnace-hot breath washes over her, not when the air grows heavy as stone.

"I accept," she says.

The hound lunges to press its forehead to her chest. Fire

erupts where they touch, igniting something deeper than flesh. Her eyes blaze molten gold, and the Wraths shriek, fleeing into the shadows.

The villagers creep out, pale and silent. The summoning pit cools, but the air stays charged. My grandmother stands in the centre, a silhouette against the smouldering ground.

She glances at me, something heavy in her eyes. Not pity. Not pride. Something else. Standing in the aftermath, I think of the same women who once taught me to string a bow. She calls hellhound summoners the amethyst inferno with a smile, as if it is a family secret.

Two weeks later, when Wraths come again, she'd be gone, slain beside her hellhound.

Mara's door swings shut behind me, but the smell of crimson dye and candle wax still clings to my skin.

I leave the village with a pack of strangers. My grandfather must stay behind, hands shaking and tears shining in his eyes. Loki, my orange tabby with a torn ear and a street brawler swagger, yowls from the neighbour's fence as I walk away.

I don't look back.

If I do, I might stay.

I follow the narrow lane toward the village centre, where a low fire crackles in a stone pit. People gather in small clusters, speaking low, glancing at me, then looking away.

That's when I see them.

There are four of them, each bearing the same crescent moon burned into their wrist. One is a boy, taller than the rest, with a shaved head and storm-coloured eyes. Next to him is a girl younger than me, hair plaited into a crown—the other two stand apart, watching me with an intensity that quickens my pulse.

"You're the new one," the boy says. His voice carries the weight of someone used to speaking for the group. "I'm Riven. That's Solene, and the twins are Ash and Arden."

I nod, uncertain whether to offer my hand for a handshake or present my wrist for identification. Solene spares me the decision. She steps forward, her fingers catching my sleeve and pushing it back to reveal the pale silver crescent.

"It's real," she murmurs, almost to herself. "Another Wolf Marked like us. That makes five now, an increase since the last summoning ritual from our villages."

Ash smirks. "Are you sure she'll survive the Binding?"

"The mark won't call her if she can't," Arden says, holding a straight face.

They speak of the Binding so casually, as if it's a trivial thing, not a vow that ties you to a Hellhound until your last breath.

Riven gestures toward the fire. "We gather here before every summoning. Those who bear the mark are bound to the Hellhound Summoners by blood and fire. You'll see soon enough."

I look around the circle, seeing the same faint crescent burned into every wrist. My grandmother once told me, "Wolf Mark means protection."

Now, staring at these strangers bound by the same fate, I wonder if it ever meant the exact opposite.

The fire pops, sending sparks into the night air. My fingers brush the edge of my mark, tracing its curve.

It doesn't feel like protection. It feels like a promise I'm not sure I want to keep.

As we wait for the guards to lead us toward the ritual grounds, all around the fire, the anticipation of what is to come makes my knees shake and my palms sweat. I rub my hands on my leather pants to dry my clamminess.

When I look at the others, I can tell I'm not the only one weighed down by worry.

The headguard sneaks up behind Arden.

"Agh! Ugh!" Arden screams as he jumps and falls off the log.

Riven, Ash, Solene, and I burst into laughter, laughing so hard we are nearly crying just from the noise. Arden makes a face. The head guard steps into the firelight, armour gleaming, posture impossibly straight.

"You are not authorized to scream," he says, his tone flat, unreadable.

Riven presses his lips together, and his shoulders are still shuddering with laughter. "You can't just appear like that," he scoffs.

"My approach was at a standard patrol pace," the guard replies. "Your lack of awareness is not my responsibility." Solene crouches beside Arden, trying and failing not to laugh again. "You scare him so badly his soul bolts first, and his body scrabbles to catch up."

Ash sighs dramatically. “Next time I’m sitting away from you guys.”

The head guard just shakes his head, mumbling, “Idiots,” under his breath. “Get ready to move out, we have a long way to the ritual grounds if we make it there in one piece. Reports of Wraths in the area surrounding the ritual grounds. I assume none of you have experience checking your surroundings. Obviously not, since I can sneak up on you. But out there, it’s a different story. Beasts are waiting in the shadows. Everyone must watch out for everyone.”

I’m not sure whether it is his mission to terrify us or the truth, but we all go quiet, grab our belongings, and put the fire out.

We march in silence, trying to catch sounds that aren’t coming from under our feet. As we inch closer to the ritual grounds, each step and snap of dried sticks emanates with dread. Then we arrive at the edge of a treacherous slope. The steep drop on our side looks as if the ground has given way and is caving in, leaving behind lethal, sharp stone that can slice your ankles if you're not careful.

I pause at the edge, fear gripping me as loose pebbles and broken soil skitter down and disappear into the mist below. One wrong step and the mountain will swallow us into the fog. Arden tests the ground with his boot, while Solene keeps her eyes on the treeline to our left, too quiet, too still. Riven lingers at the back, hands flexing uselessly at his side. All of us have a small ritual dagger, but it would not do much against a Wrath. The head guard leads the group.

He descends sideways, boots finding grip where there seems to be none, sword drawn despite the risk of losing balance. "Slow," he murmurs. "One at a time."

From what I gather, we are halfway down when the air changes.

I feel it before I see it: a pressure, like the mountain itself is holding its breath. The treeline shudders, then something is torn free from the shadows.

The Wrath bursts out of the forest with a sound like splintering wood. Its form is a blur of dark muscles and pale eyes that catch the light as it leaps at us. It moves too fast, its claws striking stone as it bounds down the slope toward our group.

"Down!" the head guard shouts.

The first impact sends rocks flying. Arden loses his footing but manages to steady himself on a protruding stone. Solene lets out a cry as the ground suddenly shifts beneath her. I drop as low as I can, fingers scraping against the stone as I cling to the slope for dear life.

The head guard plants himself between the creature and the others.

Steel rings as his sword meets the Wrath head-on, the force of the clash driving him back a step. He can barely hold his stance. The Wrath recoils, then lunges again, teeth snapping inches from the blade.

"Move!" the head guard barks over his shoulder. "Don't stop!"

We don't argue; we keep going further down the cliff.

Riven grabs Solene's arm and nearly drags her downhill.

Arden goes next, knocking stones loose as he slides. As I follow, my heart is pounding so loud it drowns out everything else except the sound of the fight above.

I risk a glance back.

Kevin is giving ground, boots skidding, sword flashing as he forces the Wrath away from the slope's edge. One misstep and they would both tumble. The creature shrieks, enraged, and charges after him again.

"Now!" he shouts.

We reach a narrow ledge just as the Wrath cripples. Kevin twists aside, using the slope to his advantage. The creature's weight carries past him, claws scraping the air before it vanishes down the mountainside with a roar that fades into nothing.

Silence rushes in to replace the clamour.

The Head Guard stands alone above us, chest heaving, sword still raised. Then he slowly lowers it.

"We keep moving," he says. "Before it decides to climb back up."

We sidestep to the safety of the cliff ridge, to solid ground that opens into a narrow path.

We continue toward the gateway, shaken, bruised, and marked with minor wounds, but painfully aware of how close we had come to losing everything. Ahead of us, the treeline looms tall, dark, swallowed by fog so it erases distance and sound alike. Mist clings to the trunks as if alive, curling around roots and limbs, blurring where one tree ends and the next begins.

Every step forward feels like crossing an unspoken

boundary. The air grows colder and heavier, and the world behind us fades until only the pale grey ahead remains.

Somewhere within that foggy forest, the path continues, the uneven ground making it difficult to walk forward; the trees watch in silence, and the haze promises nothing.

Once you enter, there is no turning back. Every sense is on high alert, watching for whatever might ascend from the shadows.

We reach the gateway to a world unknown to me, just as dawn is breaking over the woods. The gateway opens into a vast, cavernous chamber. The scent of pine and lavender incense greets us like a long-lost friend.

A sign on parchment paper with instructions includes women's rooms and the location of the men's rooms. Solene and I split from Arden, Riven, and Ash. She squeezes my hand once before disappearing into her room. The women's chambers line the left side, and the men's quarters are farther down another flight of stairs.

I enter my assigned room, close the wooden door behind me, and let out a deep exhale. I've come through precarious terrain and unfriendly creatures, and the weight still presses heavily on my chest.

A claw-foot bathtub stands in the corner, its surface gently swirling with steam.

Calling my name.

I check the water to see if it's the right temperature. Natural soap and shampoo are nearby as I strip off my leathers and corset, letting my black hair fall free like a dark waterfall.

As I dip into the tub, the warm water embraces me, and I feel my muscles slowly relax, though my mind refuses to follow. While I scrub away the smoke and grime, images of my village return unbidden, and my mind wanders.

I can only hope Mara is taking good care of Papa. Too often, I've found him wandering around the yard or the village square, searching for my grandmother. Some days, he remembers me. Remembers Loki. Other days, he calls me Elowen, my grandmother's name.

I rinse off and wrap a towel around myself.

Time to get ready. The ritual awaits.

CHAPTER 2

THE RITUAL

ELARA

The main chamber feels thick with anticipation. Flickering candlelight casts restless shadows on the stone walls, and the scent of burning sage mingles with damp moss, creating an atmosphere that is both sacred and foreboding. Tonight is the night I have been preparing for since discovering the mark on my wrist.

I draw a slow breath, steadying my racing heart. Months of studying ancient texts, half-forgotten rituals, and warnings etched on brittle pages have led to this moment. A hellhound is not merely a companion; it is a guardian, fire and fury given form. It will sharpen my power, protect me, and tether my life to its own.

I glance toward the altar: a rough-hewn slab of obsidian gleams dully in the candlelight. Upon it rests a silver dagger, a vial of my blood, and a sprig of nightshade, its dark purple petals bruised with promise. My fingers graze the dagger's hilt—the metal is cold.

A tool of sacrifice, a means of creation. I turn toward the aged mirror that hangs on the wall. My reflection stares back; long raven-black hair falls loose over my shoulders, and emerald-green eyes shine with resolve, but beneath, doubt flickers just once.

Does it turn on me? I remember the story someone told me about what happens when a bond fails. The boy is barely eighteen. When his ritual goes wrong, the hellhound tears him apart before ending its own life. They said you never forget the smell of hellfire burning flesh.

The hellhounds choose whether to accept the bond.

It's always up to them.

I swallow hard. Does it accept me, or end me?

I shake off the thought and reach for my ceremonial robe draped over a nearby chair. The deep crimson fabric feels heavy in my hands—blood and power, woven together. As I slip it over my head, energy coils through me, sharp and magnetic.

This is my destiny. I do not cower from it.

Cautiously, I shuffle to the centre of the chamber. Symbols glow dimly beneath my feet, the candlelight dramatizing their intricate lines. Solene waits with the others, eyes wide with awe. None of us has observed anything like this in our villages. Arden and Ash are from the gatherer's clan; their ritual attire must be functional. Solene's robe shimmers blue and white, beads set off-center like churning water. Riven wears deep red and black, the colours of fighters and guards. Together as a group, we move as one, slipping into the crowd, waiting for the summoning to begin.

At the heart of the chamber grows the tree of life, its branches and roots interwoven in green and gold hues, pulsing with calm strength—balance, rebirth, the promise of leaving one life behind and stepping into another, into partnership, into a clan.

Around it, the other elemental symbols burn and breathe.

I look left. A spiked flame symbol interlocks to resemble a candle flame symbol, honoring the sun gods and goddesses. It pulses with fierce crimson, hot and demanding.

The Triskelon, my favourite, catches my eye, its three spirals, eternal motion—mind, body, and spirit.

Hellhounds exist to hold the Wraths at bay. Over the years, shadows have learned to take shape, to hunt. Outer villages vanish. Children grow up with pieces of themselves missing.

Focus, Elara.

That is why I am here. So, no one else grows up hollowed out by loss, bleeding slowly until numbness replaces pain.

The ultimate symbol in the circle is the Triquetra: the trinity knot. Physical, mental, spiritual. Its pale light casts over me, soothing as warm water.

I am not alone. Forty-five other initiates fidget like me, nerves wound tight, eyes bright with fear and fragile hope. Ancient runes carve spirals along the chamber walls, pulsing faintly in uneven rhythms. Energy hums through the air, low and constant, threading anticipation with dread until I can't tell one from the other.

Not all of us will survive.

That knowledge hangs in the air, heavier than smoke curling from the torches. The chamber feels smaller now, tighter, as if the walls themselves lean to watch. The runes blaze brighter with every passing moment, their light sliding over the stone and skin alike.

The ritual begins as the leaders and elders walk through the passage, sealed off from the rest.

CHAPTER 3

THE SUMMONING

ELARA

Footsteps echo across the floor of the great chamber. A heavy hush settles over us, broken only by a slow, rhythmic pulse of the summoning circle etched into the stone floor. Shadows cling to the carved pillars like watchful specters. Every breath feels thick in my lungs, every heartbeat amplifies like a hum surrounding me. The chamber waits, and I can feel it watching me.

A figure steps forward, dark robes swallowing the torchlight. I can't look away. His presence silences the room.

"I am Helios," he says, and the sound of his voice cuts sharply and steadily. I stiffen at the name, unfamiliar but commanding, and my pulse jumps.

"You stand here to prove your worth, to call forth what will be bound to your soul until the day one of you ceases to draw breath. The bond between a summoner and their hellhound is forged in fire and blood. It can't be undone without the cost of life. Fail, and you will pay that price in full. If you succeed, you will have a companion that will fight at your side until the end."

Every word lands like a hammer. Fire, blood, bound. My chest tightens; my hands curl into fists by my side. The summoning circle pulses beneath me, slow and steady, almost like it's counting down. Soon it will be my turn.

Unease ripples through the initiates. He lets the silence hang for a heartbeat longer before going on.

"The circle will not answer to fear. It will not answer to arrogance. It will only answer to will."

His gaze moves over the group until it lands on me. For the briefest second, his eyes linger, not with warmth, but weighing. Measuring. Then he looks away from me in an almost dismissive way.

"Elara. Step forward."

My name hits the air like a challenge. My stomach tightens with uncertainty, but my feet carry me toward the circle with steady steps, the hem of my crimson ritual cloak whispering against the stone. My group gives me a weak thumbs-up for good luck, but their faces are tight with anguish. We all know this is part of the trial. The weak rarely survive it. But I keep going, climbing up the few steps toward the circle.

The air inside the ring crackles against my skin, charged with ancient power. My pulse matches the slow, molten glow beneath my feet. I raise my hands and let the magic surge through me, familiar yet dangerous. The chants spill from my lips, each word heavy with intent.

The chamber responds with a dark amethyst flame bursting high, swirling and twisting like a living thing. Heat washes over me, but I fight to stay upright, eyes locked on the heart of the fire.

Through the blaze, she emerges—fur black as a starless sky, streaks of deep violet that shimmer like oil on water. Her molten purple eyes never blink. The weight of her presence settles against my mind, sharp and cold.

I give the command: "Come to me."

The hellhound doesn't move.

Her gaze burns into me, and her voice slips into my mind. Not words at first, only disdain, and a clear, "*Kallesie.*"

Kallesie steps forward, but not fully, keeping two paces between us. Hackles high. Muscles tense. A warning as much as acceptance. As if she isn't quite sure whether I am worth it.

I swallow hard but don't look away. We are bound now, the way fire binds to fuel, ready to consume or destroy.

Helios' voice cuts through the silence.

"The bond is done. Take her to the gates."

I turn to look for my group, but all I find is Helios, watching me. Not smiling, not frowning. He's simply judging, like he evaluates a blade he doubts will keep its edge.

Kallesie pads beside me as the guards lead us from the chamber, her presence a persistent pressure in my mind, constantly shifting and watching. Almost annoying, like an unsolicited beggar.

"You don't look like much" her voice invades my mind, almost taking over. *"But I suppose we'll see if you survive the week."*

"Funny," I shoot back silently. *"I am thinking the same thing about you."*

A low, mental growl echoes in response, but it doesn't quite reach full hostility—more an acknowledgment. The corridor to the gates is long with onlookers. Some stare openly, others whisper under their palms. I keep my chin level and my steps steady.

Halfway down, I feel a heavier weight of attention. I don't have to look to know it's Helios, leaning against one of the archways, arms crossed, gaze piercing. He says nothing as we pass, but the air feels sharper, as if the moments are being marked in time.

Kallesie glances his way, then she turns to me. *"He looks like trouble."*

"Good thing I'm not here to make friends."

The other good thing is that he can't hear our conversation right now. I think and keep going, looking straight ahead until he is behind us.

Solene and the others fall into step beside me, their hellhounds pacing close enough to feel, impossible to hear unless they are your own. We all survive the summoning, hearts hammering in our chests. What's to come next is far less certain.

The path winds upward, narrowing as it climbs. Stones darken beneath our boots, worn grey to scorch-black, still faintly warm, as if the gateway itself hasn't forgotten the fires that shaped it. Wind howls through the ravine, carrying the clangs of metal and the distant roar of forges.

Arden kicks a loose stone over the edge. "Anyone else get the feeling that one wrong step sends us straight to our deaths?"

"Ah, yes," Kallesie says in my mind. *"Classic. Perhaps next he'll warn you that fire is hot."*

Ash huffs a laugh. "That's your concern? Falling?"

"This trail isn't very safe," Riven agrees.

"Neither is anywhere worth going without a bit of danger attached to it," Solene replies.

"She has a point," Kallesie adds. *"Though I admire how fiercely your heart is trying to escape your chest."*

"You're enjoying this?" I reply.

"Immensely."

Ahead of us, Ash and Riven react simultaneously, tension snapping through them. Whatever their hellhounds say, it remains trapped behind their eyes.

Arden notices it. "You two planning something…?" he pauses. "…Or do you just enjoy being unsettling?"

Ash smiles without looking back. "Both."

The climb grew steeper, the air heavier, the mountain pressing in on us, swallowing the sky a little more with every step. Kallesie moves at my side, her presence an incessant heat.

"Steel ahead," she says. *"Blood, too. Old. Try not to slip in it."*

I swallow. *"Comforting."*

"I do what I can."

I lift my chin and keep walking.

The gates of the Stronghold rise before us, black iron twisted into curling shapes.

Beyond that, the air thickens with the smell of smoke and hot metal, and each breath edges with the tang of oil and ash. The earth beneath my boots is uneven, the kind of ground that is ingrained with the abuse of years of drills, battles, and bodies.

Kallesie treads beside me, silent as breath. Wisps of dark amethyst shadow curl lazily from her smokey coat before dissipating into the air, similar to nightmares fading away at dawn. Her molten purple eyes narrow sideways toward me, watchful, weighing with some exclusive imaginary measuring scale.

I adjust the strap of my pack but refuse to look at Kallesie. The summoning ritual still echoes inside me. The heat of the fire, the binding spell, the moment her presence crawled into my mind like an irritating tenant who has no plans to leave. My thoughts are half my own, half coloured by the low hum of her awareness.

The courtyard beyond the gates quickly fills with the initiates and their beasts, crowding in a restless, snarling sea of fur, claws, and unfamiliar magic. The noise is a constant rumble: growls, metallic ringing of shifting armour, the scrape of massive paws against stone.

From the far end, a man steps forward, and silence falls. He is a block of muscle and old scars, standing easily six feet tall. His bald head catches the afternoon light, and his crimson shirt stretches tight over a chest built for breaking things. I keep watching, evaluating—brown trousers, boots beaten down from years of use.

When his gaze sweeps over us, it feels like he is grinding us against a whetstone to see who would crack first.

"I am Alasdair," he says, voice like a lover's gravestone—low, heavy, and final. "… Second in command. Out here, you do what I say when I say it. Your survival depends on it. You slack? You die. You disobey? You die faster. Understand?"

A "Yes" chorus rises from the initiates. Alasdair's eyes narrow in brief approval. "Training starts tomorrow. Dawn. We run, we fight, and we bleed until your body forgets weakness. In the afternoon, bond work. You'll learn to speak to your hellhounds without words. They already hear you, you just don't know how to listen." He paces forward, his shadow casting over Kallesie and me. "It's not about forcing them to obey. It's about trust. And trust doesn't come easily."

Kallesie's presence pulses in my mind- sharp and unreadable. I look way before she can read the same thing in me.

And then I feel it: that subdued prickle along the back of my neck, like eyes on me.

I don't have to search for them. Just past Alasdair's shoulder, Helios stands with arms crossed, as if he doesn't have a care in the world, speaking quietly with another officer. He doesn't join in the instructions. Doesn't even seem to be watching, but every time my attention drifts his way, the air shifts, like stirring too close to a storm front.

Beside me, a voice breaks the tension.

''You look like you swallowed something sour."

I turn to find a woman leaning against a fence post with the kind of ease that comes from never doubting she belongs. Lean and corded with muscle, she has the look of someone who's been fighting since before she can walk, not because she had to prove anything, but because it's simply what she does. Dark hair pulled into a careless braid, half undone like she can't be bothered to finish it. Her eyes assess me with the blunt curiosity of someone deciding whether I'm worth the effort of remembering my name.

"I'm Harlow," she says, nodding toward Kallesie. "That's your girl?"

"Something like that," I say with a small grimace.

A smirk tugs at the corner of her mouth. "Don't let her hear you talk like that. Hellhounds have pride. Treat her right, and she'll take a blade for you. Treat her wrong—" She shrugs. "I've seen worse than just a bite."

I can't tell for sure if it's a warning or her particular sense of humour.

Yet there is a steadiness in her tone that makes me feel grounded since stepping through the gates. A thin thread of calm in the chaos. I file it away. Friends will be rare here. Allies might be rarer still.

Kallesie shuffles closer, her leg passing over the top of my head. When I meet her eyes this time, I don't immediately look away as something soft thrums between us, unsteady but real.

Maybe, I thought, *this can be more than a connection.*

From the far side of the yard, Helios' voice drops low as he speaks to Alasdair. I can't make out the words, but it doesn't matter. The sense of being defined and assessed lingers within them.

What feels like ages later, Alasdair finishes speaking with Helios and calls forth a female guard by the name of Serephaire.

She takes us women to the east wing, while the men remain behind with Alasdair and are shown to their bedchambers.

The East wing is older, rougher, with cracks in the walls, and patches at different stages of completion: off-white plaster and forest-green gold-trimmed pillars that don't match. The floor is uneven, rock set with black mortar, flowing like a frozen river beneath our boots.

I slip beside Serephaire. "Where do our Hellhounds sleep and eat?"

"They go where they please," she says plainly. "They hunt if they want. Or they eat what the chef cooks."

The cobwebs stretch thick in the corners, some occupied by massive orange-and-black spiders, one the size of a dinner plate. I survived the summoning ritual, but spiders are another thing. We stop in front of each door, as Serephaire calls out each name and assigns rooms in what appears to be no particular order.

Mine sits deep within Stronghold's East wing; its massive, solid walls softened by a calm palette of creams and warm greys. A sturdy, wooden, four-poster bed anchors the space, its posts dark with age and polished smooth by time. Layers of cream-colored linen spill across the mattress, covered by a slate-grey blanket. Light filters through a narrow, arched window, catching on the grain of the wood and warming the cool stone. Grey wool tapestries hang along the walls, in mute patterns, breaking the coldness of the stone, and holding in the warmth. The cedar trunk at the foot of the bed has dull but solid iron details, and the small wooden table and a simple clay pitcher sit on it. My nostrils register the sandalwood-and-white-sage scent wafting from the twigs twisted into a neat braid, burning slowly in a stoneware bowl beside the pitcher. Across the room, I spot an old-looking wooden desk tucked in the corner of the east wall, right beside the window, and an antique wardrobe against the opposite wall.

I peek into what I think would be the bathroom. Not much. The usual finishes of a copper claw bathtub in the middle, and a few shelves hanging on the wall. Simple and practical.

I wrap up the quick inventory and turn, drop my pack on the bed, take out my nightclothes, and place them on the toilet beside the tub. The hot steam from the already prepared bath that waits for me is more than just an inviting sight. In no time, I peel off my ritual attire from my weary body. The stress of the day finally runs its course through me. The spark of today's advent leaves a mark. I soak in the bathtub and let my mind wander for a bit.

But the same thought loops in my mind, refusing to let me be. *How am I supposed to work with Kallesie? Am I ever going to get used to sharing a mind with someone who can tear me apart?*

I sink further into the water, so other than my nose, my face is under the water. Just thinking about what tomorrow will bring.

A calm feeling rushes over me once I get out of the tub and crawl into bed. Exhaustion pulls me into a heavy sleep.

CHAPTER 4

THE BOND

ELARA

I wake with the memory of warm water clinging to my skin, heavy sleep still pressing against me, but dawn in the Stronghold is never kind. No gentle gold spills over the hills, just the clang of the iron bell, the snap of cold air thick with ash, and the sense that the day is already a battle waiting to happen.

I drag myself into the training yard, my morning run still burning in my lungs. Kallesie paces beside me in perfect silence, paws barely rustling against the dirt. Shadows cling to her coat, curling off her like smoke caught in an unseen wind.

The initiates gather in a circle around Alasdair. His crimson shirt stands out in the grey morning like a wound that hasn't stopped bleeding.

"Bond work,'' he barks out orders, his gravelly voice carrying over the yard. "Today, you stop being strangers to your hellhounds. Close your eyes. Feel them. If you can't speak to them in your mind by week's end, you're dead weight." He stalks between us, all sharp edges and watchful eyes. "Your hellhound doesn't care about your pride, your fear, or your excuses. You want them to fight for you? You give them everything. That means letting them in, no walls." My shoulders tense. "Eyes closed," the order cracks like a whip.

I obey, shutting the world out, only to find the darkness behind my eyelids is not still. It moves, fogging like breath on glass. Somewhere in that shifting darkness, something awaits. Somehow, this feels different from the first time she talked to me. I'm still getting used to having a voice that isn't my own talking back to me.

"You keep staring at the walls."

I know that voice isn't mine; it slips through my mind like claws on stone, familiar from when I first summoned Kallesie, but sharper now, impatient.

"*Kallesie?*"

"Who else?" The voice is a cool ripple through my skull, with dry amusement threading through it. "*You're loud here.*"

"*I am loud*?" My jaw tightens. "*You've been stomping around my head since the ritual.*"

A low growl answers, "*And you've been bolting every door you can find. You were the one who summoned me here, Elara. Or did you think summoning a hellhound meant you get the body without the mind?*"

Heat prickles at the back of my neck. *"I never asked for—"*

The presence snaps away, leaving my mind abruptly empty.

"Elara!"

My eyes fly open. Alasdair stands over me like a tower of stone, his shadow swallowing my boots. "This isn't about what you want," he says. "It's about what you are. You and your hellhound together. Not separate anymore. Learn to deal with it, that goes for all of you!"

He moves on, the weight of his words settling deep in my ribs.

Just a few steps away, I spot Harlow, the girl I met when we arrived at the Stronghold yesterday. She kneels in the dirt, forehead resting lightly against her hellhound. The beast's molten eyes are half-closed, tail flicking in a slow, lazy rhythm.

Harlow glances up. "It's like breathing," she says. "You don't force it. You let it happen."

I want to argue that it isn't that simple. But then Kallesie blasts against my thoughts again. Not the hard shove from before. Something lighter. Cautious. A hand on the doorframe instead of a fist against the lock.

For the first time, the sensation that came through isn't irritating. It is approval, quiet, steady, and dangerous, like a fire once you stop fearing the heat.

And beneath it, just for a heartbeat, I sense something deeper. Something that tastes like the promise of power—sharp, intoxicating, and not entirely mine.

If we continue this thread and I have Kallesie's approval, it could eventually become the start of a shared strength so potent it blurs the line between us.

Strengthening me but also risking control.

Helios

I noticed her the exact moment she stepped through the Stronghold gates with her black hellhound yesterday. The way she carries herself, like she's been on her own for far too long. Most initiates wear their nerves on their sleeves. She shows her nervousness openly. She uses her nervousness like armour. Elara—that's her name.

For the last two days, I've watched her and not only been intrigued but also experienced intense, almost confusing coils in my stomach every time she looks my way.

My steel-grey eyes sweep across the training yard, taking in the usual ruckus. The clamour of steel against steel, the thud of boots in the dirt, and the sharp scent of blended sweat lingers. Vulcan trails along, a living shadow of solid black, muscles rippling under his short, bristled coat. The Hellhound's amber eyes burn like coals, fixed on Kallesie as though gauging her worth.

"Helios." Alasdair's voice carries weight, but I barely glance at him.

My attention is already on her and the other initiate, who are running warm-up drills with a blade that appears to have been forged to fit her hand precisely.

Let's see what she's got. I step into the sparring ring, sword in hand, amethyst shirt loose at the collar, black trousers tucked into my boots. I own this ring, regardless of whether anyone likes it.

Her eyes flick up, and I catch the recognition there. She knows who I am—the leader of this clan, a true alpha born, a wolf caged in human flesh.

"Elara, is it?" I ask, although I already know the answer.

She nods. "That's me."

"You're the girl from the ritual. Impressive. But surviving is easy. Fighting me…? That's another matter completely."

Her lips curve, not exactly a smile. "We'll see."

The clash comes fast. Steel echoes as our blades meet; the sound is so intense it cuts the air. She moves lighter than I expect, quick on her feet, her strikes are fierce and clean. I press her hard, testing her defenses, expecting the usual falter I get from initiates when they realize just how fast I can be.

It doesn't come.

Instead, she slips under my guard, twisting her wrist and sending my blade into the dirt. In one fluid motion, she brings hers to rest at the hollow of my throat.

For a moment, the yard goes silent.

My eyes meet hers, my pulse steady, but my pride is dented. Then, a slow smirk gradually spreads across my lips. "Not bad."

"Not bad?!" She shoots back with an arched brow and a glint of amusement in her eye, lowering her sword. "I just disarmed you."

"You got lucky," I say, though the truth is she hadn't.

Luck doesn't move like that. Luck doesn't strike with precision born of instinct.

Vulcan's growl rolls low in his chest, the hellhound bristling at the shift in his master's dominance. Kallesie's molten amethyst-purple gaze meets Vulcan's fire, her body loose but her glare daring him.

She steps back, reclaiming my sword from the ground.

"We'll do this again. Next time, I will win," I say, sounding more confident than I feel.

She doesn't flinch. "Next time, you can try."

As she leaves the ring, Kallesie pacing close beside her, I feel the subtle tug of something I rarely grant initiates: curiosity.

She isn't just strong. She has that dangerous blend of skill and defiance that makes people either great leaders or major threats.

Vulcan's thought matches my own, a wordless growl of approval and a concurrent warning.

Yeah, I think. *Just keep a close eye on her.*

CHAPTER 5

THE MEETING OF STEEL & SASS

ELARA

The sunlight filters through the canopy of trees in fractures of gold, catching motes of dust that swirl with each step. I pause, pushing a loose strand of hair from my face, unaware of the alert and wary eyes that track me from beyond the treeline. The forest feels peaceful, almost too peaceful, yet a flicker of unease stirs inside of me, like a warning I can't place—the smell of pine and warm earth clings to the air. I grip my sword, the leather hilt tacky from sweat, shoulders aching from repetition.

Alasdair's voice snaps through the clearing.

"Again. Precision before power."

I inhale, shift my stance, and lash the blade, slicing a clean arc until my boot slides on loose soil. The world tilts, dirt scraping my palms as I hit the ground.

From the treeline, a voice drops in like velvet over steel.

"Look who decided to show up."

Helios steps forward, sunlight striking the planes of his jaw and the faint curl at the corner of his mouth, while Vulcan, hulking and dark, trudges beside him, giving a faint scent of smoke.

"Here to help?" I say, wiping the grit from my hands. "Or just to flex?"

His gaze flicks down my frame and back to my eyes quickly. But before looking away, he lingers just long enough to make my skin warm. "I thought I'd check on my favourite apprentice. Looks like you can use a little help."

Kallesie, lounging nearby, cracks an amethyst eye.

"Oh, look. The muscle-bound hero." Her mental voice drips with disdain. *"What's next? A flex-off? Not impressed."*

"Someone that hot shouldn't have an ego that big," I say. *"Though ... if he flexes, I might drool.*"

Helios's brows lift slightly, like he catches a stray thought. I try to hide a smile, but I do a lousy job. His lips twitch in response.

He reaches into his satchel, pulls out dried meat, and holds it out to Kallesie. "Peace offering?"

"He thinks I'm a common mutt?" Kallesie sniffs and then plucks the treat from his hand, chewing with smug defiance.

"See?" Helios smirks, tilting his head toward me. "She's warming up to me."

"Don't get cocky," I say, stepping closer without realizing. "She's still deciding if you're worth the trouble."

His eyes sharpen, but amusement curls at the corner of his mouth. “Then let’s decide. You and Kallesie versus Vulcan and me. Tally up.”

The air thickens as we square off. Kallesie rose, ears forward.

My sword catches the sunlight, sending a bright flare across his cheekbone. “Ready to eat dirt?” I tease.

He gives a knowing smirk. “Dream on.”

“Trip him,” Kallesie purrs.

“Not that desperate.”

“Creative.”

Helios moves first, blades meeting with a loud screech that rattles my bones. The scent of steel and oiled leather floods the air. His gaze locks on mine, intense enough to harm, but there is a flicker of half-challenge, half-admiration.

I cat-step, boots whispering against dirt. He tracks my every move, my shoulders shifting like a predator adjusting to its prey.

“Footwork,” Kallesie reminds me. *“Make him chase you.”*

She sweeps low for his ankle. His stance breaks just a fraction, but it's ample enough. I close the gap, sword angling toward his ribs. He catches it, hilts grinding together.

Our faces hover inches apart. His pupils tighten, a muscle flexes in his jaw, and I feel the tension, not just from the fight.

Kallesie's voice chimes in. "*Hair flip*?"

I smirk. *"Shut up."*

His strikes come sharper, the heat rolling from him in waves. I match his energy, my movements fluid, breath syncing almost unconsciously to his rhythm. Vulcan's tail flicks in the corner of my vision; Kallesie's mirrors it, keying into her rising adrenaline.

Then I open. Trying to catch him off guard.

Helios lunges. I inch close enough to catch the faint scent of leather, steel, and something darker, like embers. Hiking my sword under his, I twist and yank. His weapon hit the dirt with a resonant clang.

My blade hovers at his chest, breath quick, lips curling into a victorious smile. "Small doesn't mean weak. I belong here."

I extend my hand. He takes it, grip firm and hot. His eyes scan my face as he rises slowly, deliberately, like he is memorizing details. Sunlight pours across his chest and shoulders, and the faint shift of muscle beneath his shirt makes my throat move with a dry swallow.

His steel-grey eyes catch the light, glinting with something unreadable, something that makes my stomach flutter in a way I refuse to name.

Wow, I thought.

"Oh, I see it," Kallesie says, dragging her words with wicked amusement. *"You're drooling. The Fallen Hero got you bad."*

"*He's just ... fit*," I say.

"Walking sculpture," Kallesie corrects. "*Dangerous,*

too."

I clear my throat. "We should get back to Alasdair. Before he sends a search party for us."

"You think he will?"

"Maybe since Kallesie and I are still new and not proven yet."

We begin walking, Vulcan and Kallesie trailing behind. Helios's stride is steady; his back broad and irritatingly easy to admire.

"Careful," Kallesie teases. *"You're two seconds from mounting him in the clearing."*

My cheeks burn. My stomach growls loud enough to draw a glance from Vulcan. "Think we missed lunch," I mutter more to myself.

Helios doesn't notice my mortification. And honestly, that makes it worse.

HELIOS

The training yard still carries the dust from the morning drills, the scent of sweat and hot iron thick in the air.

The initiates are trickling back in from their run, boots scuffing tiredly, hellhounds wading silently at their sides. Some look sharper than they did last week. Others already look like they are one bad order away from crashing.

I cross the yard with Vulcan at my right, the steel-grey gaze scanning the ring as if assessing each newcomer.

Alasdair is already in the centre, the crimson of his shirt bright against the foggy morning. His eyes find me, and he takes two strides forward. "Tomorrow, we move to mounted work," he says without preamble. "They'll learn to ride their hellhounds."

I give a single nod. "Do it."

Alasdair's mouth twitches in satisfaction before he turns and begins barking orders, but I stop mid-stage, something in the rhythm of the day clicks wrong in my head.

I pivot on my heels, my voice slitting through the yard.

"Alasdair." The man pauses, half-turn. "They eat first," I say. "A full meal. You'll get nothing from them if they pass out on their hellhounds."

Alasdair gives a slow nod. "Understood."

"And," I add, stepping closer until the words are for Alasdair alone, "you remember the rules. They are not proven until they master control and can stay on their hellhounds without breaking stride. Most of the trials ahead are Hellhound-based. If they can't ride, they can't fight. And if they can't fight—"

"They're dead," Alasdair finishes for me.

My gaze sweeps the yard, lingering a fraction longer on one particular pair, Elara and Kallesie. The girl still carries herself like someone who has already survived more than most here, but confidence without control is just a shorter road to disaster.

Satisfied, I turn and make my way to my office. The elevated chamber overlooks the training grounds through tall, narrow windows. From here, I can see every swing of a sword, every stumble, every moment when someone's courage cracks. Vulcan settles by the door, ears perked as if guarding not just the Alpha but the unspoken weight of the trials to come.

Below, Alasdair is already moving them into new formations. I lean my forearms on the windowsill, watching.

Tomorrow, the real culling will begin.

ELARA

"Well," Kallesie speaks in my head, voice slow and smug, "*… went better than expected. For him, I mean. He remained conscious the whole time."*

I wipe my face with the back of my wrist. "*You're insufferable."*

"And yet, correct. Did you see his expression when you knocked the sword out of his hand? I swear something in him broke. Something that isn't physical."

"I don't care," I mutter under my breath, more habit than intention. No one is close enough to hear.

I pace across the yard toward the outer training grounds, where things are quieter, and the stone gives way to packed dirt and scuffed practice lines. The smell of iron, stale sweat, and familiarity settles something in my chest. It always does.

Solene spots me first. She is stretching near the weapon racks, long limbs tight with tension, jaw clenching like she's been chewing on bad thoughts all morning. Harlow stands a little off to the side, fiddling with her bracers, eyes darting everywhere except where they should.

"You look annoyingly fine for someone who just humiliated Helios," Solene says.

I shrug. "He slipped."

Harlow snorts. "On purpose?"

"Gravity's unpredictable."

"She's lying," Kallesie says pleasantly in my head. "*It is devastating watching him get tripped. I'm still savouring it."*

I ignore her and grab two dull blades, tossing one to each of them. "We don't have much time. Show me what you're struggling with."

Solene hesitates for only a second before stepping forward. Her stance is strong and practiced, but stiff. Too planted. I circle her slowly.

"Move," I say.

She attacks hard and fast. She has power, no question, but she drives every strike like it has to end the fight. I wait for it, then slip inside the swing, catch her wrist, and shove her with a precise tap between the shoulders.

She stumbles and spits: "Fuck."

"You commit too much," I say, tone flush. "You won't always finish it in one blow."

Harlow shifts her feet. "Tomorrow."

I give her a look. Not angry. Just decided. "We're not talking about tomorrow."

"We are absolutely talking about tomorrow," Kallesie sighs discreetly. *"Just... silently. With dread."*

I turn to Harlow. "Your turn."

She rushes me, movements quick but scattered, fear driving every step. I block easily, watching instead of striking.

"You're staring at my hands," I say. "Watch my shoulders."

She blinks and misses the shift. I sweep her legs from under her and catch her before she hits the ground.

"Again," I say, setting her back on her feet.

We work on that for a while. I correct grips, adjust angles, and knock them down when necessary. I don't lecture. Don't explain more than necessary. Just enough to keep them learning instead of panicking.

By the time we stop, Solene is bent over, hands on her knees, breathing hard. "You're brutal."

I hand her a waterskin. "You're still standing."

"Technically true," Kallesie adds inside my head. *"Low standards, but effective."*

Harlow drinks quietly, eyes flicking toward the walls like she expects them to listen. "You're different today," she says softly. "Sharper."

I look away. "Have a good match."

Solene studies me closely. "Helios isn't easy."

"Neither are the Trials we are all facing," I say before I can stop myself.

The words hang there. None of us reaches for them.

After a moment, I straighten. "Get some rest. Eat. Don't run the fights in your head tonight. When things go wrong, and they will, trust your body. It knows what to do."

Solene nods once. Harlow tightens her grip on her blade and nods, too.

As we leave the grounds, Kallesie marches beside me in a way only I can feel her presence—warm and complacent against my thoughts.

"You don't have to caution them," she says. *"How restrained of you."*

"They don't need it from me."

"True," she replies. *"They'll find out soon enough. Still, if they live, they'll owe you. And if they don't ... well, at least Helios lost today."*

I let out a quiet breath as the sun dips lower behind the stone walls.

Success doesn't last.

Tomorrow will be tough with uncertainty.

I retire to my room, Kallesie lags steadily behind me as much as a ten-foot-tall beast can. Her strides are smaller than her normal pace. Maybe to give me breathing room. I don't know. As I make my way to my door, I sigh in relief, glad that the day is over.

The East Wing feels less lively than normal. I guess something shifted today. Another worry that can wait until tomorrow to deal with, as my grandmother would say, “Don't worry about what you can't control; worry about what you can.”

I climb into my bed and nestle my head into the pillow. Exhaustion welcomes me in a deep embrace.

CHAPTER 6

THE RIDE

KALLESIE

Elara sleeps like the world has never asked anything of her. I must wake her up with some sass, of course. I can't help it. *"If your mouth is any wider, a fly would find a hiding spot somewhere in the back of your throat."* I nearly scream in her head. Her eyes fly wide. *"By the way, your morning breath stinks like mothballs or something."*

She rolls over, annoyed, pulling the blankets over her head like I'm not dead serious about her breath stinking up the entire room. I'm surprised the pillow hasn't crumbled from the smell alone or crawled away like a caterpillar to its next meal. And her snoring from yesterday's workout? It is something that can wake the dead.

I have finally had enough of her antics. I grab the blanket with my canines and pull it off her, making sure I don't leave a drool mark, or I wouldn't hear the end of it. *The things I do for her!* I dramatically roll my eyes, b*ack to* *minding my own business.*

The shriek she lets out when the chilly morning air hits her bare legs is something out of this world. "Is that necessary, Kallesie?" she howls at me.

I give her the best puppy eyes I can pull off while secretly plotting my next move if she doesn't get up.

"It won't be my fault if we are late, and I'm not looking forward to Alasdair coming after us. So, get your behind up, or I'll nip your arse, and you won't be able to sit for a week. Move your ass!"

"You wouldn't dare."

"Fucking try me."

ELARA

After Kallesie rudely wakes me up, I have no choice but to get ready, even though I'm not feeling it.

In slow motion, I put on my workout leathers. All the initiates received a set yesterday, before the mock battles. The only light comes through the window from the moon still hanging in the sky while I get ready for what today will bring. I brush my hair and tie it into a tight ponytail, away from my face. Half-heartedly, I drag my exhausted ass toward the training grounds.

The yard smells like dirt, new leather, and the hot, wild scent of hellhounds that lack the capacity to stand still. Dawn is still emerging, but the air is already buzzing with the restless scrape of claws and the jingle of tack.

Kallesie remains beside me, her weight solid and warm. She doesn't fidget, doesn't huff, but watches the others with intense predator calm.

Alasdair's voice rolls over the yard. "Mount from the left. Grip with your knees, not your hands. You force them; you lose them. And if you fall off…" He pauses long enough for the tension to land. "You get back on. Or you walk away for good."

The first few attempts are a disaster. One boy barely gets a foot over his hound before the beast bolts, and he plummets face-first into the dirt. Another girl freezes halfway, her hound turning in a slow, irritated circle until she slides off like a sack of grain. A third one, a boy, doesn't even make it past the mounting block before his hound bares its teeth and sends him stumbling backward.

Kallesie's thoughts slip into my mind like mist. *"You're not going to do that, are you?"*

"Not planning on it."

"Good. I'd hate to waste the effort of carrying you."

I ignore the bite in her tone and step forward at Alasdair's signal. One hand on Kallesie's shoulder, a swing of my leg, and I'm up, settling my weight as naturally as I can. But my knees feel like they might lock from the tension. Kallesie doesn't so much as flick an ear.

"You're heavy," she says, though her stride is steady when Alasdair calls us forward.

We move with the pack. The first jolt of motion nearly throws me; her muscles coil and release under me like springs. The power in her gait is nothing like riding a horse. My instinct is to grip tighter with my hands, but her thought wipes mine. *"Knees. Not hands."*

I shift and find the rhythm.

Around us, the chaos climaxes, with riders tumbling, hounds veering off course, and Alasdair shouting orders that cut through the din. She keeps a smooth pace, neither pushing to the front nor falling behind, and I match her breathing without realizing it.

When the run ends, only a handful of us remain mounted. I slide down, landing gingerly on my feet. Her tail flicks once. In approval, maybe. Or just relief at having me off her back.

"Not bad," I hear her mocking in my head.

"Not bad?!" I echo.

Her violet eyes catch mine, unblinking. *"Don't get cocky. The wild hasn't come yet."*

A shiver slides down my spine, not exactly from fear, but from understanding she is right.

Tomorrow isn't a yard run. Tomorrow, the ground will be uneven, the wind biting, and there will be more than falling to worry about.

And if I fail there, I won't get back up. I tighten the straps on my pack, fingers trembling against my will. The Wilds Trail waits beyond the fence line, untamed, unpredictable, alive in a way the training yard can never be. No neat paths. No second chances. Just instinct, endurance, and whatever mercy the land decides to grant.

I check my boots. Then I check them again.

"You know?" Kallesie sneaks inside my mind. *"If you keep staring at those laces, they might start charging you*

rent."

I exhale slowly through my nose. "*Now is not the time, Kallesie."*

At my side, my hellhound stretches, massive paws digging into the dirt. Her dark hide ripples slightly, purple oily fur with sparks of defiance in her stance. On the outside, she appears silent, just another beast waiting. Inside, though, she is anything but.

"Correction," Kallesie says, "*now is exactly the time. High stress situations are my specialty. That, and biting things."*

I swallow, eyes drifting toward the jagged line of trees. "The Wilds doesn't care how prepared I am," I whisper, even though no one else can hear me. "One mistake out there—"

"And yes, yes, dramatic doom, eternal failure. Very grim," Kallesie chimes in. "*Honestly, you're exhausting when you spiral. It's annoying. Stop it!"* Despite the tightness in my chest, I almost smile. *"Look,"* Kallesie goes on, her mental voice lowering just a notch: "*—you're not doing this alone. Even if I can't shout witty commentary out loud, which is frankly unfair, I'm still with you. Every step. Every bad decision."*

"That's reassuring," I mutter.

"It should be. I'm excellent at survival. And violence. Mostly violence."

The wind snaps through the clearing, sharp and cold, bearing the scent of the Wilds with it. I straighten, shoulders squaring, fear still heavy but no longer paralyzed.

"And tomorrow," Kallesie boasts self-righteously inside

my skull, "*we prove the Wilds picked the wrong girls to mess with.*"

I close my eyes for a moment, then open them, gazing around the surviving area, as if I have already decided how tomorrow ends.

Tomorrow, I will make it through?

Stronghold gates yawn open at dawn, spilling us into the Wilds like bait tossed to predators. The air is cold enough to bite; the ground is still damp from the night fog. Kallesie's breath steams, her muscles quiver under my legs like a coiled spring.

"Ready?" she asks, though I can feel the answer she wants.

"As I'll ever be," I reply.

Alasdair rides at the front on a lean black hellhound that moves like smoke over the ground. "This isn't a race," he calls back, "but if you fall behind, you will get left behind. Stay on, keep your hound under control, and remember out here, nothing waits for you to catch up."

Kallesie lunges forward as soon as the command comes, like it is all she has waited for. The first stretch is open, a blur of pounding paws and snapping wind, but then the ground tilts and breaks into gullies and stone-strewn slopes. My knees burn from the grip it takes to stay one with her.

She takes a jump without warning, two strides and a leap, and we are airborne. My stomach lurches, but I land with her, miraculously with breath still in my chest.

"Better," she says, and there is something almost like respect in her mind-talk.

The others aren't faring so well. The boy ahead of us loses his seat and hits the dirt hard. His hound doesn't even look back. Another rider clings desperately to his hound's neck while the beast veers dangerously close to a drop.

By the time Alasdair raises a hand to halt, only six of us remain mounted.

Kallesie slows under me, head high, chest heaving. I slide off, legs trembling.

"You stayed on," she says.

I don't have the breath to answer, but I can feel her approval as a solid, steady weight in my chest.

HELIOS

From the ridge above the trail, I watch them, a thread of riders half already on the ground, the rest barely clinging to their hounds.

My scrutinizing eyes find her easily. Elara rides low, knees tight, body moving with the hellhound instead of against her. Not perfect. Her grip is raw but strong, not skilled yet, but she stays on when the terrain turns treacherous.

Vulcan shifts beside me, heated eyes tracking her too. The big hound sends a flicker of wordless approval, though it has the aftertaste of a warning.

I'd told Alasdair the truth: until they can ride and control their hounds, they aren't proven. And most of the trials ahead aren't about swords or fists; they're about the bond.

Elara clears a rocky rise without losing pace. I feel the corner of my mouth lift, just barely.

Not bad. But it's not enough.

Tomorrow, I'll see if she can do it when the wilds aren't empty, when something is chasing her.

CHAPTER 7

TRIALS BEGIN

ELARA

The morning starts wrong when Kallesie decides entirely on her own that I deserve to be woken up in the worst way possible. It appears to be turning into a nasty habit.

She grabs my linens and blanket and yanks them off me. Again.

The cold air washes over me, and I gasp awake.

"Looks like I'll have to get used to this," I mutter, shivering and sleepy.

Kallesie chuckles, *"About time you woke up. I thought maybe the dead got you before I did."*

I rub my tired eyes. Today is going to be challenging if Alasdair has anything to do with it. I know this much. I slide into my training outfit and tie my hair back in a ponytail, strap on my boots, and leave the east wing, toward the training yard.

The smoke hits first. Acrid, stingy, clinging to my lungs like it wants to drown me from the inside. The training grounds look different today, not the open space I know, but a war zone waiting. The obstacles loom like the bones of some terrible beast, blackened wood and twisted metal waiting to burn.

Alasdair stands in the centre, still as stone, his shadow long in the low morning sun.

"Today begins the Trials. Many of you will not see the next sunrise."

Forty-five of us stand shoulder to shoulder. Not a single foot shift. No one draws a full breath. I feel the silence pressing against my skin.

Helios steps beside him. The fire reflects in his steel-grey eyes, making them look like liquid silver. His voice travels through the quiet suspense floating in the air.

"Your hellhound is your life. Without trust, without command, you're already dead. This test is simple. You fall? You burn."

At my side, Kallesie's flames flare higher, coiling in amethyst whirls along her ribs. She rumbles in my head, a low, dangerous purr. *"Let's see if you can keep up, little summoner."*

I tighten my grip on my bow, trying not to let the shake in my hands show. I've never shot my bow from her back before, not while she is moving, and certainly not when the fire tries to swallow us whole.

The first whistle splits the air.

"The culling has begun," comes to mind.

Chaos hits instantly.

To my right, a rider barely makes two strides before her hellhound twists and clamps down on her leg. The scream is cut short when the beast shakes once and drops what is left of her into the dirt. A spear flies from the sidelines, ending the hellhound before it can lunge at anyone else.

Two riders ahead, a hellhound turns on another, jaws locked around the rival's throat. The sound is wet, raw—blood spraying in the firelight. Both go down in a snarl of claws and flame.

And then the sabotage starts. The rider on my left shoves the man in front of him off his hellhound. The man hits the ground hard, straight into the fire that has just burst from a nearby pit. His scream rises above the roar of flames, then reduces to silence.

Kallesie's muscles tense beneath me, ready to leap into the fray, but I lean forward, pressing a hand to her neck. *"Not yet."* She hesitates. Barely. That is trust.

When the smoke clears, nearly half of us are gone.

The second whistle screeches, and the course comes alive.

Flames roar from hidden vents, forming rings that pulse with heat. Ramps sway overhead, chained to posts that groan under the weight. Wooden targets spin in dizzying arcs, and some burst into flames without warning. The dirt smokes beneath our feet, patches of sudden fire blooming like hungry traps.

Kallesie charges forward, and the world around me skews.

The first flaming ring comes too fast. I launch an arrow midair and miss by inches.

"You do better, or you'll fall," Kallesie snaps.

We hit the ramp, claws ripping on the wood as the chains above creak. Ahead, a rider loses his balance, and the entire structure shudders. The front half of the ramp gives way, and both rider and hellhound plunge into the fire pit below. The smell strikes me instantly: burnt fur and something far worse.

Kallesie doesn't slow. She vaults over the collapsing section, and I drop another arrow, hitting the spinning target dead centre.

Screams echo behind us where two hellhounds are locked in combat on the course. Their riders shout and pull at their beasts to no avail. One goes down in the flames, dragging its rider with it, while the other rider and their beast veers right of us.

Ahead, Harlow and Zinnia are a blur of black-and-gold flame. Every leap is perfect; every arrow is a bullseye.

The next obstacle is a hanging bridge spanning over a pit that spits embers into the air. Wooden planks sway, already weakened by fire. Halfway across, the rider in front of us kicks backward, aiming for my leg. Kallesie snarls, claws raking the boards, and springs past them.

The rope on the side snaps, sending the kicker and another pair sliding into the pit, howls fading into oblivion.

We hit solid ground and run straight into an ambush.

A hellhound with eyes wild and flames guttering black breaks from the course's edge and lunges for Harlow's side. Without thinking, I draw and fire. The arrow slams into its shoulder, sending the beast off course before it vanishes into the smoke.

“Don’t get it into your head that I owe you!” Harlow yells, her grin quick, bright, and real.

Kallesie barrels toward the next ring. Mid-leap, another rider’s hellhound comes from the side, aiming to knock us off balance. Kallesie twists midair, claws raking at nothing as she kicks the attacker away. My stomach flips, but we land hard and keep sprinting.

The final stretch proves to be beyond absurd: two rings ablaze, one already collapsing, and the last target swinging so fast it’s blurry.

“Ready?” I whisper.

Kallesie doesn’t answer; she keeps running.

We hit the first ring; fire writhing so close, I feel my skin tighten. Two strides later, we leap through the second one just as it cracks, flipping inward. I shoot the arrow mid-jump, and it strikes dead centre, snapping the chains. The target tumbles into the flames below.

We land in a shower of dirt and ash. My lungs burn, my arms shake, but we remain upright.

The final whistle blares through the smoke.

Out of forty-five initiates, only eight of us finished the trial. The rest are nothing but ash and bone scattered in the fire pits.

HELIOS

From above, the course burns like a living thing.

The weak fall first, torn apart by their own hounds or shoved into the fire by the strong, desperate to survive. They adapt fast, fight back, and keep moving, even when the ground under them gives way.

Elara is unrefined. Her first shot is shaky, but she doesn't break. She pulls Kallesie back from the kill in the culling, survives sabotage on the bridge, and even saves Harlow mid-run. That kind of grit is rarer than perfection.

By the end, the survivors are more ash than flesh but still breathing.

That's all the Trials demand.

Tomorrow, though… tomorrow, they'll face something worse than fire.

ELARA

My lungs are full of smoke. My clothes stink of fire and ash. Solene, Ash, Arden, Covin, Harlow, Neria, and one I barely know, and myself. We line up, faces streaked with soot, carved hollow by exhaustion.

For a split second, I think maybe they'll give us time to rest.

It doesn't take long to realize how wrong I am.

Alasdair paces in front of us like a wolf stalking its prey.

His voice carves through the haze in my brain.

"You survived the flames. Now we'll see if you can survive with nothing but your teeth," He says. "From this point on, you live or die by what you can find."

One by one, we return weapons, placing them on the rack beside Alasdair. Each clang echoes through the yard. I feel the weight of going into the pit unarmed. My hand twitches. My stomach tightens. I swallow hard, telling myself to remember that surviving the Trials is the only thing that makes my sacrifices matter.

Anticipation builds as the gates at the far end of the ground creak open.

The sound that comes through isn't a roar; it is a rumble, low and deep enough to make my bones vibrate. Hellhounds march into the arena in pairs, their eyes catching the torchlight. These aren't our bonded hounds. They are leaner, meaner, and clearly more than just half-mad. The kind that they don't trust anyone to ride.

Just muscles, flames, and teeth.

Alasdair's smile spreads across his face. An incisive sneer. Arrogant.

"You have no bows. No arrows. You fight with what you find. Survive for three minutes, and you pass. Fail, and your body feeds the training pits."

Kallesie's flames flare beside me, her snarl rolling like thunder in my head. *"Stay close. I'd rather not have to drag you out in pieces."*

The whistle blows.

The first hellhound hits the line before I can move. Its

flames, dark red, almost black, and its eyes lock on a rider at the far end. It leaps, jaws snapping, and the sound that follows is a gurgle. Final. The rider goes down screaming, one leg almost severed between those teeth—his hellhound barrels in, both beasts hitting the dirt in a blur of claws and inferno. The chaotic energy radiates from the encounter as fire and fury intertwine, each creature vying for dominance in a battle where only one can emerge victorious. The ground trembles beneath the weight of their struggle, the air thick with smoke and the growl of primal power.

Something slams into my side. I stumble, catching myself against Kallesie's flank as a second hound lunges past. Kallesie meets it head-on, teeth flashing, air sizzling where their flames collide.

In the chaos, I see Harlow duck under a swipe from another hound and roll toward a discarded spear. She drives it into the beast's side, black smoke billowing from the wound as it screeches.

Kallesie knocks her opponent sideways, giving me an opening. I grab the broken half of a spar from the dirt, swinging hard as the hound lunges again. The wood cracks against its muzzle, and it recoils, snarling, before diving at my legs.

"Left!" Kallesie barks in my head.

I spin as her claws rake the hound's shoulder, sending it limping back into the mayhem.

Everywhere I look, I see teeth and fire, riders locked in frenzied grapples. Hellhounds slam into each other hard enough to shake the ground. The smell of blood is everywhere.

A scream pierces through the din, and one of the survivors goes down under a hound's weight, his bonded hellhound too far to help. The beast's flames flicker bright, and in seconds, there is nothing left but charred bone.

"Two minutes!" Alasdair shouts over the chaos.

I never knew two minutes could feel like forever.

Another hound comes for me, flames guttering low like it is saving the worst strike for last. I raise the staff, but Kallesie is faster, launching forward in a blur of purple fire. She hits it mid-leap, jaws locking around its neck. Both crash into the dirt, rolling in a storm of heat and sparks until Kallesie tears free. The other hound doesn't rise.

By the time the final whistle sounds, the arena is littered with smoking bodies, some hellhounds, some humans.

Of the eight, only six of us are still standing.

HELIOS

They stumble from the Trial by Fire straight into the Fangs of Death, and that is deliberate.

The weak break, fast, and their screams are short-lived. The strong adapt and use debris as weapons, covering each other, keeping their hounds close.

Elara fights like someone who knows she can't out-muscle her enemies. Smart, fast, and stubborn. When Kallesie isn't enough, she uses the terrain, the scraps of wood, and even her opponent's momentum.

By the time the whistle blows, the six left aren't just

survivors. They are killers.

Good!

They'll need to be.

CHAPTER 8

THE ONES WE LOST

ELARA

In the aftermath, the arena lies quiet, its fires long since extinguished, but the smell of smoke still clings to my hair, my clothes, and my skin.

I watch as the bodies from the massacre are hauled away, while the others burn where they fell, ashes scattered across the training grounds as if they never existed. The smoke hangs in the air, thick and bitter, a reminder that no one survives this by luck. This is a test.

Pride should fill my chest. Relief should follow. Instead, there's only a hollow ache sitting heavy in my ribs.

I keep replaying it, the boy with the dark braid, so close before that hellhound takes him down. Close enough that, if I had been faster… if I had just done something, maybe I could have reached him in time.

Kallesie is quiet in my head, which is rare. She knows I

don't need her sass tonight. She walks beside me, close enough for her warmth to soak into my shaking legs.

By sunset, the village's torchlights are lit in the great hall. Long tables covered in platters of roasted meat, bread still warm from the ovens, and mugs of dark ale. The survivors are ushered in, and our arrival is greeted with cheers and raised cups.

It feels wrong.

I sit beside Harlow, facing Ash and Arden, sitting across from us. We sadly lost Riven in the first trial, along with his hellhound. When the sabotage started, they targeted him, and he was too far from me.

I barely eat, pushing food around my plate, even though I am starving. The others try to eat, to laugh, to pretend the empty chairs at the table don't matter.

Harlow nudges me with her elbow. "You survived, Elara. They didn't… but we did. That must mean something."

I try to smile. It feels like glass cracking in my face. "It doesn't feel like anything right now."

The noise around me fades until a shadow falls across the table.

Helios.

He doesn't sit. He doesn't speak right away. His eyes sweep the table, lingering on me for a fraction longer than anyone else. Then he discreetly jerks his head toward the door, as if signaling me to `come'.

I follow him out into the cool night, cheers and music fading behind us.

The training grounds are empty, the dirt scorched from the trial.

Helios stands there for a while, his back turned to me. He looks out over the arena as if the ghosts of the day still linger there, and he can see them.

When he finally speaks, his voice is low. “You can’t save everyone.”

The words make something inside me snap. “I should have done more.”

He turns, stepping so close that I have to tip my head to meet his eyes.

“If you had, you’d be dead. And then who would Kallesie be stuck with?”

Against my will, a tiny laugh slips out. More like a whimper. Fragile, but real.

Helios’ mouth curves. Not quite a smile. He reaches up, sweeping soot from my cheek with his knuckles. The touch is light and fleeting, but it sends a shiver through me.

“You survived,” he says quietly. “And that means the others didn’t die for nothing.”

I swallow hard, the lump in my throat making it impossible to answer.

He then lets his hand fall and steps back.

“Get some rest, Elara. Tomorrow… we begin again.”

And just like that, he is gone, striding toward the hall, leaving me standing in the moonlight with my heartbeat far too loud in my ears.

Despite how weary I feel, sleep refuses to come. When it finally does, it comes in scraps, flashes of fire and screams, the reek of blood, and burnt fur.

I wake up with Kallesie's muzzle nudging my shoulder, amethyst eyes glowing faintly in the dark.

"Up, little spark," she murmurs in my mind. "*Your chief wants you on the grounds."*

The word chief makes me groan, but I yank myself up, throwing on my boots and gear.

Moonlight silvers the training grounds, the air stings with the scent of pine. All six of us stand in a loose circle, hellhounds restless beside us. Helios and Alasdair remain in the centre like carved pillars, one dark and severe, the other broader, his grin wolfish even in the cold.

Helios' steel-grey gaze passes over us, lingering a bit too long on me. The kind that makes the back of my neck burn. Then his voice breaks the silence.

"Tonight, you hunt." Alasdair steps forward. "You'll be dropped in pairs deep in the wild. There are things out there that don't care if you've got a hellhound. If you can't work together, you'll die."

A low growl rips from somewhere in the dark, too far to see but close enough to make my stomach knot.

Helios' eyes find mine again. "Stay on Kallesie's back. Keep moving. Don't stop to think, don't stop to breathe unless you're sure it's safe."

I want to ask, Safe?! From what?

But the answer comes right away, as one of the handlers

releases a captured creature into the wild. Bigger than a man, skin pale and stretched, and way too many teeth for a mouth. It vanishes into the trees without a sound.

Pairs are appointed, and Harlow ends up with a tall, scar-faced rider named Corvin. They exchange a brief look, measuring and accepting, and step together.

Then silence stretches. Nothing follows. A murmur ripples through the yard. I feel it before I hear it, eyes turning toward me. Beside me, the black mass of muscle and heat shifts. Kallesie lifts her head, eyes glowing beneath her hide, her tail flicking once against the dirt.

Solene shifts beside me, a faint frown pulling at her mouth. Arden glances toward Helios, clearly waiting for a correction that never comes. Instead, Helios speaks, voice even and final.

"Kallesie is worth two of the others."

The words land hard. I blink, not sure if I'm hearing him right. Kallesie lets out a low sound in her chest, not a growl, not quite approval either. Pride, maybe. Or a warning.

Helios doesn't look at me when he continues. "She doesn't need balancing. She doesn't need reinforcement. Pairing her would dilute what she already is."

My stomach tightens. Is that praise, or am I being set apart because I'm too difficult to place?

"Elara does not require Solene's precision or Arden's strength. She functions more effectively without divided command."

Divided command. Like I'm a problem that can't be shared.

Helios turns away, the decision sealed as cleanly as a snapped bone.

I remain where I am—just the other person, both equally confused. And Kallesie pressed warm and solid against my leg. Whatever Helios sees when he looks at us puts us outside the rules. And I don't know yet whether that makes us dangerous or disposable.

We are taken to the edge of the forest. The shadows are thicker here, and the air colder. Alasdair raises a horn to his lips and blows it.

The hunt begins.

Kallesie launches forward, her paws barely touching the earth. Branches whip past, moonlight flashing in broken shards through the canopy of trees. My bow is already in my hand, an arrow knocked, though my pulse is hammering so hard I can barely keep my aim steady.

Something moves to our left fast.

"Not prey," Kallesie warns. *"Predator."*

I draw and fire, but miss as the thing blurs past a smear of bone and sinew. Kallesie lunges after it, her claws gouging deep furrows into the soft earth.

The forest erupts in snarls and shouts. Somewhere behind us, a hellhound screams, a sound that makes my blood turn to ice.

We aren't hunting tonight.

We are the ones being hunted.

The thing is fast. Too fast.

Kallesie zigzags between trees. Her body coils with every stride, the muscles under her dark coat flexing as she springs forward, and I can feel her heart thrumming in my knees.

I risk a glance over my shoulder—big mistake.

Two shapes have joined the hunt, pale limbs catching moonlight, teeth gleaming. Their movements are wrong, too smooth, and too silent, like they are gliding over the ground rather than running.

"Faster!" I gasp, though Kallesie is already pushing herself.

"Hold steady," she says, voice calm despite the fire in her stride. "*You have one shot before they're on us. Make it count."*

We burst into a clearing, and Kallesie pivots hard to face them. The first creature charges, mouth stretching wider than it should, claws reaching for her throat.

I barely have time to aim but shoot deep into the thing's skull. It drops with a sickening thud, twitching once before lying still.

The second shrieks so loudly it makes my ears ring and launches at me. Kallesie twists mid-air, her massive jaws snapping shut around its neck. Bones crack, and she drops it, panting, her fur smoking faintly with heat.

"Two down. More are coming."

From the woods comes the sound of chaos, another hellhound crying out; a rider's scream cut short. My stomach twists at the thought. *This isn't a trial. It's culling.*

We push forward, weaving through roots and underbrush until the trees thin and the smell of smoke reaches my nose. Ahead, firelight dances through the trunks.

We break into another clearing and freeze.

In the centre, a hulking shadow is crouched over what remains of Corvin's body. Only a few feet away, also just a corpse, lay his hellhound.

Harlow's voice cracked somewhere beyond the flames. "Zinnia, now!"

Her hellhound leaps, amethyst flames bursting from its jaws. The beast roars and spins, its hide blistering under the flames.

Kallesie doesn't wait for my command; she lunges. I fire arrow after arrow, each one sinking into the beast's ribs, its neck, and its eyes. Finally, with a strangled roar, it collapses.

Then silence falls. One by one, the remaining pairs emerge from the treeline: Harlow, Solene, Ash, Arden, and me, with all our hellhounds. All breathing hard and exhaustion nipping our asses.

HELIOS

I find Elara standing alone near the edge of the clearing, bow still in hand, knuckles white from the grip. Her hellhound paces at her side, ears flat, tail lashing.

There is blood on her cheek, not hers. Her eyes are too

wide and too bright in the firelight.

"Breathe," I advise, stepping close enough for my shadow to fall over her.

She doesn't look at me at first, just stares at the body being carried away. "I should have been able to save him."

"No," I say, my voice gravelly. "You'd have died with him." Her jaw tightens, but she doesn't argue. "Come," I say, resting my hand at the small of her back, not pressing, just there—a shred of steady heat in the night's cool. "You'll make it. That matters."

She finally meets my gaze, and for a heartbeat, I think she'll say something bold. Instead, she nods.

And that is enough for now. As we ride back to the Stronghold, I can't help but sense that something has changed between Elara and me. I don't quite know if it's for better or worse. Summoners are meant to strip themselves of weaknesses, and love is a weakness no leader can afford.

CHAPTER 9

ASHES AND SHADOWS

ELARA

The gates of the Stronghold loom ahead, their iron edges catching the moonlight. We ride in silence, our hellhounds' paws thudding dully against the dirt. The quiet weight of absence swallows the usual sounds of the night.

Eight of us began this endeavour, but only five remain, and I have a feeling it's not over yet.

The guards at the gate step aside without a word, their eyes flicking to the empty spaces in our ranks, then look away.

By the time we reach the central square, the air is full of the smell of roasting meat and wood smoke. A feast is prepared, long tables groan under platters of venison, bread, and berries, but no one moves toward them. It feels wrong.

Kallesie presses her head into my side as I dismount.

"*You did well.*"

I want to believe her. But every time I close my eyes, I see Corvin's hand twitching as life leaves him. I see the young girl with the pale braid, Mira? Miri? Slip from her Hellhound's back into claws and teeth from the Trial by Fire.

The others begin to sit at the tables, speaking in low voices. I stand at the edge of the firelight, watching the flames bend and crackle. My bow hangs from my shoulder. My hands will not stop trembling.

HELIOS

By the time I reach the central square, the air is thick with the smell of roasting meat and wood smoke. A feast has been prepared; long tables groan under their platters of food. I notice that no one moves toward the food. And then I spot her. She stands rigid, unmoving, her eye fixed somewhere far beyond the bustling scene as if none of this exists. The others linger near the tables, staring at the food like starving men, yet none of them dares touch it. She doesn't touch anything.

Alasdair joins me, his voice pitched low. "She is in shock? It will get her killed in the next trial."

"Not if I break it out of her," I reply.

He lifts a brow. "You?"

"She made it this far without losing her head. She just needs it sharpened."

Alasdair smirks faintly. "Or you're just looking for an excuse to keep her in your shadow."

I don't answer.

I cross the square, weaving between tables, until I am standing beside her. "You're not eating."

Her eyes don't leave the fire. "Don't feel like celebrating."

"This isn't a celebration. It's survival. You eat, or you'll fail the next test." Still, she doesn't move. *Fine. If she wants to wallow, I'll drag her out of it.* "Tomorrow, you train with me. Sunrise. No excuses."

That makes her glance at me, just for a heartbeat. "Why?"

"Because," I say, leaning in until the firelight catches the steel in my eyes, "you're too stubborn to die, but not yet good enough to live."

I don't wait for an answer. I turn and leave her there, knowing the words will follow her into the night.

ELARA

Sunrise is almost peaceful. The smell of baked bread drifts from the village kitchens, and for once, the clang of the training grounds feels distant and muffled. Kallesie sprawls in a patch of sunlight, eyes half-lidded, tail wagging lazily.

Across the yard, Helios speaks with Alasdair, his voice low, his posture relaxed. For a moment, I allow myself to think maybe, just maybe, we'll see a day without blood.

The thought barely forms before the air shifts.

Kallesie's head snaps up, and her ears flatten.

"Elara." Her tone is razor-sharp. *"They're here."*

A sound tears through the village, the kind that scrapes against bone. A scream warps into something inhuman—the ground trembles.

Helios's head whips toward the tree line. I follow his gaze. Shadows spill out between the pines, moving too fast to count. They hit the open ground, and the light catches them in jagged shapes, all claws and teeth, with the wind carrying the smell of decay towards us.

Wraths.

"Mount up!" Helios' voice booms through the panic like steel. "Form lines. Now!"

Kallesie is under me before I even register that I am moving, her body taut with energy. The first Wrath slams into the outer barricade, splintering wood. Two guards go down before they can draw breath and are dragged screaming into the swarm.

The air fills with fire. Hellhounds leap to meet the creatures, jaws clamping onto scaled throats. The stench of burning flesh hits me, and I force my bow up, arrow nocked.

Helios' hellhound growls beside us, black flames curling off his shoulders. Helios is already in the middle of it, blade flashing, slashing anything that comes within reach.

A Wrath breaks through the line, lunging straight for me. Kallesie spins, and I shoot without thinking; the arrow buries in its eye. It collapses in a convulsion of black ichor, spraying the ground.

"On your left!" Helios shouts.

I turn in time to see another leap for me, but Helios is already there, his sword splitting its skull in one clean strike. The momentum throws him close, so close his shoulder grazes mine.

"Stay with me," he says, voice low and commanding.

We move together as one. He carves a path through the thickest of the flock. Behind him, I pick off anything that slips past his defense. Kallesie and his hellhound fight in sync, their movements mirroring ours. Vulcan takes the lead, and Kallesie picks off anything that gets past his defenses.

But the Wraths don't stop. For each one we kill, two more take their place.

"They're after the guards!" I speak. "They're thinning our numbers!"

Helios' jaw tightens. "Then we hold until they break or we do."

A Wrath lunges for the enforcers behind me. I spin and shoot an arrow, but I'm too slow and miss. Helios' arm rushes past my shoulder, his blade taking its head clean off. The force of it spins me halfway around, close enough to feel his breath on my cheek.

Our eyes lock for a moment. Fire and ash swirl around us, the roar of battle crashes around me, each clash and scream hammering in my skull. Then he is moving again, pulling me with him, our hellhounds matching their pace, fighting as one.

By the time the last Wrath falls, my arms ache, my fingers are raw from the bowstring, and the ground is littered with the still bodies of Wraths and our own.

The peace is gone. The realization hits me. The Wraths know where to find us now. Something in the way Helios' hand lingers on my arm confirms somehow that this isn't over.

I exhale as the training grounds finally come into view, my shoulders sagging now that the attack is over. But the scar of human lives lost and hellhound alike, stays more alive than ever before today.

"You hesitated," Kallesie says.

I scowl. *"I didn't."*

"You did. Again. And one day that's going to get you killed."

A few steps away, Helios snorts softly, clearly having his own private argument with Vulcan. His jaw tightens, his grip clenched like he's still holding his weapon.

I straighten my spine despite the ache in my bones. Whatever mistakes I made today, I'm still standing. Still chosen. Still bound to a hellhound who expects more from me.

As we step back onto the training grounds, I lift my chin in determination. *Tomorrow I won't hesitate. Tomorrow I'll do better.*

CHAPTER 10

ASHES AND SILENCE

ELARA

I lift my chin and draw a steadying breath, letting the ache in my bones remind me that I survived.

Smoke hangs low and heavy over the training grounds, smouldering my lungs and stinging my eyes, blurring my vision. The echo of the battle still pulses in the air, shrouded in the scent of burnt flesh, torn earth, and shallow breathing rises from every corner, the wounded pressed close.

Bodies lie scattered, the line between the human and hellhound hazed by ash and blood. My stomach knots as I move among them, searching for faces, praying I don't find any I know.

I find them anyway.

Neria, the youngest of us. She was barely fifteen. Her hellhound is still curled around her as if it intends to protect her even in death. Both are gone. I drop to my knees, fingers trembling as I wipe the soot from her cheek.

"I could have…" My voice cracks. The end of the sentence dissolves in my throat.

Kallesie presses her nose against my shoulder. "*This isn't your fault, Elara.*"

It feels like a lie. Every death feels like my fault. "I should have seen the Wraths coming. I could have aimed faster. I should have." The sheer panic is hitting me with the force of a bull.

"Enough." The word comes from above me, small but sharp.

I look up into Helios' steel-grey eyes, darker than I've ever seen them. His sword sheathed. Blood still streaked across his knuckles. "You fought," he says. "You lived. That's what you were meant to do."

"I could have saved them," I whisper.

His jaw tightens. "No one can save everyone." His voice softens, almost imperceptibly. "But you saved who you could."

He holds my gaze while I push myself to stand. I sway, and without hesitation, his hand catches my elbow. Strong, grounding, the heat of him winning through the cold smoke.

At nightfall, the survivors gather in the great hall. It's supposed to be a feast of victory, but only a few sit at the long tables, much less than the room can contain. Bowls of venison stew and bread sit untouched. The silence between clinks of cutlery hangs heavier than any war drum.

Helios stands at one end, saying nothing for a long time, like he is trying to find the right kind of words. When he finally speaks, it isn't in the commanding voice I expect; it's softer, more meaningful.

"We mourn our dead," he says. "We honour their bravery. And we live because they cannot."

No cheering. No pounding of mugs. Just quiet, solid nods of people who understand that survival is both a privilege and a burden, and nothing is a guarantee.

I sit near the end of the table, Kallesie curled at my feet as much as her massive body can, my bowl of food untouched. I don't see him approach, but suddenly Helios is there, easing into the seat beside me.

"You haven't eaten," he says.

"I'm not hungry."

"You should be. Tomorrow will be worse."

"Then maybe I won't be here tomorrow." The words slip out before I can give them a second thought.

His gaze sharpens. "Don't ever say that again."

The firmness in his tone stings. But there's something else under it, something that makes my pulse skip.

He leans in, voice low so only I can hear. "If you fall, Elara … Who the hell is supposed to watch my back?"

For the first time since the Wraths arrived, I nearly smile. Almost. Then he walks away, and Kallesie and I head back to our room.

I'm still under the blankets when the heat comes. Not sound. Not footsteps.

Just that familiar pressure behind my eyes, like claws scratching around my dreams.

"Elara," Kallesie's voice purrs, a low vibration inside my skull, *"I swear to fuck, if I have to wake you up one more time, I'm flipping this bed and letting gravity handle it."*

"I hear you," I grumble, pulling the covers higher.

A pulse of irritation slams through my mind.

"No," her voice is sharp. *"You're still horizontal."*

Before I can say anything else, her paw tangles in my hair just behind my ear. Not piercing, never piercing, but tight, possessive. The sudden pull rips a scream from my throat.

"Hey. Stop. Kallesie!"

"Too late."

The grip dies just as suddenly as it appeared.

Then the world bends as the bed wobbles violently, defying gravity for half a second before flipping completely. I shriek as the mattress goes over, sheets sliding, the motion tossing me sideways before landing on the stone floor in a tangle of blankets and limbs. The impact knocks my breath clean out of me.

I lie there gasping, heart pounding, eyes wide.

The heat looms closer.

She stands over me, jaw tight, her form casting an enormous shadow, his claws flexed, her tail swaying slowly. Deliberately.

"Look at that," her voice whispers inside my head, smug and satisfied. *"You're up."*

"Ugh, Kallesie! That isn't the wake-up call I need."

"You're welcome."

My boots feel heavier than usual, and so does my chest. Every time I blink, I see flashes of the Wrath attack: teeth like sharp obsidian ridges, the smell of burning fur, and the sound of screaming. We lost people. People I should have been able to help.

By the time we navigate into the training yard, the morning frost has burned off, replaced by the heat of open flames roaring in the pit. Helios is already there, a shadow moulded from steel and firelight, giving orders to Alasdair and guards.

His steel-grey eyes find mine immediately. No smile. No welcome. Just that assessing gaze, like he's measuring what I have left in me today.

"You finally decided to join us, little archer," he says as I step into the ring.

"Oh, sure. I didn't realize punctuality is the most important survival skill. Who knew, Helios? Not me," I shot back, with more bite in my voice than I intended.

“It’s not,” he says, stepping closer. “What matters is that you’re ready for it.”

The initial drill is brutal. Kallesie and I weave through flaming barricades while I shoot arrows at moving targets with my bow from my back. I've practiced archery for years, but never while firing from a moving mount and leaping through fire. I survived the Trials by luck, but in this ring, I don’t think luck was on our side.

The first arrow misses. The second barely clips the target’s edge. By the third, my grip tightens with frustration.

Helios watches from the side, arms folded, giving no hint of approval or irritation, just an unreadable stare.

By the fourth round, he steps in. “You’re fighting her movements instead of working with them.” He gestures to Kallesie. “Loosen your hips. Trust her footing. If she fails, you fail. If you fail, she burns.”

His words slice through me, conjuring that memory of a rider screaming as her hellhound goes down in the Wrath attack, both swallowed by flames. My breath hitches, and I nearly fail the shot again.

Helios proceeds to demonstrate, but not before peeling his amethyst shirt over his head in one smooth motion. The heat of the fire kisses his bare skin, making every scar stand out, pale lines against tanned muscle. His chest rises and falls steadily, shoulders broad enough to block the flames behind him.

I don’t mean to look. God help me, I don’t. But my gaze traces the defined contour of muscle down his abdomen before I look back up.

Too late.

His mouth curves slowly, infuriatingly smug. "If you're done staring, maybe you can keep your guard up."

Heat rushes to my face, but before I can snap back, he's already mounting Vulcan. The next moment, he's low on his hellhound, every motion fluid and in sync. He fires arrows without hesitation, each one striking dead centre even as they vault over walls of fire.

When it is my turn again, he stays close enough to correct my posture, his hand briefly touching mine under the pretext of adjusting my aim. Every time I falter, he pushes me harder, making me loop the course repeatedly until my arms burn and my fingers throb from the bowstring.

At the end, sweat runs down my skin, and Kallesie's flanks heave with exertion. Helios's shirt still hangs abandoned over a fence post, and he stands before me bare chested, just a faint sheen of sweat on his torso.

"You're not there yet," he says quietly. "But you will be. Or you'll break trying."

It should sound like a threat. Instead, it feels like a promise.

HELIOS

The morning air is sharp, the kind that twists in the lungs and quickens the blood. Good training weather. My clan needs to feel their muscles ache, and their minds honed, especially after the Wrath attack.

And Elara? She needs it most of all.

She comes into the yard, her appearance weary, and her hair in all directions. The guilty glance of her hellhound tells me she must have dragged Elara out of bed. There is a heaviness in her step. Loss does that. Grief puts stones in your boots. I've seen it before, on warriors twice her age.

Her eyes meet mine. She fumes, trying to mask the slump in her shoulders with attitude. *Good. Let her use it. Anger burns longer than pity.*

"Look who finally decided to join us, little archer," I say, letting the words grind just enough to sting.

She snaps back, and I can almost see the flicker of fire in her again.

The first drill confirms what I suspect. She can shoot, but she isn't riding with Kallesie yet. The hound compensates for her rider's stiffness, which is a fast way to get them both killed in a real fight.

I let her fail. Again. And again. *She needs to taste frustration before she opens herself to correction.*

By the fourth round, I step in close enough that I can see the subtle tremor in her hand on the bowstring. "You're fighting her movements," I say. "Loosen your hips. Trust her footing. If she fails, you fail. If you fail, she burns."

Her eyes flicker with pain, memory, and the kind of fear that you can get as a fighter mid-battle while watching your friends die in front of you. I know the demons are haunting her. We all have them. But you either make them work for you, or they drag you down.

She still isn't letting go. So, I decide to force her to focus.

I pull my shirt over my head and toss it onto the fence. Heat from the pit kisses my skin, highlighting old scars. Of the demons from my past, of the violence I got to walk away from when others didn't. Her gaze snaps at me before she realizes it, and when she jerks it back up, I let the corner of my mouth curl.

"If you're done staring, maybe you can keep your guard up."

And the glare she gives me is worth it. Better than the blank look she walked in with.

I mount Vulcan and show her the way she should run the course with Kallesie. Every movement in sync, every shot clean. I stay on Vulcan; I don't give her time to overthink.

"Again," I order.

This time, I stay close, correcting her posture with brief touches, making her run until her arms tremble and her aim steadies out of sheer stubbornness.

By the end, she is flushed and sweating, strands of hair plastered to her temples. She looks at me like she wants to throw her bow at my head, but there is a spark in her eye that wasn't there this morning.

I step closer, lowering my voice so no one else can hear. "You're not there yet," I tell her. "But you will be. Or you'll break trying."

And as I walk away, leaving my shirt where it is, I know I've just set the hook deeper.

CHAPTER II

THE EDGE OF CONTROL

ELARA

The heat from the training pit curls against my skin, but it isn't just the fire that makes my pulse quicken.

Helios still hasn't put his shirt back on. He stands across from me in the sparring circle, his muscles taut, scars with stories I haven't learned yet. My stomach twists. Something about him today feels… different. I can't say why, but I know I can't hold back.

Kallesie paces beyond the ring, hackles elevating, like she can sense my nerves.

"This isn't about hitting hard," he says, circling me. "It's about control. Lose that, and you're just another corpse waiting for the Wrath to finish the job."

"I'm not losing control," I say, trying to keep my voice even.

"You're already distracted," he counters, and before I

can retort, he lunges.

Steel meets steel as I bring my blade up in time, the jolt running through my arm. He surges forward, not with brute force but with precision, every movement designed to push me exactly where he wants me.

I hate that it works.

"You're thinking too much," he says, grasping my wrist and twisting it until my blade clatters to the ground. He doesn't let go. "In an actual fight, that hesitation gets you killed."

I push him away, my cheeks burning with frustration, not from his touch.

"Again," I say.

HELIOS

She comes at me faster this time, teeth grinding, blade flashing. *Good.* The fighter in her is waking up.

But her footwork isn't what it used to be. Not because she forgot how, but because something in her hesitates now. Her balance slips when she pushes too hard, as her body second-guesses itself. The Trails left demons in her head, and sometimes they surface at the worst moments.

I let her drive me back, let her believe she's gaining ground. Then, when she overcommits, I pivot and sweep her legs out from under her.

She hits the sand with a thud and a "Fuck, Helios!"

"Sloppy," I say as I step into her space while she

scrambles up. The defiance in her eyes fades away, and it makes the corner of my mouth twitch.

I can smell the adrenaline on her and see the tremor in her grip, not from fear, but from holding back.

"Stop protecting me," I say.

Her eyes widen. "I'm not…"

"You are," I parry, knocking her blade aside and catching her by the back of the neck, holding her still. My voice drops to a low snarl. "If you can't bring yourself to hit me, you won't survive what's coming."

Something changes in her gaze. The hesitation wanes, replaced by fierce intensity and something sharper.

She twists free, drives her elbow into my ribs, and for the first time, I feel the sting of her blade nicking my arm.

Better. I smile with slow and dangerous intent. "There you are."

Her blade skims my ribs, and I don't give her time to savour the win. I hook her around the waist, momentum carrying us both into the sand hard.

She twists mid-fall, trying to pin me, but I roll us, ending with my weight braced above her.

Her chest presses against mine. Her hair is a wild mess between us—the scent of smoke and something sweet wraps around me.

"Still think I'm protecting you?" Her voice is jagged but shaky.

My gaze drops for a heartbeat to her mouth. *Dangerous*. I shift my grip, one hand curving around her wrist, the other pressing into the sand beside her head.

"You fight like you want to prove something," I rasp, "but you're still afraid of what happens when you win."

Her eyes locked on mine, softened and unflinching. "I'm afraid of what happens if I lose."

The space between us feels like a fuse burning down. The firelight dances on her skin, highlighting the gold in her eyes. For a moment, I can't tell if my racing heart is from the fight or from her.

She shifts beneath me, her knee contacts my hip, and heat shoots straight through me. My fingers squeeze on her wrist, not hard enough to hurt, but enough to remind us both who is still in control.

"Careful, little wolf," I utter, my mouth inches from hers. "You keep looking at me like that, and I'll forget we're supposed to be training."

Her lips part, not quite a smile, not quite a challenge. "I'm counting on it."

Kallesie's sudden bark breaks the moment; the sound echoes in the silence surrounding us. I push up, offering her a hand, my expression unreadable.

But as she takes it, I let my thumb brush against her palm once.

"Again," I say, but my voice is rougher now, and we both know this isn't over.

ELARA

I struggled to sleep last night, and the exhaustion still drags at me, dulling the sharp edge I usually carry. A memory surfaces unbidden of Helios's weight pressed against me, solid and steady, his warm breath brushing my skin as his low, smoky voice murmurs a warning to be careful. The echo of it lingers longer than it should.

Kallesie is pacing in the dark, her mind touching mine with restless energy.

Now, in the dim light of the morning, the training yard feels colder than usual. Helios is already here, wearing the same loose black pants as yesterday. The morning sun highlights the contour of his shoulders and back. He doesn't look up when I approach, but I know he is aware of every step I take.

"Late," he says, not bothering to look my way.

"You said dawn," I reply, keeping my voice even. "This is dawn."

He turns, steel-grey eyes pausing into mine. "If you are mine to train, you know *dawn* means before the sun."

A flash of heat stirs low in my stomach, and I hate that my body responds before my brain catches up. "Then you should actually start training me instead of—"

He moves fast. One moment I am standing, the next I'm on my back in the sand, his hand braced beside my head, his body caging mine in.

"Instead of what?" he says in a soft voice.

My heart pounds so loud that I am sure he can hear it.

"Instead of trying to intimidate me."

The corner of his mouth lifts close enough to a smile to make my pulse falter. "If I want to intimidate you, little wolf, you will know."

Before I can answer, Kallesie's voice comes through the bond, dripping with sarcasm. *"If you two are going to roll around again, I'm going to need a warning."*

I move Helios back, though the feel of his hands lingers long after he lets me go. "Let's train."

HELIOS

I told myself I would not touch her today. That yesterday's sparring had been too close, too dangerous, that I can put distance between us with discipline and focus.

And yet, every time she moves, I notice. The way her hair catches in the wind. She tilts her chin defiantly, movements intense and precise when she shoots an arrow.

She is better this morning. Her aim is steady, and her form has improved. After witnessing countless riders torn from their hellhounds during the Trails, their screams still echoing in her mind, it's no surprise she hasn't tried shooting from Kallesie back again. Every time the subject comes up, I see the hesitation creeping into her shoulders.

"Mount up," I tell her.

Her eyes flick to me, uncertain. "While moving?"

"That's the point."

She climbs onto Kallesie, and I swing up behind her

without asking. My hands skim her hips as I saddle, and she tenses.

"You'll have to learn to work with your hellhound," I whisper in her ear. "That means trusting the person behind you to cover your blind spots."

Her breath hitches. For a moment, I wonder if she knows how many kinds of blind spots I'd be willing to cover for her.

We navigate the course rings of fire, swinging targets, and I sense her heartbeat through her back against my chest. Her tits bounce with Kallesie's movements going over jumps. I don't even notice when she misses the first two shots. I am too busy checking out her amazing figure beneath the training top and tight training pants. By the third time, though, she got her groove.

When we stop, I don't immediately dismount. I stay close, my hands still resting on her hips, my mouth just a whisper from her ear. "Better."

Her pulse kicked hard against my fingertips, frantic and uneven. My hands rest on her hips, but carefully, feeling the tension that runs through her like a wire. I can sense the hesitation coils inside her, the echoes of fear she can't shake, and I hold her tighter not to control, but to steady, to remind her she's not facing it alone. I almost leaned in further.

ELARA

By the time the session ends, I am more worn from the training than he is. Every moment is a struggle. It's not about hitting targets or clearing jumps. It's more about resisting the urge to look and see how close his face actually is.

We should discuss our strategy for the next attack. Instead, we find ourselves at the weapons rack. His arm brushes against mine as he grabs a blade.

"You're unfocused," he says.

"You're distracting," I shoot back before I can stop myself.

His eyes held mine, sharp and unguarded for a second, and here comes that dangerous pull again. He takes a slow step closer, the air between us charges enough to set the torches flickering.

"Careful," he says in a gentle tone. "You start talking like that, and I'd think you actually want me to distract you."

And the worst part? I'm not sure I'd hate it.

CHAPTER 12

BETWEEN FIRE & TEETH

ELARA

Kallesie's breath blows warm against my cheek before my eyes even open. I groan and try to burrow deeper into the linens, but her paw presses down harder, heavy and deliberate and brimming with exasperation. "*This is the last fucking time I'm waking your ass up,*" Kallesie snarls, her tone sour and utterly unimpressed. *"Last time I flipped the bed, I'm running out of furniture."*

I groan again, burying my face in my pillow. Some mornings, I swear she enjoys making me suffer. My muscles ache from yesterday, my mind still tangled in the memory of Helios' words, and yet, despite everything, I can't help but smirk. Maybe some mornings are meant to hurt… or maybe they're meant to remind you that you're alive.

The air is sharp and cold, clinging to my bones. Outside the window, the sky is like black glass, dusted with stars, and the camp is quiet. All you can hear is the low growl of a hellhound now and then or the pop of the dying fire. And right there, leaning against a post, is Helios.

He looks up as I get closer. His steel-grey eyes catch the torchlight like shards of metal. "You're late," he says, though his mouth quirks, suggesting he's not truly angry.

"Blame her," I nod toward Kallesie. "She is the one who snores like a thunderstorm."

Kallesie huffs, and I can swear Helios smirks before pushing off the post. "Come on."

HELIOS

The night air slices, but the fire stirring in me when she's close isn't the weather. It's her pulse, her presence, dragging something I shouldn't let wake. I keep my steps measured, slow enough for her to match, even though I can cover twice the distance with ease.

We slip into the treeline, our hellhounds ghosting ahead. Every shadow looks deeper tonight. Wrath territory is close, and their scent rides the wind with cinder and putrefaction.

She stumbles over a root, and my hand shoots out without thinking, gripping her forearm. Her skin is warm even through the sleeve. Too warm. I should let her go. But I don't.

For one heartbeat, she looks up at me, and it feels like standing on the edge of something I can't afford to fall into.

Don't make me want this more than I already do. I release her before I do something I will regret.

Elara

We move in silence for a while, and the only sound is the crunch of frost beneath boots and paws. My bow hangs against my hip, and every time I think about raising it from Kallesie's back in an actual battle, my stomach knots.

Helios stops suddenly and crouches low. I drop beside him, trying not to notice how close his shoulder comes to mine. "We'll watch from there."

For a while, we watch and listen to the forest for any signs of danger. Then, he gestures to move ahead. The climb is steep and slick with frost. My boot slips, and before I fall, his arm snakes around my waist, hauling me upward like I weigh nothing.

For a second, my back rests against his chest, his breath warm against my ear. The world narrows to the press of him and the steady beat of his heart.

I don't move. Neither does he.

"If you stay like this, I'll fight everything inside of me and still want you to stay."

HELIOS

I release her the moment we crest the rise. The night stretches over dark hills, bare tree branches, and distance. Something shifts.

I can't tell yet if it's Wraths or the wind stirring through tree limbs. But every instinct says it's the former.

We settle in, Elara at my side, Kallesie and Vulcan sprawled low. The cold gnaws at exposed skin, so I strip off my shirt and drape it over her shoulders.

Her eyes widen, and for a second, she forgets to breathe. I can feel it.

"Better you stay warm than I," I say, but my voice is lower than I mean it to be.

ELARA

Helios has no right to look so hot right now. Not without his shirt. Not in the torchlight that shines on his bronze skin while he sits next to me, scars glistening along his ribs. Heat coils low in my stomach, and my mouth goes dry.

"You're distracting," I mutter.

His smirk says he knows exactly what he's doing.

We're quiet again, but it's not the comfortable silence from before. Every movement feels heavy as his knee touches mine. The way his hand rests near mine on the ground, close enough to touch but not quite, stirs my confusion.

Then I catch him looking at me, and the moment feels so piercing, it nearly hurts.

Helios

The line I keep almost crossing keeps looping back. I've been on battlefields where the danger was lower than it is right now.

Vulcan's growl comes like a warning.

Kallesie rises, ears flat, teeth on display. The air changes with sudden intensity, feeling electric.

In the dark below, two points of red light flicker. Then, another pair. Then, a dozen.

"Elara," he says, his voice all command now. "They're here."

Elara

The forest shifts, alive with the sound of claws on frozen ground. Shapes detach from the shadows, massive and wrong, eyes burning with Wrath light.

I grip my bow, my pulse drumming in my ears. Helios steps forward, sword flashing into his hand, his back against mine.

The first Wrath lunges, and the night shatters as it bursts through the undergrowth, its body a blur of shadow and bone. I shoot my arrow before I even register the motion, but it's too fast; my shot buries in its shoulder, not its heart.

Helios is already moving.

Steel glints in the moonlight as his blade swings in a sharp, deadly arc, cutting the creature's snarl short. Black smoke hisses from the wound, curling into the frosty night.

Kallesie leaps past me, slamming into another Wrath with a sound that's half roar, half hellhound fury.

The air is buzzing with activity. Shadows dart from the trees, jaws snap, and the ground shakes beneath their weight.

HELIOS

I keep Elara at my back, Vulcan at my side, and I strike down anything that dares to get too close. But Wraths hunt in packs, and this one is larger than most before today.

"Stay with me!" I bark, pivoting to block one that tries to flank her.

She moves well, better than she thinks, but the rawness in her stance tells me she's only faced them twice, hardly enough to be battle-hardened. Every arrow she fires finds flesh, but not always the kill shot. I fill the gaps.

Then I spot the largest Wrath yet, pushing through the line, eyes fixed on her.

Elara

Its size steals my breath—twice the mass of Kallesie, with fangs resembling ivory scythes. I notch an arrow and fire, but it shows no reaction.

Instead, it charges at me.

Helios slams into me, knocking me aside as the Wrath's claws rake the space where I stood a second ago. We hit the ground hard, tangled together, his arm around my waist, my hand fisted in his shirt.

His heat is blinding. For one impossible heartbeat, it's only him. His weight holds me down. The air fills with the smell of smoke and steel, and something that clearly reminds me of Helios.

Then his voice jolts me back.

"On your feet, Elara!"

Helios

I don't give her time to think. I haul her up, plant her behind me, and meet the Wrath head-on.

It hits like a battering ram, but I hold my ground, and the sword sinks deep into its neck. The beast thrashes, claws tearing at my side, but I drive the blade in again, harder this time.

Vulcan barrels into it from the flank, Kallesie snaps at its throat, and together we bring it down.

I don't even stop to breathe. More are coming.

ELARA

I don't have time to process the blood on my hands. Helios and I fight in sync, moving like two halves of a whole.

But there are too many. The Wraths are pressing closer, a living tide.

"Helios," I start, but my words die as the treeline beyond them flares up with more red eyes.

Dozens. Hundreds.

My grip tightens on my bow.

We are not going to survive this.

HELIOS

I step closer to her, close enough that our shoulders touch. "Stay with me," I say again, softer this time. It's a promise, not an order.

Wraths advance, gaining toward us.

And then the night is nothing but teeth, claws, and fire growls.

CHAPTER 13

Torn from You

Elara

The same teeth and claws hit us like a storm breaking over stone. Kallesie lunges forward and bites through a throat before the first scream escapes. Her force pulls me sideways, and my feet scramble for grip as firelight flickers over snapping jaws and black fur.

I keep firing, arrow after arrow, each shot a blur until a shadow bigger than the rest clashes between us.

"Helios!" I roar, but he's lost in a wall of moving bodies, his sword flashing once before vanishing.

The Wrath before me attacks. I duck, my fingers scraping the wet soil as I roll beneath it, coming up with another arrow already loaded. But more are coming. Always more.

The world narrows to survival: dodging, firing, breathing, and staying alive.

Then something slams into my back. My bow goes spinning into the dark, and claws close around my arm.

Helios

I hear her shout, and every muscle in me locks.

"Elara!"

But the Wraths surge between us; the snapping and cracking cut me off. Vulcan tears a path open, flames boiling from his jaws, but it's like trying to keep a hurricane in check. Every time we hack one down, two more take its place.

I see her for a split second; her hair catches the firelight, her bow gone, her body jerks as a Wrath's claws drag her backward.

Something inside me breaks.

I carve through the creatures with raw force, my sword an unending arc of steel, but I'm too far. I will not reach her in time.

Elara

Kallesie's snarls are the only thing that keeps me from going limp. She's on the Wrath instantly; her weight rips it off of me, but it's chaos, heat, blood, and snarling shadows.

I scramble for my bow, my heartbeat deafening my ears. My fingers grip the wood just as Kallesie lets out a shrill yelp. The sound freezes me mid-breath.

She hurts.

And if Kallesie falls, I fall with her.

HELIOS

I push forward, every step a fight through muscle and shadow, until I'm almost there.

A deep roar rips through the woods ahead.

The ground shudders. A heavier, older, darker growl rolls through the air, and the Wraths themselves falter, glancing toward the shadows.

That's when I see it. Not Wraths. Something worse.

And Elara is still too far from me.

ELARA

Sound comes back in pieces. First, the ringing. Then the dull pounding thud of my pulse. Then the screaming.

I blink hard, but the world stands still, smeared in firelight and shadow. Kallesie's growl cuts through the haze, but it distorts as though she's underwater.

I push up onto my elbows. The ground sways under me, heat licking at my skin from a burning Wrath corpse feet away. My vision clears enough to see him.

Helios.

He's sprawled on his back, half in shadow, half in light, chest still. Too still. Vulcan is down, attempting to rise with a faint growl, but clearly injured.

And between us? It.

The new Wrath crouches low, limbs contorted unnaturally, coiling with the quiet menace of something that shouldn't exist. Its eyes, like fractured amethyst shards, fixed on me. The whispering in my head swells again, grinding against my skull until it makes my stomach heave. It wants me to move first.

Kallesie slips behind it, slower than she should be, her flames dim and unsteady. She shouldn't be fighting like this, but she waits for my signal.

I tighten my hold on the bow. I could call her back. Buy us a few seconds. Run. "But Helios damn you." I huff, the words bitter on my tongue, and I'm not sure if they're meant for him or for me.

I stagger to my feet, legs like water. The Wrath twitches at my motion, claws dragging through the dirt with a sound that makes my teeth ache.

Every instinct in my body screams that I won't reach him in time.

I see his fingers twitch. Barely, but it's enough. The Wrath chases when I move, its limbs bend in that impossible way as it barrels toward me. Kallesie hits it from the side, flames blooming into a purple light, the heat so intense it steals my breath. I dive over Helios, the ground slamming into my ribs, and I grab his collar.

"Come on, come on."

He groans. The relief is so sharp it almost knocks me out

again.

The Wrath screeches and knocks Kallesie aside. That's when I notice it. The wound where my arrow hit is splitting wider, and something is moving beneath the skin.

It's not dying.

It's changing.

I don't have time to think. I hook my arms under Helios's and drag, praying to whoever God or Goddess will listen that the others see us with this creature on our asses.

The Wrath straightens. The shift spirals at an incredible speed. Spines push out along its back. Its jaw splits wider than it should. More shards of light appear where eyes should be.

And then it steps toward us.

Slow.

Purposeful.

As if it knows we can't stop it.

The Wrath's shadow swallows us.

I lift my bow, but my arms are trembling so hard I can't even keep the string steady. Kallesie is up again, but limping, her flames flaring with rage more than strength. My lungs burn, my muscles scream, and the monster's whispering fills every space in my head.

Then a hand clamps around my wrist.

"Elara," Helios rasps, voice low and ragged. His eyes lock on mine, and there's no room for argument. "Move."

Before I can react, he yanks himself upright, sways, but

quickly reaches for the black-handled axe at his hip. The movement is fluid, a terrifying speed for someone who was down just a minute ago.

The Wrath plunges.

Helios meets it head-on.

Steel bites into its spine and shards, forming a sound that turns my stomach. Yet the creature doesn't waver. It twists in midair, claws raking across Helios's ribs. His shirt tears, crimson blooming over skin, but he doesn't flinch. He twists the axe and splits the creature open in a spray of unnatural amethyst light.

"Back!" Helios barks at me without looking.

I want to argue. I want to plant my feet and fire until my quiver is empty. His movements, each strike countering the Wrath's incredible speed, show me I'd be more of a liability than help. And the damn thing is already regenerating in front of our eyes.

"Great," Kallesie snaps in my mind. *"Next time, aim for something important. Like all of it."*

Kallesie shoves her upper body into my side, pushing me back. My attention never leaves Helios. The Wrath is already stitching itself back together, with sounds of ripping and crackling as it does so. The sounds make my stomach lurch just from the sound, but witnessing it makes it worse. He's fighting like a man who knows exactly how quickly this can go wrong.

The Wrath shifts mid-combat, stretching its arm. Claws carve twin lines in the dirt, while spines rattle like bone chimes in a storm. Helios shifts his stance, blood dripping down his side, jaw clenched.

And then the ground behind the Wrath splits. Something else stirs beneath.

Helios freezes for half a breath, eyes flicking at me. “Run, Elara.”

The Earth bursts open.

Another one climbs out.

CHAPTER 14

HELP ARRIVES

ELARA

The Wrath that climbed from the shattered earth attacks. Not the one knitting itself back together behind Helios, this one is new. Its limbs snap and twist at impossible angles, like its joints were shaped from nightmare instead of flesh. Its skin shifts between shadow and slick, gleaming bone. The air around it reeks of rotting iron and burning hair. Its head, if that thing deserves the name, splits into three jagged jaws lined with teeth like broken glass.

I barely breathe, my eyes glued to the wrath as it twists and strikes, impossible limbs snapping in every direction. My stomach knots, and my fingers tighten on the bow as if gripping it harder could somehow make it less real.

"Kallesie...can we even handle this one?"

Kallesie's hackles rise under me, muscles bunched tight as bowstrings.

"Little busy here, Elara," she growls, eyes locked on the thing. *"Unless you want to be chewed up, we move."*

Helios steps in front of us, sword down. "Stay on her back. Don't get off for anything." His voice is sharp enough to pass through the terror squeezing my lungs.

The Wrath shrieks, the sound knifing straight into my skull. My vision swims, and for a second, I swear I see shapes inside its shadowy mass. Faces scream silently, then melt back into the dark.

It strikes.

Helios meets it head-on, blade arching with a sound like a whip crack. Sparks explode as steel meets claw, and the impact sends dirt and ash spinning around us.

"Kallesie, move!" I shout. We bolt sideways as a tendril of black flame whips toward us, searing the ground and leaving it scorched, looking like a spider-cracked mirror.

And then, a blur of gold and white flames tears through the chaos.

Harlow.

Zinnia crashes into the Wrath's side with the force of a meteor, her amethyst eyes blazing. The creature screams, staggering, black ichor spraying across the dirt. Harlow is already firing. Each arrow bursts into flecks of light that prick deep into its shifting hide.

"Thought you could use a hand!" she shouts over the commotion, her expression fierce and wild.

Another blow—this time sharper and faster. Alasdair's hellhound charges at the Wrath from the other side, his voice a low, menacing command as he thrusts his spear into one of its twisted limbs. "Hold the line!"

The Wrath thrashes, its form crumpling and reforming like living smoke. It shoves the hellhounds back, shrieking when a low whistle rises above everything.

In a split second, the air changes.

Smoke rolls aside, and a figure steps through the haze: tall, broad, and clad in weathered black leathers smeared with dirt and time. His hair is dark, sprinkled with silver, eyes cutting and cold as moonlit steel.

Ciaran Vale. He's part of the Legendary Summoners clan east of the Stronghold.

"When did you crawl out of your hole, you fucking grotesque creature?" Ciaran says to the Wrath, his tone almost amused, as this whole thing excites him a great deal.

Next to him walks a hellhound like no other; its fur is a deep midnight with shiny reflections like moving constellations, as if the night sky itself blended into its skin. Its eyes glow white, star-bright, and every step makes the earth reverberate.

The Wrath recoils.

"Go," Ciaran says without elaboration.

The constellation hound surges forward, every star in its fur flaring. It crashes into the Wrath, light and shadow colliding in an explosion of heat and force.

The battle turns savage. A huge group of Hellhounds bite and burn. Steel carves through twisting limbs in a last-ditch effort, sweeping dozens of hellhounds and riders off it and throwing a bunch right into the trees, killing them. More Hellhounds are on The Wrath as it gives one final squeal before it retreats into the darkness. Its shape unravels, leaving only smoke that tastes like nightmares.

Silence falls.

But it's not the silence of safety.

Helios's gaze stays fixed on the treeline where the Wrath vanished. His jaw ticks. "It's not over."

Ciaran meets his eyes. "No. It will be back."

And somewhere in the dark, I swear I hear the faint scrape of glass teeth.

Suddenly, the night feels too still.

The only sound is the crackle of dying flames and the faint groans of the wounded. The Wrath is gone, pushed into darkness by sword, fire, and by the fierce pack of the hellhounds and their riders. Yet its absence feels like a lie. The air still tastes of that unnatural cold laced with something putrid.

My bow is slack in my hands, the bowstring gnaws at my fingers, raw and bleeding, and every tug reminds me I can't afford a single mistake. But I can't stop scanning the shadows. Kallesie's massive frame feels tender at my side, her low growl vibrates through my boots. She smells the same thing I do. The evil hasn't left.

Alasdair stands nearby, barking orders to the older summoners. He wants them to move the dead summoners and hellhounds alike, not from their group, but fallen Legendary Summoners. His features are carved from granite, but there's grief in the tightness of his jaw. Harlow kneels next to Zinnia, checking a deep gash along the Hellhound's side. Her lips move, giving solid reassurance.

The battlefield is quiet now, safe for the low murmurs of the surviving Summoners. Alasdair moves among them, barking orders with the same authority as before, though the weight of loss presses in around his shoulders. The bodies of the fallen Legendary Summoner and their hellhounds lie scattered across the field. The bodies of the fallen Legendary Summoners and their hounds are slowly brought towards the group. One by one, the summoners wrap the dead in their cloaks, in which they died. The Hellhounds, too, are covered, their loyal forms carefully tucked beside their riders. Each movement is methodical, precise, and a grim choreography to honour the fallen.

When the preparations are complete, the group forms a slow procession back toward the Stronghold. They carry the cloaked bodies, hounds included, over the rough ground, careful not to disturb what little dignity remains. The weight of each body is a silent reminder of the battle that took so many lives, and of the legends now lost to history.

Helios and I hang back, giving the survivors their space. There's nothing for them here except observation and quiet respect, and we allow it. The procession moves steadily, the stronghold looming closer with every measured step, ready to receive its fallen and grant them the burial rites they earned.

Helios is a different kind of stillness. He stands in the middle of the training grounds. His shirt is torn at the collar, and his steel-grey eyes remain fixed on the treeline. He doesn't blink, doesn't speak. Just listens.

When Alasdair calls a war council, we gather in the great hall. The air inside is filled with smoke and the copper sting of blood. Torches spit and pop along the stone walls, casting uneven shadows across the table.

"It wasn't random," Alasdair says without preamble. "That was a test. It came close enough to breach our lines and then retreated before we could trap it."

Ciaran leans forward, eyes narrowed with skepticism. "You're saying it is evaluating us."

Helios braces his hands on the table's edge. "No. It already knows our strength." His voice is low and dangerous. "It's assessing our weaknesses."

The silence that follows is heavy.

I don't see him at first. Then his gaze locks on me, and I look up. When I see his eyes, the rest of the room blurs. Something sharp passes between us, like he's searching, and impossibly heavy, like he's looking for something I don't even know exists.

The meeting wraps up with quick orders. Double the patrols, strengthen the south wall, and keep the initiates inside after dark. Everyone scatters—everyone but him.

"Stay," Helios says as I turn to leave, and I know it's not a request.

Kallesie stiffens, muscles coiling as she struggles to rise. He takes a step closer, slow and deliberate, and still, he doesn't flinch. The air between us tightens, electric and dangerous.

"You froze out there," he says. "Not long, but long enough."

My chin lifts. “I still took the shot.”

His mouth warps almost into a cruel sneer. “Barely. And what if you had missed?”

“I didn’t.” My voice is tighter than I want it to be.

He studies me like he’s peeling me apart, layer by layer. “Your hellhound can’t carry both your weight and your hesitation. Next time, there won’t be the luxury of missing.”

I swallow hard. The truth of his words burns, and so does the heat in his eyes. It’s not anger; it’s more significant.

For a moment, neither of us moves. The noise of the hall fades until all I hear is my heartbeat. Then he steps back, and I can breathe again, though it doesn’t feel like a victory.

Later, Kallesie and I wait in the courtyard as the scout riders return. Dust swirls behind them, nails scraping against the stones. Their faces are dark with anger, eyes blazing, legs tight around their hounds. It’s more than unease; something dangerous simmers beneath the surface. They shout in clipped tones, sharp words snapping through the air, and even from back here, I can feel it as a tension that makes my chest tighten. Kallesie’s growl rumbles under me, hackles raised, sensing it too. “There’s more than one set of tracks,” one says, voice rattled. “It isn’t alone.”

The cold that floods my veins occurs instantly. My hand finds Kallesie’s fur.

From somewhere beyond the gates, a sound rises low at first, almost part of the wind, then it grows, many more growls, layered, all wrong. The kind that scrapes at your spine.

Helios steps out of the shadows at my side. His hand lightly touches mine before settling on his sword hilt.

“They’re closer this time,” he says in a low whisper.

And then silence.

The kind that means something is watching you.

CHAPTER 15

SHADOWS THAT DON'T BELONG

ELARA

Kallesie wakes me up before sunrise, not with her usual tail swat or impatient huff, but with a sharp growl that vibrates through my spine. I sit up, rubbing sleep from my eyes. *"What now?"* Her ears are flat, every muscle is tense, nose lifted toward the door, as if she can smell something creeping over the horizon.

The air feels amiss. Thick.

It's not the kind of chill that seeps into your bones; it's the kind that presses on your ribs, making it harder to breathe. The torches outside flicker and hiss, their flames too small and too orange.

I throw on my jacket and follow Kallesie outside. The fog rolls in heavy waves, twisting low and slow, as if it's searching for something.

Shapes ripple inside it. Not anything that belongs here.

My skin prickles as the village's usual morning sounds come from the training grounds. Hellhound barks. The clink of armour fades into a muffled, underwater hush. Only Kallesie's low, persistent growl splits the silence.

I hear it then.

A sound I can't place, a deep, low hum more in my chest than in my ears. It builds, slow and steady, until my stomach knots. The shapes in the fog move closer. At first, they are only taller shadows. Then they stretch, limbs bending in the wrong directions, moving in skips instead of steps. The fog clings to them like skin, peeling away in wet strands when they lurch forward.

One pauses at the edge of the light. I shouldn't be able to see its face through this much mist, but I do.

A jaw too long, teeth sharp like glass shards, eyes—two dying embers buried deep in an almost human skull.

Kallesie shifts, ready to vault, but I can't move.

The thing tilts its head like it's listening to something I can't hear, and before I can process, it's in motion.

It snaps forward, reality stuttering with each inch, and closing the distance in a heartbeat.

The torch nearest to us explodes in sparks.

Something massive slams into Kallesie and me, knocking the air from my lungs.

The fog swallows us whole.

I can't see. Can't breathe.

The fog presses against my skin like a wet robe, clinging, pulling at my clothes and hair as though it were alive.

Kallesie shoves against me, snarling, but something is dragging her sideways. Her claws score the earth, muscles strain under the pull of whatever is inside the mist.

Shapes flicker in the dark, too many to count. Tall, crooked silhouettes squirm in impossible arches. Their movements aren't random; they're circling us.

Hunting.

A flash of ember eyes to my left, then something screams.

Not a human scream, not an animal's either. It's high and cavernous, like metal tearing underwater. The sound spikes through my skull, and for a split second, my knees buckle.

The fog shifts. No, it's shaping itself. The swirling mist compacts and thickens until it forms a massive torso and head without legs and a void where its mouth should be, filled with teeth all the same. Its arms are streams of black vapor that split into clawlike fingers. Every part stretches as it stems from the screams it creates.

"Kallesie!" I don't know if I'm yelling at her or trying to hear myself.

She attacks and snaps at one of the claws. Her fangs bite into what should be nothing, but fog solidifies where she strikes. The claw jerks back, hissing like steam against hot iron.

Suddenly, others move, and the shapes in the mist close in. I fumble for my bow, but the string catches on my jacket. My hands are shaking so violently that I nearly drop them.

Something dark darts through the fog, right at me.

Steel flashes. Helios bursts through the fog like a storm given flesh, his amethyst shirt open at the chest, eyes lit with a fury that doesn't belong to a man.

"Elara, stay behind me!"

"I can't. Kallesie—"

Another claw comes for us. We both dodge under the claw. Helios springs up mid-swing, collides with the Wrath's arm, and detaches with sprays of ichor. The mist writhes in pain. It echoes through the fog.

Then Alasdair's war cry booms through the suffocating quiet. His hellhound slams into one of the smaller shapes, pulverizing it in a spray of ash. Harlow emerges on Zinnia's back. The hellhound's amethyst flames puncture holes in the fog, only for them to seal back within seconds.

Even with them at my side, the mist feels endless. Every time a Wrath falls, two more appear. Like clockwork. A pattern I have learned. The massive shape, the one the others seem to answer to, lets out a long, low rumble that rattles in my ribs. Its ember eyes fix on me as if it knows I'm the weakest link.

I notch an arrow and aim; my first shot goes wide. The second hits, but the fog only parts for a moment before knitting itself back together. My third shot dies against the thing's chest like I'd fired into water.

Helios glances at me over his shoulder, jaw set. "You can't kill. Not today."

Strike after strike, the legendary summoners force the fog to recoil. To slink away in shreds until the unnatural weight in the air lessens.

The shape retreats, folding into the mist as if they'd never been there at all. But the fog lingers at the edges of the clearing, pulsing like it's breathing. It hovers at the treeline, slow and deliberate, as though it's breathing in unison with my own shaky lungs.

Watching.

The air tastes metallic.

Kallesie presses against my side, but her hackles stay high. She is not fooled. Neither am I.

The Wrath isn't gone.

It's… waiting.

CHAPTER 16

ASH BETWEEN US

ELARA

I stay awake in the dark. Kallesie's warmth presses along my side. The steady rhythm of her breathing is the only anchor in a world fraying at the edges. The air is damp and cold, with the smell of smoke and earth.

A shift in the shadows makes my pulse jump.

"You're awake." Helios's voice arrives low through the gloom. A tone that slides under my skin and finds the places I don't let anyone near.

I push up on my elbows. "You move too with such silence."

He steps closer, the torchlight from outside hugging enough of his face to make the angles sharper, more serious. He's shirtless again, and I try not to notice the ripple of his muscles across his abdomen, the way his shoulders look carved from something older than stone.

"You are staring," he says.

It's not a question.

I scoff. "You wish."

He keeps moving until I must tilt my chin up to meet his eyes, those storm-grey irises fastened on me like they know exactly what I'm thinking. "You've been avoiding me since the training grounds."

"I have been busy surviving."

His mouth curves, but it isn't a smile. It's sharper than that. "You can't avoid me forever, Elara. Not out there—" He gestures toward the world beyond the walls without much clarity, "—and not here."

My heart is pounding, though I can't decide if it's irritation or something far more dangerous.

He lifts a hand, gently flicking a loose strand of hair from my cheek. The touch is light, but the air between us feels electric. We're one breath from crossing a line we won't be able to uncross.

Helios leans in, his voice low enough that only I can hear it.

"When the fire comes for you, I'll be the one who decides if you burn."

The words crackle through me, heat heaving in my chest, and then the night itself rips open.

A sound like metal screaming against stone shatters the air. Kallesie jerks upright, her hackles flaring, a guttural snarl rolling from her throat. The ground trembles under me.

Helios is already spinning toward the door in one fluid motion; every muscle coiled for violence. "Stay behind me," he snaps, and this time there's no teasing in his voice, only the steel of a commander bracing for war.

Outside, the fog isn't fog anymore. It's shaping itself. Long, jointed limbs like broken scythes creep through the mist, glistening wet. The Wrath is here; a new, wrong, and incredible form is now complete. It's bigger than the others and more unpredictable.

And it's coming straight for us.

The Wrath lurches into full view, the fog peeling away to reveal a nightmare that shouldn't exist.

Its body is too long; spine arched in unnatural peaks beneath skin that ripples like wet leather. A head, or something pretending to be one, tilts toward us. The maw splits not into a mouth but into jagged seams of teeth that grind in slow, calculated hunger. The sound of it is worse than its shape. Wet. Scraping.

Helios doesn't hesitate. One moment he's in front of me, the next his amethyst flame erupts, turning the mist into violent, swirling light. The Wrath jerks back, limbs folding wrong, then springing forward again.

Kallesie launches her body, a streak of violet in chaos, teeth snapping for the thing's spine.

I draw my bow. Breath shallows in my lungs. Every lesson my grandmother drilled into me snaps to life: stance, aim, focus. The arrow flies, burying deep into where its shoulder should be. Black fluid hisses out, eating the grass beneath it.

"Again!" Helios's voice booms over the roar, but it's not

the same kind of authority as before. This one is life or death.

The Wrath swipes, a limb defacing a wooden post like it's nothing. Another arrow sings from my bow, but it keeps coming.

A second flame flashes through the fog. Alasdair charges in with a blade wreathed in crimson fire. The older Legendary Hounds thunder behind him, snarling, their jaws lock onto the Wrath's limbs.

Zinnia's magic snaps in the air like breaking glass, deep green wrapped around the creature's torso, holding it just long enough for Harlow's whip to lash across its back. The sound it makes is completely wrong. Almost human.

Still, it doesn't die. It stumbles, shreds of mist pouring from its wounds, and then it's gone, vanished into the darkness as quickly as it came.

Silence drops, heavy and trembling. The scent of blood and scorched earth fills the air.

My bow arm lowers, muscles aching, but my chest is tight for an entirely different reason. Helios looks at me, a storm brewing in his eyes. For a moment, it looks like he will say something about what happened between us.

But he only says, "This isn't over."

And the worst part is … I don't think he's talking about the Wrath.

The hall is quieter than it should be. The air carries the faint scent of blood and smoke, combined with the heavy weight of exhaustion. Survivors gather in small, tired groups. They tend to wounds, share quiet conversations, and keep their voices low. They know the Wraths might hear us if we speak too loudly.

I sit in the far corner, examining my bowstring. While I focus on avoiding the faces we lost.

Footsteps approach, unhurried, heavy, and deliberate.

I know it's him before I raise my lashes. Helios stops in front of me, close enough that the faint heat radiating off him seeps into my skin.

He's fresh from the training yard, shirtless, his skin still damp from exertion, with superficial nicks that haven't been bandaged yet. The low torchlight glimmers on his chest and shoulders, catching the sweat sliding down his skin.

I try to focus on my bow, but I fail.

"You've been hiding," he says, voice low-pitched not for secrecy, but because it cuts deeper.

"I'm not hiding." My voice is steady. Mostly.

Actually, I am hiding from him as I try to process what we just saw with that Wrath changing forms.

His gaze dips to my mouth, then back up to my eyes. He tilts his head, resembling a predator deciding whether you are worth the chase. "You don't look at me when you lie."

My pulse jumps. "I'm not lying."

He steps closer. Not close enough to touch me yet, but close enough that the pull of his presence draws me in like a moth to a flame. "You could've sought me out. You didn't."

I set my bow down with haste.

"We've all been busy."

He leans in a fraction more, his voice dropping to something almost daring. "Don't make excuses, Elara. You're better than that."

The words hit harder than they should have. I tell myself it's Helios being Helios—blunt, commanding. His fingers casually touch my forearm. It feels like he's testing how much contact I'll allow before I pull back. And I don't move.

"Next time," he says in a low voice, "find me first."

And then, when I'm ready to step forward and close the space between us, he steps back and walks past me. His shoulder rubs against mine as he

leaves, slow, and for some reason, it feels full of intent, as if he isn't the reason my heartbeat is going haywire.

He is gone before I can breathe again.

The heat he leaves in his wake lingers far longer than it should.

Kallesie and I make our way to our room. My thoughts are all jumbled. Kallesie, all smug and knowing, *"I've seen more effort put into hide-and-seek, Elara."*

She won't let this go, and neither will Helios.

CHAPTER 17

TANGLED

ELARA

The training grounds smell of sweat, dirt, and the faint tang of steel. I'm still panting, my body pressed against Helios's. Kallesie paces beyond us, tail wagging restlessly. As we are working on hand-to-hand combat. His arm locks around my waist, holding me in place from our sparring maneuver. We sit here not moving, just breathing heavily.

"Not bad," he says, the words blazing through me like fire, warm and tormenting. His breath wafts on my temple, and I swear my pulse is louder than the clatter from the initiates' weapons.

I open my mouth to fire back something clever, something that will put space between us, when a voice comes through.

"Well," Harlow drawls, "either I walked in on the slowest disarm in history, or I'm interrupting something much more interesting."

My head snaps toward her. She's leaning against the fence, arms crossed, her grin far too satisfied for someone who claims to be an observer.

Helios doesn't move. If anything, his grip on my waist tightens enough that I feel it. "Training," he says, voice flat, but there's a flicker of something dangerous in his eyes. A warning. Or a promise, maybe?

I nudge his shoulder, though he's slow to release me, and I scramble to my feet. "It's not like that."

Harlow's smirk deepens. "If you say so, Sunshine."

Helios rises with infuriating calm, dusting himself off. "We're done here."

He says, though his eyes linger on me for a heartbeat too long, firing a flush right into my cheeks.

Later, the weapons are put away, and the others have gone. I'm leaning against the courtyard wall, trying to breathe past the tangle in my chest. The village feels quieter than it should. Everyone's moving slowly, mindful of the bruises and wounds—both seen and unseen—from the last battle.

Harlow sidles up beside me, offering a skin of water. "You fight well," she says, then after a beat adds in a quieter tone, "and you're not fooling me."

I frown. "About what?"

"About him." She doesn't have to say his name. "You think I don't see the way he looks at you? Like he'd take on every Wrath in the Highlands if it meant you keep breathing?"

My throat goes tight. "It's not," I say. The words feel awkward and misleading.

Harlow pats my shoulder. "Whatever you say, Sunshine."

And then she's gone, leaving me alone. I can still hear the distant clang of the blacksmith's hammer. Helios's fading warmth lingers on my waist, like a mark on my skin, while the village falls silent, bracing for whatever is coming next.

The corridor is dim and narrow, its stone walls stealing away the last of the firelight from the main hall. My boots have little time to stop before Harlow's hand grabs my arm and pulls me into the alcove by the spiral stairs. "Don't even try to run," she says, her tone light but the grip on my sleeve firm. "You've been dodging me for three days, Elara."

"I haven't been dodging," I lie, because it's easier than the truth. My heart is already pounding, and not because of her.

She leans in, eyes narrowing like she's trying to read the thoughts right off my face. "You've got that look again."

"What look?"

"The one that says you are thinking about him."

I almost choke. "Harlow…"

"Oh, don't you 'Harlow' me." She folds her arms, satisfaction written all over her face. "You're not fooling anyone. The way you watch him and the way he watches you…"

Kallesie's voice seeps in from behind us, dripping with mischief. *"I knew it. I told Vulcan you are swooning over him."*

I groan, *"Kallesie, please…"*

She slides between us, all smirk and sharp eyes. "*Oh, don't worry, I'm not judging. I want to know when you're going to stop pretending. You're less than two seconds away from combusting every time he stands too close."*

I groan aloud.

Harlow says, "You're getting it from Kallesie and me, aren't you?"

All I do is turn crimson.

"Mm-m." Kallesie tips her nose toward the far end of the hall, where someone has cracked open the training ground doors. "Speaking of storms—"

I glance before I can stop myself. He's there, leaning against the stone frame as if the scene is painted just to ruin me. The torchlight makes his steel-grey eyes look as if they could penetrate anything.

Kallesie catches the way my gaze lingers and grins like a cat catching sight of cream. *"Oh, that explains it."*

Harlow folds her arms tighter. "Admit it, Elara. You like him. You more than like him."

The air feels too thin in the alcove. I shake my head, but the fever in my cheeks gives me away. "It's… complicated."

Kallesie gives me a mental picture of her rolling her eyes. *"Translation: "Yes, I'm deeply into him, but I'm going to wrap it in twenty layers of denial."*

Harlow steps closer, her voice softening but still relentless. "You can't keep it locked down forever. He's not the kind of man you keep at a distance."

I press my lips together, searching for some way to escape without handing them the victory. "It's not that simple."

Kallesie smirks. *"It's exactly that simple."*

What I don't see … what neither of them notices … is that Helios has moved closer. Silent. Patient. Close enough to catch the thread of our words, leaning on the shadows like he was born from them.

Harlow doesn't notice him yet, but I do.

The way his presence seems to pull at the air makes it impossible not to. He stands in the shadowed archway a few steps away. Hands in his pockets, he looks unreadable except for a faint smile tugging the corner of his mouth. He knows exactly what's happening. And he's not leaving.

"Ohhh. This is getting interesting," Kallesie purrs in my head. "*Now you can humiliate yourself in front of him and me. Two birds, one mortified Elara."*

"I don't—" My voice catches. I force my eyes back to Harlow. "It's not like that…"

"You don't flinch for anyone else," Harlow says softly.

"So why him?"

"Or under your clothes in your daydreams," Kallesie chimes in with a wicked tone.

"*Kallesie, shut up."*

My cheeks go red because both have a point.

"To be clear," Harlow says, her brow lifting, "I'm not talking to her."

Helios shifts his weight against the archway, the sound soft but enough to draw Harlow's glance. She freezes for a moment of recognition, then her mouth curves in a slow, knowing smile.

She doesn't call him out. She doesn't have to.

"You know what," she says, stepping back just enough to give me some space, "you should tell him yourself."

"Yes," Kallesie croons in my skull. "*Yes, please tell him. I'll supply the dramatic background music."*

Helios stills without a word. He's content to let the silence stretch and to let me stew in it. Slowly, he straightens from the archway. Each step toward me feels like he is deciding how much space to take.

"That's an interesting conversation to overhear," he says, voice low, running down my spine. "Makes a man wonder what else is being said when he's not in the room."

I open my mouth, but all I can manage is some nonsense blabber.

He stops shy of touching me, eyes locked on mine, steel grey and unblinking. "Careful, Elara," he murmurs, the faintest hint of a smirk arching his lips. "If you keep talking like that, I might start believing you."

My pulse is in my throat. I hate the thought of him hearing it.

Harlow grins like she's seen her favourite scene in a play.

"Ohhh, he's good," Kallesie sings in my mind. "*And*

you're hopeless."

Helios doesn't wait for my defense. He leans a fraction closer, his breath hot in my ear. "We'll finish this later," and then he's gone, leaving heat in his wake and my thoughts in shambles.

CHAPTER 18

IN HIS HANDS

ELARA

I wait a beat longer than I should before moving. Kallesie, a familiar presence, presses against my thoughts, sharp and unimpressed. *"If we're late again, they're going to start placing bets on whether you froze or died."*

A breath slips out of me as half a laugh. I push off the wall and start walking.

The corridor stretches ahead, dim and narrow, torches burning low enough to drag the shadows into claws. Kallesie walks along on my left, her presence warm and watchful in my mind, even when her paws make no sound on the stone. One ear flicks back toward me.

Harlow falls into step on my right.

"Well," Harlow says brightly, clapping her hands once. "That was fun. Nothing like a near emotional collapse in a hallway to really get the blood pumping."

"I'm fine," I mutter.

She hums. "You are upright. That's a technicality."

Kallesie snorts into my thoughts. *"You stop responding. I consider biting someone. Possibly you. For science."*

"Don't," I think.

"Rude," she replies. *"I'm trying to help."*

"I am thinking," I say aloud.

"Ah. That explains it," Harlow says. "You should put up a warning sign."

I glance at her. "Why are you like this?"

"Because if I don't say it," she replies easily, "you'll shove it down and pretend it isn't happening. And I don't have the patience to watch you implode later."

The corridor curves toward the main hall, and the sound swells; voices overlapping, boots scraping stone, the low hum that always comes right before everything goes wrong.

"I hate this part," Kallesie says in my mind. *"Right before the doors open and everyone pretends they're not afraid."*

"*Wow,*" I say, "*Optimism is really your brand today.*"

I slow down when the doors come into view. The hall isn't full yet, still breathing, still calm, but it won't stay that way. The restless pulling under my skin tightens.

Harlow notices. Of course she does.

She steps half a pace ahead, forcing me to stop. "Hey."

"What," I say, already bracing.

Her sarcasm drops just enough to sting. "When he walks in, don't do anything stupid."

"I never do anything stupid."

Kallesie cuts in immediately. *"Objectively false. I have notes."*

"You're both traitors," I say.

"You don't let anyone else get under your skin," she says. "Don't start now."

The words land more heavily than they should.

"I won't," I say, because it's easier than unpacking the truth.

"Good." She steps back, all casual again.

"Because I really don't feel like dragging you out by your hair today."

I reach for the doors. Noise, smoke, and anticipation rush to meet us.

Behind us, footsteps echo measured, unhurried. I don't turn.

Not yet.

Helios doesn't announce himself. He closes the gap, every step is careful, until I'm pinned against the cool stone and his solid body.

"You looked like you wanted to say something earlier?" he says, voice low, rough at the edges. "I'm giving you the chance to say it now."

I have to steady my voice. "I don't know what you thought you heard…"

"I know exactly what I heard." His palm braces against the wall beside my head, caging me in without even touching me. "And you've been holding it in long enough."

"Oh, you're cornered now," Kallesie hums in my head with mischief. *"I need some popcorn."*

My pulse trips over itself. "It's … complicated."

"Complicated is a word people use when they're afraid to say the truth." His gaze is ruthless, catching every flicker in my expression. "So, tell me. Am I wrong?"

Harlow's voice drifts from the next archway, amusement hidden. "Careful, Helios. If you push too hard, she might bite."

His eyes never leave mine. "I want her to."

Suddenly, the air feels suffocating. I can sense something risky between us—something like a too-easy-to-cross fine line separating backing off and getting closer.

"Say it," Kallesie presses. "*Or I swear I will do it*."

Something in me snaps. "Fine. I want you, Helios." The words tear free before I can choke them back, sharp and hot. "You're in my head, in my skin. Half the time, I can't think straight because of you. There. Is that what you want to hear?"

Silence floods in, heavy as smoke. His jaw flexes. And then, slow as molten lava, that infuriating, knowing smile curves his mouth.

"Exactly," he murmurs.

Harlow's mouth is wide open in shock that I admit to it after it took her and Kallesie about a half hour to get it out of me.

His smile hangs there, lazy, before he closes the last inch between us.

The wall at my back is all cool stone. The heat in front of me is all Helios. His chest touches mine as he leans in, his voice low enough to reverberate in my bones.

"You have no idea how long I've wanted to hear you say that."

My breath stutters. "Why?"

His fingers curl around my wrist, just enough pressure to make my pulse leap beneath his touch. "Because," he says, "now I know. And knowing means I get to take my time."

"Ohhh, that's cruel," Kallesie all but purrs inside my head. *"I approve."*

"Time?" My voice comes out unsteady, half challenge, half plea.

His gaze drops to my mouth and hovers there until my skin burns under it. "Time to see how much you mean it. Time to make you say it again and again."

I swallow hard. My whole body feels wired tight, as if moving in either direction would shatter me. "Helios…"

He leans close enough that his lips graze my ear. "Not yet."

Then he pulls back enough for the air between us to rush in and cool my fevered skin. His eyes gleam, smug and unreadable all at once, like he's set something in motion that only he knows the pace of.

"You'll come to me," he says in an uncomplicated manner. "And when you do, we'll see just how far we burn."

He turns, leaving me against the wall. Nothing holds me there but his echo. My breath is unsteady, and my pulse won't slow.

"He's going to be the death of you," Kallesie hums, *"far too pleased. And I strongly support it."*

By the time I make it back to the main hall after we meet with Helios, my pulse is still an uneven drum in my ears.

The others are gathered. Maps spread across the table; the air is heavy with strategy. I should focus. I'm not.

Because he is here.

Helios is leaning one hip against the table; head bent toward Alasdair as they speak in low tones. His hair shines in the lamplight. His sharp expression is commanding until his gaze meets mine.

It's not a look.

It's a touch.

A deliberate sweep from my eyes to my mouth and back again, slow enough to make heat coil low in my stomach.

Kallesie's voice threads through my mind like silk. *"Ohhh, he's playing with you. That's a hunter's stare if I've ever seen one."*

I grip the back of the nearest chair like it's an anchor. *"Don't start."*

"Too late, sugarplum. I'm already halfway through the popcorn."

Harlow slides up beside me, passing me a cup of water like she's doing me a favour. "You're flushed," she murmurs, eyes flicking toward Helios. "Battle adrenaline?"

I take the drink, trying not to choke on it. "Something like that."

Across the room, Helios says something to Alasdair, then straightens. He slowly crosses the space, not looking at me until the last moment. Then, he smiles at me so faintly that it feels like our little secret.

"Everything all right?" he says, his voice smooth and overly casual.

"Yes." The word comes out sharper than I mean it to, which only makes the corners of his mouth curve higher.

"Careful," Kallesie warns with mocking gravity. "*That man knows exactly what kind of spell he's weaving."*

Helios glances toward the table. "Good. We'll need you in shape for the next move." His gaze stays just a moment longer than needed. Then he turns away, leaving his scent in the air, and my thoughts are jumbled.

Harlow leans in, whispering loud enough for me to hear over the shuffle of papers. "You really need to do something about this matter."

"Agreed," Kallesie says smugly. "*Preferably something that involves a locked door."*

I take a slow breath, forcing my attention back to the plans for the patrol schedule. However, my body hums with the memory of being cornered. I remember his breath against my skin, and the promise in his voice.

This is not over.

Not even close.

The meeting drags on longer than it should. Patrol schedules are rearranged, routes redrawn, and names shifted between watch rotations. I listen, contribute when needed, but my attention keeps snagging on Helios across the table—calm, focused, unreadable. If he notices me watching him, he gives nothing away.

Alasdair leans back, arms crossed. "The borders have been too quiet," he says. "That never lasts."

Helios nods once. "Agreed. We don't wait for an attack to remind us what we should already be prepared for."

My spine straightens instinctively. "Additional training cycles," I say. "Not just combat coordination. Response drills. If something hits us, it won't come politely."

A flicker of approval passes through Helios' eyes before he hides it away. "The clan needs to move as one," he says. "We perfect our skills now, while we have the luxury of time."

Alasdair exhales through his nose, already convinced. "Then it's settled. More training. Harder rotations. No complacency."

Murmurs of agreement ripple through the room.

The meeting breaks soon after, chairs scraping back, voices overlap as people filter out. Duty settles over everything like a familiar weight—steady, grounding, unavoidable.

As I rise, I feel it again.

The pull.

And that somehow makes it worse.

Helios says, "We'll start at dawn."

I internally groan. I hate early morning training. "Good," I say. "I expect our group will be exhausted."

His eyes hold mine longer than necessary. "I wouldn't expect anything less."

Then he turns away.

And the air he leaves behind feels thinner than before.

By the time they finally leave me alone, I'm wrecked. Every muscle aches, my head pounds, and my thoughts feel like they've been dragged through fire. I barely make it to bed, plopping on it harder than necessary.

"Well," Kallesie murmurs from somewhere in my exhausted mind, *"that went terribly bad. Ten out of ten for emotional ambush, though."*

I don't have it in me to snark back at her. That alone says too much.

His name still glows under my skin, stubborn and warm, no matter how hard I try to smother it. I press my palms into the mattress, grounding myself in the pain. My chest feels too tight. Too exposed.

"You could stop pretending," Kallesie adds. I can hear the smirk in her voice. *"Just a suggestion. You're exhausting even me."*

"Shut up," I whisper, but there's no firmness in it. She settles, an invisible weight behind me—calm and real. Protective. Present. The kind of gentleness she only offers when I'm on the edge of breaking.

I close my eyes, breath shuddering out of me. I don't have the strength to deny it anymore. Not to her. Not to myself.

"Took you long enough," Kallesie says gently. And that's when I realize I'm not scared of what I feel for Helios. I'm scared of what comes next.

Kallesie draws closer, her presence tender yet solid, like she's bracing for impact. *"Tomorrow's going to be unpleasant,"* she says.

"You're enjoying this," I mutter.

"Immensely."

I close my eyes, knowing rest is the only thing standing between me and completely unravelling. The truth is already awake inside me. It doesn't need my attention to exist. Then sleep takes me.

CHAPTER 19

LONG GAME

ELARA

When morning arrives, I know Harlow will be absolutely thrilled to remind me that I finally came clean about my feelings for Helios.

But I'm no longer in denial.

The hall feels changed, somehow quieter and less busy, no guards running around. The air isn't suffocating with tension. There are fewer wounded guards. Instead of whispers, there's more purposeful movement. Plans are being decided.

Helios stands at the head of the table. He scans the room, and his rough, commanding voice makes people listen.

Unfortunately, it also makes my stomach knot in inappropriate ways.

"…Elara will be on the perimeter with me," he says, like it's the most logical thing in the world.

My head jerks up. "Since when?"

"Since I decided," he replies calmly, his eyes lock on mine. "Problem?"

"No."

Yes.

Absolutely yes.

From somewhere near the doorway, Kallesie's voice purrs in my head. "*Ooooh, paired duty. How'd that happen?*"

Helios walks around the table. He explains routes with hand gestures, nearly touching mine as he goes by. It's nothing. Completely innocent.

Except it is not.

He knows exactly where my skin is and exactly how close he can get without obvious contact.

When he leans over the map beside me, his arm cages me in without quite boxing me. His voice drops low, pitched so only I can hear. "You're distracted."

"I'm not," I whisper back.

He smiles, that slow, deliberate smile that makes my pulse stutter. "Good. Stay that way, and you'll miss the flanking pattern."

"Flanking pattern, my tail," Kallesie mutters. "*He's about to besiege your walls.*"

I ignore her and focus on the map, except my body is far too aware of the warmth that radiates from him.

In a perfectly public and professional tone, Helios says, "We'll need to move quickly, Elara. I trust you can keep up?"

Half the room chuckles at the jab. He's given them no reason to suspect anything else, but the glint in his eyes tells me exactly what he's doing, turning our private tension into an unspoken game in front of everyone.

And damn it, I'm already losing.

The forest is quiet in a way that makes you listen harder.

Every step on the damp ground feels louder than it should be, though that could be the blood pounding in my ears.

Helios walks ahead of me. The afternoon light glints off his dark hair. His tall figure is hard to miss. He could be a shadow or a storm; either way, I'm the idiot standing in the path of it.

"You're quiet," he says without turning.

"I'm watching for movement."

"Mm." A hum that is not in agreement. "You'rc watching something."

I don't answer. He slows until we're side by side. He smells of smoke, pine, and something warmer that wraps around me like it's got claws.

"Want to tell me what's got your attention?" he murmurs.

"Not really."

"Then I'll guess." He steps closer, the kind of close where you feel the heat before you see the shift. His steel-grey eyes lock on mine, and my breath snags.

From somewhere deep in my skull, Kallesie's voice rolls through like lazy thunder. *"Finally, it took you long enough."*

He tilts his head, studying me like I'm something he's been tracking for hours and caught in his sights. "Your heart's giving you away," he says in a gentle tone. "It's fast."

"It's cold," I lied.

"It's not cold." His hand grazes my arm. His fingers trail down until his palm circles my wrist. It's light but strong, saying I won't move unless he allows it. "It is fast because of me."

The admission hovers on my tongue, stupid and reckless.

His gaze drops to my mouth. That's all it takes for my body to lean in before my mind can stop it. The space between us feels empty, the forest could burn down around us, and neither of us would notice. The only thing I can focus on is him.

He closes the last inch. Not a kiss, not yet, but the scrape of his breath over my lips is enough to set every nerve on fire.

"Say it," he murmurs.

My heart trips, stumbles, and tries to recover. "What?"

"That you want this."

From the back of my mind, Kallesie has a vicious grin. "*Do it, huntress."*

I don't say yes. I don't say no. Instead, I grab his collar and drag him the rest of the way in.

The kiss is not polite; it's the clash of heat and teeth that steals air and leaves no room for sense. His hand fists in my hair, tilting my head, taking more. Mine digs into the muscle of his shoulder, holding him like I'll fall otherwise.

When we finally break, both breathing hard, he rests his forehead against mine.

"This changes everything," he says.

"I know," I whisper.

The night air rolls cold off the hills, the grass whispering beneath Kallesie's paws as she pads ahead. Her amethyst eyes flick back at me now and then, like she knows where my mind is. It's definitely not on the patrol route.

"You're thinking about him again." Kallesie's voice purrs through my mind, all smug and knowing.

"I am not."

"Oh, please. You've been tracking his movements instead of the treeline for the last mile. If you're going to drool, at least try to keep your jaw shut before a bug flies in."

I glare at her ears, but it's pointless. Her tail flicks with wicked enjoyment.

Vulcan's heavy steps keep pace with ours, the deep rumble of his breath blending into the silence. Helios rides beside me, calm, controlled, impossible close.

He walks in step so close that our knees almost touch. His arm hangs loosely at his side, but I can feel the heat in each careful movement.

"You drift when you're distracted," he says, voice low, almost a growl. "Out here, that gets you killed."

My jaw tightens. "I'm not distracted."

He glances at me, his eyes catching the moonlight. "No? Then you won't mind me testing that."

Before I can fire back, he leans slightly, and the world narrows to the warmth of him beside me. His scent drifts through the air. His shoulder presses against mine, every movement a quiet claim.

"He's hunting you," Kallesie sing-songs, she's enjoying this far too much.

"Helios," I warn, though my voice sounds nothing like a warning.

He smiles, not just a quick grin. It's almost predatory, like he knows just how deep he's under my skin.

"You're quick with a bow," he murmurs, "but how long would you last with me this close?"

The air sizzles between us. Our steps pull us closer until Vulcan's growl slices through like a knife.

Kallesie freezes; her muscles coil.

My pulse slams from desire to instinct in a single beat.

Something's out there. Watching.

His hand drops to the hilt at his hip, his body shifting so he's between me and the dark forest. The heat between us doesn't vanish; it changes. Sharper. Ready.

Kallesie's voice loses its teasing edge. *"That's no deer, Elara."*

The shadows ahead twist, and the forest goes still.

CHAPTER 20

Teeth in the Dark

Elara

The calm before the storm comes to mind, and it strikes worse than the sound—every leaf and every blade of grass is still. Vulcan's hackles rise, amethyst flames licking along his spine. Kallesie's stance mirrors his: low and lethal. *"It's circling us,"* she warns, her voice razor-sharp. *"It knows you're distracted."*

Helios's eyes lock on mine for a second, but it's enough to send that electric pull surging again. Even now, with something out there, the connection between us is like a live wire.

"Stay on my flank," he orders, moving forward without breaking eye contact. My breath hitches because his tone isn't commanding; it's possessive. I fall beside him, bow in hand, arrow ready. My senses split between the night and his presence, wrapping around me like warmth before a storm.

A shape slips between the trees, too large for a wolf, too fast for a bear, and my heart staggers.

"Not natural," Kallesie hissed. *"Not alive, either."*

The thing comes again, closer this time, its eyes glowing like coals. The smell hits—rot and wet earth, and bile rises in my throat.

Helios doesn't hesitate. His hand comes out, catching my wrist, steadying me.

"Breathe, Elara."

"I am breathing."

"Not enough." His grip tightens, and it's infuriating that in the middle of this, the heat in his touch still sets fire to my veins.

The creature attacks from the shadows, all bone and black sinew, a twisted mockery of a wolf. Vulcan roars forward, fire spilling from his jaws. Kallesie is right behind him, a blur of flame and fang.

"On my mark," Helios growls.

I draw, the bowstring bites into my fingers, every muscle thrumming. He doesn't look at the target; he looks at me.

"Now."

We release together. My arrow strikes the wrath in the chest, and Vulcan's fire swallows it, the air filling with the acid stench of burning corruption.

Silence crashes back, broken only by our ragged breathing.

Helios steps so close that my bow gets stuck between us.

His voice is low and dangerous. "Still think you are not distracted?"

I swallow, pulse hammering for more than one reason. "A little."

His smirk is slow and wicked. "Good. I like a challenge."

Kallesie groans in my mind. "*Oh, for hell's sake, can you two save the flirting until after we're sure there aren't more of those things?*"

The night feels too open, like the dark is holding its breath, waiting for another chance.

Kallesie's mind-voice is all sharp edges. *"Two more out there. I can smell them. One to the east, one trailing."*

Vulcan rumbles, his flames guttering like he's ready to explode.

Helios looks toward the treeline, then back at me. His steel-grey eyes reflect the soft purple glow of the fire.

"East first," he says, stepping so close that our shoulders nearly touch. It's a casual move on the surface, but the heat that rolls off him isn't casual at all.

We move together, hellhounds fanning out in silent formation. My bow is ready, every finger gripping the string, waiting.

"You're still rattled," he murmurs.

"I'm fine."

"Liar." He dips his head closer, his breath a whisper along my ear. "You think I didn't hear your heartbeat change back there?"

Kallesie snickers in my head. *"Oh, she knows you did. She doesn't want to admit why."*

A snap of branches cracks through the charged air. Something is moving fast. Too fast for a deer.

Helios doesn't break stride. He circles behind me, glides his hand down my arm until it rests at my elbow, guiding my aim. "Don't think, just feel it."

The creature bursts into view, a second warped wolf-thing, its body stitched with shadow. Before I shoot the arrow, Helios speaks again, his voice intense, "Show me what you can do when you're not holding back."

I release. The arrow pierces through its skull, and Vulcan's flames reduce it to ash.

Silence again. Except for the thud of my pulse. Helios steps in front of me, close enough to blot out the rest of the world. "Better," he says, his voice rough. "Much better." His smirk curves with a deliberate slowness. Kallesie groans in my mind. *"If you two keep this up, I'm charging rent for the front-row seat."*

The night wraps around us, heavy and dark. The forest smells of damp, pine, and burnt flesh, the remains of the Wrath smoldering quietly.

Kallesie's voice flicks sharp in my skull. *"One left. Close. Feels like it's waiting for you to find it."*

Vulcan growls softly. His flames are tight and controlled, as if he's holding himself back.

Helios tips his chin toward the shadowed, coated trees. "We flesh it out together." His tone is all command, but the careful alignment of his movements with mine says anything but.

The trail leads us into a narrow forest. Branches snag at our shoulders, and shadows press close. Helios stays by my side, heat radiating from him with every step.

"You're walking too openly," he murmurs near my ear. "Narrow your stance. Keep your balance."

I shift, and his hand settles on my waist for a moment, steadying me. The contact is searing. Kallesie hums in my head. "*He's either training you ... or hunting you.*"

My pulse kicks. "Helios…"

Something moves ahead, a blur between the trees, at a speed that makes it difficult to catch clearly. We freeze, listening to the faint scrape of claws on bark.

Helios leans in, lips nearly brushing my temple. "It's stalking us."

I almost laughed. "Us?"

"Fine," he says, his voice low and dark. "It's stalking you. I'm just the one who's going to take it apart."

Before I can answer, the shadow lunges. Helios already moves his arm and sweeps it around my waist, pulling me close. Then pivots us away from the strike zone. Vulcan slams into the creature from the side, and Kallesie's fire snaps after him in a bright arc.

The thing snarls, but it's already burning. We're still

pressed together when the forest goes quiet again. Neither of us moves.

"You're breathing fast," he says.

"That was too close," I answer, forcing my voice to steady.

A slow, knowing curve touches his mouth. "You'd be surprised."

Kallesie sighs in my mind. *"I'm telling you, one of you is going to combust before the enemy even gets the chance to kill us."*

The hunt should be over, but it isn't. The scent is still there, faintly, and moves against the wind. Kallesie growls in my skull. *"Not the same kind. Bigger. Meaner."*

Helios doesn't speak, but his gaze flicks to me, telling me without words to stay close. Vulcan's flames burn hotter now, casting jagged shadows against the trees.

The forest narrows around us, leading into a ravine choked with rocks and tangled roots. My boots slip once, and his hand shoots out, gripping my arm before I can stumble. He doesn't let go, even when I find my footing.

A low rumble rolls through the dark, and before I can pinpoint it, the ground shakes. The thing is here.

"Move." Helios shoves me sideways into the brush. The space, which is just wide enough for one person, now accommodates two. We're pressed chest-to-chest, his breath hot against my cheek, his arm braced over my head to keep us both wedged in. The creature's claws scrape over the stone right outside.

Kallesie's voice is a smug whisper. *"Oh, now this is*

interesting."

His eyes look into mine in the narrow light. Heat flows through them like a fuse ready to explode. "Don't move," he murmurs, but the words sound like a promise more than an order. I try to control my breathing. I fail.

Outside, Vulcan's growl deepens, and the sound of tearing wood echoes. The creature drifts further away. Still, Helios doesn't move, and neither do I

"You're shaking," he says, his tone both teasing and predatory.

"Adrenaline," I whisper.

His mouth curves in a gentle arc. "Sure, it is."

The danger passes, but he doesn't step back right away. Instead, his thumb grazes the inside of my wrist with intention. When he finally does move, the cold rush of air between us feels worse than the threat outside.

Kallesie sighs in my mind. *"If he doesn't finish what he's started soon, I'm filing a complaint with the universe."*

The creature isn't alone.

The sound comes first, cutting through the air… a ragged, wet snarl echoing through the ravine. Vulcan's flames flare, bathing the rock in light, while Kallesie's voice is sharp in my head. *"Two. Three. All of them are hungry."*

Helios doesn't hesitate. He steps in front of me, steel flashing as he draws his blade, but I move right with him, my bow already nocked and ready. The scent of him and the underlying warmth wrap around me even as the danger surges closer.

The first one bursts from the shadows.

It's bigger than the last, its hide mottled with scars, eyes burning red. Helios meets it head-on, his strike brutal and clean, forcing it back, while I pivot to cover his flank—the second one lunges from the opposite side, all teeth and claws. I bury an arrow into its chest before it can reach him.

The ravine turns into a blur. Both Vulcan and Kallesie jerk, flames flare, and steel splits the dark. Somewhere in chaos, Helios's back finds mine.

"Left," I warn, feeling him shift in perfect sync.

"Right," he counters, his voice low and edged with the same heat from before.

We move as one, his blade a deadly arc, my arrows finding every weak point. Each time I shift, his presence shadows mine, solid and unyielding. Every time our shoulders touch, it ignites something risky and distracting in my chest.

The third one tries to flank us. Helios spins, pressing into me as he drives his sword home, the heat of his body a wall against my back. My next arrow buries itself in the skull of the first, dropping it.

The fight ends in a rush of silence; the air is covered with smoke and the scent of the fresh blood lingering behind it. Vulcan and Kallesie stalk the edges, their eyes still bright, their breaths hard.

I'm still catching mine when Helios turns. His hands catch my jaw, tilting my face toward him; his thumb sweeps the faint smear of blood along my cheek.

"You fight like you are created for this," he murmurs.

"Or I am keeping you alive," I fire back, but the words lose their edge.

His smile is sharp and predatory. "Either way, you're mine out here."

Kallesie's mental snort is immediate. "*And maybe in there too, if he gets his way.*"

CHAPTER 21

AFTER THE FLAMES

ELARA

The air crackles from the fight.

Vulcan and Kallesie pace the edges of the ravine like they're daring anything else to try its luck. The smell of smoke clings to me. So does the thrum of adrenaline, that sharp, electric hum since Helios's back pressed against mine.

He's watching me now, not with indifference … with a strong desire for me. Every step he takes on the blood-streaked stone is careful. My pulse stutters. My body is still in fight mode, but it's shifting, not spiraling into something hotter and heavier.

Kallesie says, "*Oh, he is drawn to you, and you know it.*"

I don't get a chance to tell her to be quiet before Helios stands in front of me. He's so close, I feel his heat wrapping around me like a second skin.

"Are you all right?" he says, with the kind of tone that coils through you and refuses to let go.

"I'm fine," I manage, but it's a lie. Fine isn't the word for this. I'm trembling, and my heart pounding is out of control, barely able to steady myself.

His hand finds my wrist, fingers gripping, not hard, but firm. He draws me a fraction closer. "You looked good out there." His gaze drops to my mouth for a moment. "Too good."

My breath catches. "You're still riding the adrenaline."

"Or I like watching you fight."

Kallesie hums in my head. *"Translation: he wants to pin you against the wall and..."*

I choke on a sound that's part laugh and part warning, but it fades when Helios closes the gap between us. My back hits the ravine wall. His hand braces beside my head, his other sliding down my arm.

"You're still shaking," he murmurs. "Is that from the fight… or me?"

I'm about to answer, about to give in, when Vulcan's head snaps toward the tree line. His growl is low and guttural.

Helios goes still.

So, do I.

Then Kallesie stiffens under my hand. "*We're not alone.*"

A shadow shifts at the edge of the ravine, far enough to

blur against the darkness. The air changes, becomes colder, heavier, and predatory in a way the beasts from before weren't.

Helios angles his body in front of mine. The heat between us replaces something sharper and more dangerous.

"Stay behind me," he orders.

The shadow moves again.

It's silent… too silent. Even the wind seems to hesitate, like the trees are holding their breath with us.

Vulcan lets out a deep growl. His sound echoes in the ravine, and Kallesie crouches into a low position, sensing danger. *"That's no straggler from the pack earlier,"* she hisses in my head. *"This one's clever. Patient. And I don't like patient hunters."*

Helios doesn't take his eyes off the treeline. His arm comes back, presses across my middle, forcing me flush against him. His heat is like a brand through my leathers, sharp and inescapable. "Stay close," he murmurs. The command washes over me, hinting at something deeper than just danger.

My breath comes quickly, half from the thing out there, half from him being this close.

A low scrape of claws on stone filters through the air, distant but methodical. Whatever it is, it's circling. Helios tilts his head enough to speak without losing sight of the threat. "On my mark, you move when I move."

"And if it's faster than us?"

"Then I make damn sure it doesn't touch you." He says his voice is pure steel, but there's a heat under it…a possessive promise that twists low in my stomach.

Kallesie mutters in my head. "*Oh, if you live through this, you two are going to combust.*"

A shape flickers between the tree's massive shoulders, the gleam of eyes that are far too intelligent. The scent of it hits next: wet earth, copper, and something acrid that makes my skin crawl.

The thing steps into the light. It's not like the other beasts; it's taller and leaner with limbs too long and a grin full of teeth that don't belong to any animal I've ever seen. It looks at Helios… then at me… and that grin widens. Helios shifts, his body caging mine completely. "You're not going to get her."

The thing moves with blinding speed. One second, it is in our line of sight, and it's gone. Next, the creature is bursting toward us with a shriek that pierces the night. Vulcan and Kallesie launch and intercept it mid-leap. The impact shakes the ground beneath us.

Helios seizes my hand. "Move!" with desperation lacing his voice.

We sprint, hearts pounding. Jaws snap nearby; our breath comes fast. Whatever chases us craves flesh, but it also senses our fear and desire.

Helios yanks me off the trail. Before the ravine curves into open ground, his grip is unyielding as he pulls me between two slabs of rock. The space is narrow, more like a cleft in the earth than a shelter, and the jagged walls force us close.

CHAPTER 22

BREATH IN THE DARK

ELARA

Too close.

I can feel every inch of him. The firm press of muscle, the steady beat of his heart against my chest, and the warmth radiating from him in the chilly night air. My back meets the cool stone, but the warmth that cages me in is all Helios.

Outside, the creature's shriek splits the air again. Stones rattle loose from above as the creature stalks past.

He doesn't dare speak, but his hand stays on my waist, fingers splayed, holding me exactly where he wants me. His eyes lock on the gap in the rocks, watching for movement.

Kallesie's voice slinks dry and amused. "*Hmm. Narrow space. Racing heartbeats. Breathing the same air. I'm saying, Elara, if you two don't kiss now, you're wasting an*

Oscar-worthy opportunity."

I stifle a groan, not from my words, but from the way Helios moves against me. Whether it's for balance or not, the consequences are deadly to my lower area.

The creature's shadow slides across the narrow entrance, and every muscle in Helios goes taut. His head dips, his breath blows hot at the edge of my ear as he whispers, "Don't move."

Like I could.

Its steps are slow, sniffing. Searching. The silence is a vice, squeezing tighter with each second. My lungs ache from holding my breath. Helios's chest presses harder into mine, his warmth wrapping around me like a shield.

For a heartbeat, I think it's going to find us. But then there is a crash in the distance. The predator hears the sound and slips into the dark. Its pursuit fades into the hills.

We stay frozen, pressed together, long after it's gone. When Helios finally looks at me, his eyes are all heat and intent. It's the gaze that leaves no doubt about what he wants.

Kallesie hums in my head. "*You can flirt later, you know.*"

The forest has gone still. Too still. Only our breathing breaks the silence. Mine is fast and shallow, his is slow and steady. Vulcan and Kallesie are at a distance where their bonds tug with little strength. Still, it doesn't pull my focus away from where he is standing, almost touching me.

His gaze pins me in place. Steel-grey eyes catch the dim light, sharpened by something that feels like hunger.

"The threat's gone," he said, his voice low. The words should be a relief. They are not. They curl through my chest like smoke. The danger is still here. Only now does it live in the way Helios looks at me. He steps forward. Not quickly. Not cautiously. Like this moment was always going to happen.

A hunter who knows exactly where his prey will run.

My pulse hammers a wild rhythm against my ribs.

"You…" I start, but my voice breaks on the word.

The air between our mouths feels alive—hot, restless, drawing us closer. "Me what, Elara?"

Every inch of myself tells me to retreat, and every inch of me betrays myself. I lean into the warmth of him instead. His hand moves up, fingers pushing a stray lock of hair back from my cheek. His knuckles graze my skin like the softest touch of flame. The contact itself almost undoes me.

His eyes darken. "Still think you can hide it?"

My breath catches, a soft hitch that tightens my chest. My shoulders draw back, as if my body is reaching before I realize it, with my fingers flexing once at my sides. And then I don't know which of us moves first, but the moment snaps, and his mouth is on mine.

There's heat there, something hungrier beneath it, kept carefully in check.

I melt and fist the fabric at his shoulders, letting him set me alight. His hand moves to the back of my neck, holding me there. The kiss deepens, and everything else fades away.

When he pulls away, it isn't out of mercy; it is precision. The final touch leaves me breathless, reaching for something that's already gone.

His mouth curves not in mockery, but in something far more dangerous. "You feel it too."

My lips tingle. My heartbeat is a war drum. I couldn't answer, but he doesn't need my words. He already knows.

And in the quiet that came next, the forest feels like it is frozen in time. Yet, it is my own racing pulse that keeps the hunt between us alive.

CHAPTER 23

BREAKING POINT

ELARA

The forest has gone too still. No whisper of wind through the trees, no hellhound growl, no sign of the threat we've been tracking. Vulcan and Kallesie are gone scouting ahead. Now, only the crackle of heat hung in the air between us.

He moves first, each step slow and purposeful. I follow, backed against the rough bark of a tree. A trap he set with precision. The last few feet close between us, inevitable and undeniable. A predator is closing the last few feet, knowing there is nowhere left to run.

"You're still trembling," he said, his voice low and dangerous, as if the sound alone could pin me there.

His palm lies flat against the tree beside my head, and the last of my resistance melts away. His other hand traces the line of my jaw as if he is choosing the perfect spot to bite. My pulse spikes, a sharp staccato I am sure he can feel.

Kallesie's voice purrs in my head, wicked and amused. "*Oh, sweetheart ... this is the part where you stop pretending you don't want him to catch you.*"

He leans in, his scent curls around me. His gaze falls to my mouth, pauses, then moves back up as if he is noting every flinch and breath.

When he passes his thumb over my lower lip, it isn't smooth. It is a pressure test that sends heat plunging low in my belly. And when he kisses me, it isn't cautious.

He claims me.

His mouth presses against mine, slow and deep, as if he's savouring the moment. The scrape of his teeth pulls a gasp from me; one he swallows whole. He presses into me, pinning me against the tree; every shift of muscle is deliberate. There are no mistakes in him; he can hold me here with ease, take what he wants, and I am utterly consumed by the desire for him.

My hands fist in his shirt, dragging him closer to me. He angles my head with a firm grip, deepening the kiss until my thoughts scatter into static.

When he pulls back, it is only far enough to let the cool night air sting my swollen lips. His forehead rests against mine, breath ragging, and his voice is nothing but gravel.

"This changes everything," he murmurs, as a promise.

My reply is a faint whisper. "I know."

We remain in each other's embrace, neither daring to move. It feels like pulling back would extinguish the spark that's come alive between us.

The forest doesn't seem so silent anymore.

Not after that kiss.

I can still taste him, the smoke, the danger, and the heat of him lingering in my chest. Every step back to Stronghold is careful and slow. Neither of us wants to rush toward safety.

Helios walks close enough that his arm caresses mine with each stride. His presence is a weight, a shadow that moves with me, keeping me within reach.

I try to focus on the path ahead, but his gaze is a constant pull at the edge of my vision. Every time I look at him, those steel grey eyes are on me, watching, measuring, remembering. It is the same look he'd given me moments before he kissed me, the one that makes me feel hunted.

Kallesie's voice links into my head. "*You're not walking back ... Someone is escorting you.*"

Heat crawls up my neck, and I quicken my pace. He matches it with ease, a faint smirk, as if he knows exactly what I am thinking.

Vulcan and Kallesie rejoin us halfway back. The hellhounds fall into step ahead. It should have broken the spell, but it didn't. Helios stays nearby. His hand sometimes touches my lower back as we step over roots or duck under branches. Each touch is fleeting and yet feels like sparks against bare skin.

The Stronghold's outer torches flicker in the distance, but he doesn't speed up. His steps slow, as if he wants to stretch the moments before others can see or hear him.

When they reach the gate, he leans close enough that his breath brushes my ear.

"This isn't over," he says in a low voice, the promise curling around me like smoke.

My reply comes without thinking. "I know."

And then we step inside, carrying the heat of the forest with us—unspoken and unfinished.

Dawn came, but the night still clings to my skin. I hardly slept, replaying every beat of last night's patrol. Helios walking beside me like a predator who had already claimed his prey. His eyes held a promise that hangs between both of us.

The Stronghold is awake. The clang of steel on steel echoes across the yard as initiates begin training. The smell of baking bread drifts from the kitchens. I move through it all like a shadow; Kallesie walks behind me with an exaggerated yawn.

"You look like you crawled out of a dream you don't want to wake up from," Kallesie's voice teases in my head. *"Is he in it? Oh, wait, he doesn't have to be, does he? He's in your bloodstream."*

I try to keep my face neutral, but my pulse betrays me. I spot Helios across the yard, speaking with Alasdair. Even at a distance, I can feel him. His eyes lift and find mine with immediate focus, holding me.

It isn't a look; it is a pull. A reminder. A challenge.

My fingers tighten around the strap of my quiver.

Helios gives Alasdair a nod and walks toward me. He walks with an unhurried but purposeful stride. People step out of his way without thinking, sensing the shift in his focus. I had seconds to prepare myself, and I'm not ready when he stops in front of me.

"Elara." He says his voice is low, but not soft. "You're with me today."

I don't protest. Truthfully, I don't want to.

"Oh," Kallesie purrs, *"this day is going to be fun."*

The training yard is a storm of movement, pairs clashing with blades. The thump of boots against dirt and the dull impact of fists hitting pads targeted. Helios leads me toward the centre. The noise around us seems to fade into something distant and unimportant.

He doesn't pick up a practice sword. Neither do I.

This isn't going to be a normal spar.

He begins circling me, hands loose at his sides, his eyes locking on mine the whole time. It is about tuning in to my body, checking my stance, spotting the tiniest openings, and helping me feel it both physically and mentally.

"You're distracted," he says, his voice calm but with an edge to it. "That'll get you killed."

I mirror his movements, keeping my breath steady. "Or it'll keep me alive," I shoot back. "You'd be surprised by what people miss when they underestimate a distraction."

One corner of his mouth lifts dangerously, knowingly. "Are you calling yourself a distraction, Elara?"

"Oh, you are so outmatched," Kallesie's voice hums in my head. *"And you like it."*

Helios closes the circle between us, enough that I can feel the heat radiating off him. He doesn't touch me, but the air feels charged. It's as if one wrong move can turn this into something no one should see.

I feint to the right. He doesn't bite.

He steps in instead, catches my wrist with one swift move. He uses my momentum to throw me off balance, forcing me to meet the full weight of his stare.

"That's better," he murmurs, low enough that only I could hear. "Now you're paying attention."

My pulse kicks hard. Breaking his hold would be easy, but I don't.

Helios knows it. He keeps hold of my wrist. His grip tightens, strong and steady. He knows how much strength it takes to keep me in place.

I twist, trying to break free, but he moves with me like a shadow, anticipating, closing every gap I create.

"You're fast," he says, circling behind me, our arms still linked. "But speed without control?" His voice drops lower, near my ear. "That's chaos. You want precision, Elara. You want the strike to land exactly where it needs to."

I spin, hoping to shake him off. But he grabs me with his other arm, pinning me for a heartbeat. Then he releases one arm, catches my waist, and pulls me closer.

"He's hunting you," Kallesie croons in my head, smug

and utterly unhelpful. "*And you don't even want to run.*"

The yard blurs. I focus on his faint breath, the shift of his weight, and how his eyes hold me in place without a word.

I lash out again, driven by instinct and pride. He blocks it. Their bodies collide enough for me to feel the strength hidden beneath his skin.

"Better," he says in a soft voice, conveying approval, though there is heat beneath it. "You're thinking less. Trusting more."

I should be furious at the implication, but I can't bring myself to be. I lean into his forearm, pressing against mine. The closeness feels like a threat and a promise.

"You're enjoying this," I accuse.

His smile is a deliberate, predatory expression. "Only because you are."

My pulse spikes. I can't tell if I am the prey or the predator anymore.

He guides me back with careful steps until my boots scrape the edge of the sparring ring.

"You keep letting me close," he murmurs, his gaze fixed on my mouth.

"That's because you're crowding me," I shoot back, though the bite in my tone is weak as I don't step away.

"That's the point."

He feints left, and when I counter, he catches my arm and spins me into him. My back is against his chest. His arm slides across my front, possibly to restrain me or something different.

Gasps ripple from the onlookers, but no one steps in; it remains a spar. Technically.

"Now," he says, his voice curls against the shell of my ear, "tell me you'd rather have space."

My heartbeat beats wild and heavy, rattling my ribs inside. I yell at myself to break free, but I grab his forearm. I pivot enough to meet his eyes over my shoulder.

"Say it," Kallesie hisses in my mind, sharp with amusement. *"Or kiss him. I dare you."*

Instead, I push back against him. It's not hard enough to break away, but it aligns our bodies for a reckless second. Close enough for his breath to catch, for mine to falter, and for every trained fighter in the yard to feel the shift.

I slip away, stepping back before the moment breaks. He stands there with an unreadable look and a faint smile. I almost lose focus because of it.

The match is over. But something else started.

The spar ends without another word. No victory is declared. No crowd cheers. A heavy silence settles over the onlookers, people who haven't seen enough to know what they have witnessed. They aren't sure whether to call it a fight or something else.

Helios doesn't linger for commentary. He crosses the yard, Vulcan's massive form falls beside him, molten eyes fix ahead. I follow a moment later with Kallesie sneaking to my side. Her tail flickers as if she enjoyed the show.

"You let him get under your skin," She murmurs in my mind, each word thick with satisfaction. *"And under*

everything else, if you had half a chance."

I clench my jaw and keep walking—the path from the training grounds to Stronghold twists through a narrow forest. The trees press close, their branches catching the fading light of dusk. The air smells of damp earth and familiar wood smoke. It feels grounding, but the tensions tighten with every step.

He moves just ahead of me, slow and unhurried, but every step draws us closer. The gap between us shrinks, and I feel it in my chest something dark, something familiar, waiting.

Vulcan drifts ahead with Kallesie, leaving us on the narrow gap between shadows.

"You're too fast," Helios says behind me, his voice low and dangerous.

"You're the one moving too slow."

My words get lost in the forest, but he leans closer, voice deepening. "Or," he says, "you're afraid of what happens if I catch up."

My pulse leaps, betraying me. I don't look back. I only feel his presence faintly at the edge of my awareness. When I do look over my shoulder, his gaze is already locked on mine.

He has that same look from the spar. He moves in slowly, knowing just how close he can get before I break.

I turn forward again, lengthening my stride.

He matches it.

Step after step, neither rushing. The tension between us is so thick it seems to pull at our skin.

When the walls loom near, he moves to my side, our elbows touching. I feel the heat of him like a brand, every nerve on high alert.

"Next time," he says, eyes glinting in the half-light, "I won't let you walk away."

The words linger in the air, sharp as a blade and warm as a promise.

The path ahead is quiet. Neither of us is speaking. Our hellhounds are farther ahead. Birds call softly, our boots whisper against dirt, and that moment should have been peaceful. Instead, his threat burns beneath my skin. He won't let me walk away, turning the silence into a challenge. By the time Stronghold comes into view, I'm braced for what waits behind the gates.

CHAPTER 24

THE CATCH

ELARA

The gates loom ahead, torchlight spills across the earth like molten gold. Vulcan and Kallesie slip through the courtyard, fading into the shadows. Only the creak of the gate hinges and the whisper of night air remain.

I keep walking, my pulse loud in my ears. I can feel him behind me, that steady rhythm of steps, each one drawing him closer.

I don't need to look to know when he closes the gap. The air shifts. Heat presses against my back.

"You've been making me chase you all the way from the training grounds," he says, every word breathed against the skin of my ear.

"I'm not."

The denial breaks as he moves in front of me, forcing me to stop short. His eyes are darker now, catching the torchlight in flashes.

"You are," he states.

My feet don't move even though they should. I stand there, caught in his magnetic pull, every nerve screams with the same wild rush I have in the ring.

He reaches up, fingers caressing my jaw, in slow motion, like giving me time to pull away if I want to. But I don't want to.

And then there is no more space.

The kiss hits sharp, claiming, the kind that leaves no room for doubt. I catch his shoulders to anchor myself against the surge of heat and want. He tastes like fire and the cold bite of night air, a contradiction I could drown in.

"You're not running anymore," he murmured.

I almost smiled, chest still heaving. "Who says I was running?"

He answers with a look that says he doesn't believe me.

We linger, letting the heat between us coil and thrum, the Stronghold slipping from the thought for a few stolen moments. My pulse hammers in my chest, quick and uneven, each shallow breath a taste of him. Every glance, every subtle shift in space, vibrates with conscious energy, something alive. Whatever it is between us will not be contained again.

Then the world widens again.

The Stronghold swallows us in shadows and torchlight. The heavy gates shut behind, sealing the night out.... or sealing us in. Helios doesn't step away from me right away. He stays close, the heat of his body warming my side. His stride matches mine—slow, unhurried—daring anyone to notice or to question.

The courtyard is quiet, too quiet. A handful of sentries cross the ramparts, their eyes sharp, their movements crisp. The scent of smoke and oiled steel hangs heavily in the air.

I feel Kallesie in the back of my mind, her tone smug with satisfaction. *"About time."*

My jaw clenches, lips betray me with the weakest twitch. My shoulders stiffen, and I shift my weight, running my palms down my sides. A gesture too small to matter—but Helios notices. His eyes trace the tension from my mouth, catching the tension I can't hide. Predatory. Patient. That edge spreads faster than patrol ever could.

Heat pools along my side where his body pressed just a fraction closer than necessary. I nod once, pulse quickening, and fingers brushing against the stone at my side as I scan the darkening edges of the courtyard. "It's like the shadows are listening."

His hand rubs the back of mine. It's enough to make my pulse stumble. "Then let them. We'll give them something worth hearing."

Before I can respond, a prickle runs along my spine. The air feels heavier, pressing against my skin, and my chest tightens as if the shadows themselves are holding their breath. My fingers curl at my sides, nails bite into my palms, and I realize my pulse has jumped, too loud in the quiet. Then a sharp howl splits the air from somewhere beyond the inner wall, a Hellhound's call, urgent and guttural.

Helios's expression shifts quickly. The simmering heat cools, replaced by the lethal focus of a hunter ready for the chase.

"Looks like our night isn't over," he murmurs, turning toward the sound.

The heat between us still burns, but now it twists with a sharp pull of the hunt. Every heartbeat feels like a drumbeat pushing them toward whatever is lurking in the dark.

The path narrows, shadow pressing in from all sides, the forest floor damp and heavy beneath our feet. A sharp tang of moss and fallen leaves. Each step feels heavier, the silence almost solid, as if the darkness itself is leaning closer, watching. My fingers itch near my weapon, and every sense stretches thin. Kallesie prowls at the edge of my awareness, her presence sharp and alert.

"Focus," she murmurs. *"This thing knows you're coming."*

Helios moves beside me without a sound. He matches my pace like we have learned the hard way. All those practices in the sparring ring have started to pay off. The closeness is deliberate and dangerous. If I turn my head, I know exactly what I will find—his attention locked on in the dark, his body coiled as if he were already mid-strike.

Vulcan growls low, every muscle taut, every ear flickering to some silent signal. The pressure in the air thickens with it. Whatever he senses has me wound tight.

"Don't rush," Helios whispers the words only meant for me alone.

I almost laugh. "You're the one vibrating to hit this headfirst like always."

The corner of his mouth twitches, but his eyes never leave the treeline. "Because this isn't prey. It's a challenge."

The words settle into my chest and stay there.

Kallesie bares her teeth in my mind. *"He's right. This one won't run. It wants people to see it."*

The forest opens, and shadows pull back like it is holding a breath that hasn't been released. My pulse kicks harder, instincts screaming even as my feet keep moving.

Whatever waits out there is watching us, and I notice it before it shows itself.

The howl rises low, ancient, close enough to rattle in my bones.

CHAPTER 25

THE CALL IN THE DARK

ELARA

The howl hangs in the air as Helios moves.

The ground seems to close beneath his steps as though the Stronghold itself bends to him.

I keep pace, bow in hand, eyes scanning the shadowed gaps between the trees. The sound comes from beyond the training yards, lost in the darkness of the west gate. My chest tightens, every breath sharp, pulse spiking with each step.

"Something's in here." Kallesie's voice coils through my mind, a low growl beneath every word. *"And it's not one of ours."*

The torches along the ramparts burn low, their flames bending as though some invisible wind passes through, though my skin feels no chill. Every instinct screams that we are not alone, and a shiver runs along my spine.

Vulcan rumbles ahead. For a heartbeat, I see him massive, dark as midnight, with amethyst eyes glowing in the gloom. Muscles coiled, gaze fixed on a deeper shadow between two storage halls. My stomach tightens, every nerve stretches taut, breath caught somewhere between awe and caution.

Helios runs his hand over my hips, the grip solid, anchoring me to him. “Stay close.” His voice is low, deliberate, each syllable vibrating with the quiet command that brooks no argument.

My pulse kicks harder, the night thick around me, listening, my arms prick with goosebumps, and my fingers curl into a fist around the bow.

Then the shadow moves.

It slips along the stone, low and sinuous, too fluid to be human, too wrong to be a beast. The torches closest to it sputter out, drowning the space in black. My stomach lurches, and my chest constricts. I swallow hard, breath hitching involuntarily.

We move in unison, taking measured steps that widen the gap between us and the Stronghold’s heart. Things in the dark follow. My legs coil like springs, ready to react before my mind fully processes the danger.

The further we lure it, the thicker the shadow grows, until the walls loom far behind and the only light is the faint shimmer in Vulcan’s eyes ahead. My pulse hammers, heat pooling low in my stomach, tension sparking along every nerve.

Then, like lightning, the creature lunges.

I shoot an arrow as Helios intercepts, his blade catching

moonlight before driving deep. The thing shrieks, a sound that scrapes the air and dissolves into black vapor. My hands tremble, breath ragged, a shiver runs through me as adrenaline buzzes in my veins.

Silence.

Vulcan pads forward, sniffing the spot, ears flat. Kallesie stays tense in my mind, buzzing taut wire.

Helios straightens slowly, and his gaze finds mine in the dark. No need for words; the fight has pulled something primal to the surface, and it isn't going away. My chest heaves, lips tingling, pulse still staccato from the encounter.

"That," he says, stepping closer until the heat of him wraps around me, while staring directly at me, "Isn't what I came out here hunting for."

A shiver runs through me, stealing my breath. His eyes hold me there, the space between us tense with something that has been building for far too long. A shiver of heat races along my spine, making every nerve stand alert.

Vulcan and Kallesie melt into the night, leaving us in a silence teeming enough to burn.

His hand comes to my jaw, rough and sure, pulling me into him. The kiss strikes like flint, sharp and dangerous. I don't hold back. It is claiming. I meet it without hesitation, every shred of restraint snapping under the weight of the moment. My pulse gallops, breath coming in shallow bursts, fingers digging into his shoulders as if I could tether myself to the sensation.

The world narrows to heat, breath, and the pounding of our hearts, the taste of him tangles with the echo of battle still in her blood every nerve alight.

When they finally break, barely an inch remains between our lips. Neither of us steps back.

Somewhere, far off, the Stronghold waits. But right now, they are nowhere else, caught between heartbeats.

The night doesn't soften. If anything, it presses harder against us, with the scent of rain on stone and something darker, like the air after a wildfire. My lips still tingle, my pulse stubbornly refusing to slow.

Helios doesn't release my jaw right away. His thumb lingers, dragging faintly across my skin like a mark, not a touch. Only when Vulcan's low rumble ahead does he pull back, before continuing to let his fingers trail down the side of my neck, claiming new ground.

We start toward the Stronghold at an unhurried pace.

Every few steps, his hand strokes my hip or my shoulder, the barest contact, but each one carries a weight I can't ignore. The way he moves beside me isn't protective; it is possessive. My breath hitches slightly with each touch, my stomach tightens, and my pulse pounds.

The torches along the path burn low, casting molten edges into his profile. His steel-gray eyes flick toward me once, slow, as if cataloging something already his.

Kallesie hums in my head. *"You feel it too."*

I don't answer. I don't need to.

We pass beneath the arch of the west wall, shadows clinging to the stone like they don't want to let us go. Vulcan pads a few paces ahead, tail low, ears flicking at every sound. Kallesie follows, a steady hum in my mind, but neither hellhound nor breaks the silence.

Helios leans close, his voice low enough for me alone.

"You know this doesn't go away now."

It isn't a question, and it isn't a statement either. My breath hitches, my throat tightens. "I know."

His gaze drops to my mouth for half a heartbeat before he straightens again, the faintest curve tugging at his lips. That almost smile feels more dangerous than a drawn blade.

We move through the training yard, our steps echo in the stillness. Somewhere above, a sentry shifts on the ramparts, but the sound feels distant and unimportant. Every inch toward the Stronghold's heart is another step with that heat still wrapping around them, quiet but impossible to ignore.

At the heavy doors, Helios stops behind me. I can feel his presence at my back, close enough that the warmth of him bled through my coat. He reaches past me to push one door open, but doesn't move to go inside.

Instead, he dips his head, lips inching close as if to let me feel the words without hearing them clearly.

"This isn't finished between us."

I step back, letting him walk ahead, though every part aches to close the space he leaves behind. The heat of him lingers along my jaw, my hip, where his hand paused, and it sets my blood thrumming in ways I can't quite tame. My pulse races, chest tight, breath shallow, as if the night itself presses in on me.

Kallesie hums in my mind, steady and grounding, but she doesn't let me wallow. *"Oh, bravo,"* she quips, voice dripping with mock admiration. *"You two are really subtle. That public display of desire? Almost tactful. Almost."*

I roll my eyes at her, fingers brushing where his hand has been, but the warmth lingers. "Thanks, Kallesie. That really helps." I mutter out loud.

"You're welcome," she snaps, quick as ever. *"I'd say 'get a grip,' but clearly that ship has sailed. Enjoy your scorched nerves and tingling lips."*

Her sarcasm makes me grin, even as the ache in my chest refuses to ease. Every step toward my chamber is deliberate, but my mind keeps circling back to him, the press of his hand, the steel in his gaze.

By the time I reach my bed chamber, the corridors are quiet, the torches flickering low. I drop my bow and sink onto the edge of my bed, pulse still racing, stomach coiled with tension I can't shake.

Kallesie circles, landing beside me with a soft thump, her presence warm and grounding. *"Try not to burn the place down thinking of him,"* she teases, though there's a sharp edge to her warning. *"He may be entertaining, but he's not harmless."*

I close my eyes, letting the sensation settle; heat, desire, and the echo of battle still thrumming through me. Somewhere beyond me, he awaits, too. And the ache of him is still here, coiled under my skin.

"Honestly," Kallesie mutters, more to herself than me. *"Humans are ridiculous. And predictable. Especially this one."*

I can't help the laugh that escapes, even as my pulse slowly begins to ease. The night presses against the window, silent and patient. I know it isn't empty. Something shifts just beyond my sight, and I feel it watching.

CHAPTER 26

THE LINE BETWEEN FIRE & ASH

ELARA

The Stronghold's torches burn low, shadows stretching long across the courtyard. The night is still except for the soft thud of Vulcan's claws and the faint scrape of Kallesie's tail against the flagstones as the Hellhounds move ahead.

"Finally," Kallesie's voice slides into my head, dripping with sass. "*Alone. The universe must really want to see you two combust.*"

I roll my eyes, cheeks warming. "*Shut up.*"

"What? I'm just saying ... The man's been looking at you like you are dinner, dessert, and the fine wine in between."

Helios' steps fall beside mine, close enough that the heat of his arm bleeds into her own. His presence wraps around me like the scent of rain before a storm, heavy, electric.

His steel-gray gaze flicks down to my mouth, lingers for a fraction too long, then he deliberately slides away. Predatory.

"You're quiet," I murmur, my voice smaller than I intend.

"I'm pacing myself," he says, voice low, dangerous in a way velvet could be dangerous if it hid a blade beneath.

Kallesie snorts in my head. *"Translation: He's winding you up on purpose."*

We reach the steps to the inner hall, the air between us thrumming. He stops, letting Vulcan and Kallesie prowl ahead into the darkness.

He doesn't follow.

Instead, he steps closer, slowly, until the world shrinks to the rhythm of my heartbeat and the rasp of his breath.

"Elara." His voice is almost a growl, and my stomach twists.

Her fingers curl against the urge to grab his shirt and pull him closer. "Helios."

He leans in, mouth so near I swear I could feel the curve of his smirk. "If I start, I won't stop."

My pulse stutters. "And if I don't want you to stop?"

Something in his control has slipped. His hand rises, fingers sliding over my throat until his palm rests there, warm and firm. not to claim. Just enough to keep my interest. My breath shortens. His thumb slides under my jaw, tipping my head back slightly, leaving me no choice but to meet his gaze. They have a somber, controlled look about them, but only barely. The touch is not aggressive.

It's a reminder. And that makes it worse.

The kiss is slow, deliberate, and consuming. The heat coils through me until breathing becomes an afterthought. I melt into him, into the precise, dangerous rhythm, of his mouth on mine.

When he pulls away, it's with a deep, steady breath. "Not here," he says, his voice fraying around the edges.

But the look in his eyes promises that it will burn later.

The courtyard awakens to a quiet hum. There is no hollow wind tonight, just a pulse of torches ringing the enormous ring, flames shooting skyward like strands of gold and violence in the breathless darkness. The air itself pulses to a rhythm older than the mountains and the clan's own name.

The full moon hangs heavy above, and silver spills across the gathering of every member of the Hellhound Clan. A hundred cloaks shift in the firelight. The growl and huff of hellhounds rolls through like distant thunder.

I stand among the surviving initiates, Harlow on my right and three more on my left. Kallesie prowls beside me, massive and magnificent, amethyst flames curling lazily around her paws as if the night owes her favors.

A great horn sounds, its note stretching long enough to shiver through my ribs. Then the chanting begins, a language I've never heard; the mountains speaking, river sloshing over stone.

"Veythra sahl, veythra mor.." From fire we rise, to fire

we return.

The crowd's voices weave together, rolling and deep, each phrase a drumbeat against my chest.

"Kelroth alen, kelroth ahren…" Bound by ash, forged by shadows.

Kallesie slides into my mind, amused. *"That part's basically saying you're married to me now. Shh…. Don't fight it."*

I keep my face still, but the heat flares in my chest. Helios steps into the ring, steel-gray eyes catching the torchlight like molten metal. When he speaks, the chanting falls away.

"Do chrúba sa talamh ár súile sa lasair…" Our claws on earth, our gaze in flame. He looks at each initiate, but when his gaze finds me, it lingers. The crowd seems to fade.

"Tharven a'sahl, karrven a'mor…" We guard in life; we hunt in death.

A ceremonial dagger, black and etched with curling runes, is pressed into his hand by Eldest Keeper. One by one, each initiate steps forward, lightly cutting their palm. Blood hisses against the shallow obsidian bowl at the center of the ring. Steam lifts from its surface, as if the stone drinks deep.

When it is my turn, the air thickens.

Kallesie's whisper against my thoughts, like silk and mischief. "*They're watching your hands. They don't know I already claimed your heart.*"

I press my palm over the bowl, and my blood falls into the dark liquid. When I lift the bowl to my mouth and drink, the metallic taste floods my tongue—hot, electric—like a tether pulling taut inside me. Helios's voice lowers, steady and commanding. It feels meant only for me, yet the words carry across the entire circle.

"Var shalven, varmourlen, hellath draem." Through the rising flame, we dream eternal.

The crowd answers as one. The torches bend toward us, fire approving. Hellhounds tilt back their heads, roaring flames into the night sky.

The oath-seers and settlers, sparks ignite in my veins. When the chanting fades and the crowd disperses, Helios steps close. Firelight catches the edge of a smile on his face. Now the ancient tongue slips away like armour.

"You're one of us now, Elara." There's no warmth in his voice, only the quiet weight of a promise.

The hall hums with fading chants, murmurs of the clan. Flames lean low, hissing, and smoke curls toward the vaulted ceiling. Initiates shift nervously, whispering oaths. The faint scent of sweat, ash, and leather thickens the air. I straighten the crimson-and-black beading sewn by the village seamstress, glinting in the torchlight. Harlow laughs quietly with Zinnia at her side, but the tension in her shoulders betrays her.

I move among them, crimson cloak hugging my waist, the black beading catching the torchlight, each step a whisper across the stone. Every glance toward him sends heat skimming over my skin. Helios is watching. I feel it: a pull in my chest, my heartbeat stuttering. Steel-gray eyes, fixed entirely on me.

Kallesie nudges my thought. "*Oh boy, he is staring at you like you're the last steak in the Highlands.*"

I scan the initiates, noting proud, scared, and awe-struck expressions alike. Some try to hide it, some can't. All of them are marked now, bonded to their hellhounds and the clan in ways they can barely articulate.

Helios parts the crowd without a word, moving toward me in measured steps. Black and gold drapes his shoulders, silver torque at his throat catching the dim light, and runic embroidery smudged with ash.

"And here comes the minister, tall, dark, and smoldering, looking like he's about to devour you. Please tell me you at least brushed your hair."

When he stops before me, the murmurs and glances fade to a distant hum. Harlow glances between us, then nudges Ash, whispering something I can't catch. The moment is thick, charged. Every heartbeat seems louder than the last.

"Come," Helios says, his voice a command that cuts through lingering chatter like a blow.

"Oh, he used a command voice. You're doomed." Kallesie murmurs.

We slip down a side passage, leaving the hall behind. The torches flicker, shadows bending over stone. Laughter and whispers of congratulations, murmurs of oaths trail behind us, reminders of the public world we are leaving behind.

He comes to a halt at the thick wooden door and lays his hand on the middle of my back as he guides me forward. The latch clicks shut behind us, and the space between us seems to hum with a heat from his presence, the strength behind his hand a tangible thing, as he pulls me along without a single word. The door closes with a final thud against the wall, sealing away the hall, the clan, and all the eyes that were on us.

The room is dim, lit only by a single torch burning low in its sconce. Firelight glides along the stone walls and gilded carvings, the fireplace flame casting a warm glow over the room. The huge bed looms beside us, but the space still feels impossibly small. He stands close, his hand resting in the middle of my back, and there is nowhere for my attention to drift but only him.

My pulse is loud in my ears. Too loud.

He doesn't move at first. Just watches me, steel grey eyes dark, measuring. The oath still clings to him, to both of us smoke and heat and something feral beneath it.

"Well," Kallesie murmurs, far too pleased. *"No witnesses. Efficient man."*

I swallow; my throat feels tight, exposed, still remembering the weight of his hand there earlier.

He circles me, stopping in front of me at last. Each step draws him closer, until my spine comes against cool stone. My arousal of him circling me like I'm prey he can't wait to devour.

"Elara," he says, and my name lands heavily, stripped of ceremony.

I tilt my chin up without thinking. If he notices, he

doesn't comment. His gaze tracks the movement, lingers at my throat, the pulse beating there.

"The room is quiet," he says quietly. "But I wouldn't be sure about the night."

I shift slightly, feeling the space tighten between us. "Then the night is ours."

He leans in just enough for his heat to wash over my skin, causing a shiver of arousal to wash over me. "The night... maybe," he says, voice dark and slow, "but the rest of you is mind to find."

Kallesie hums. *"Point to him."*

Heat pools in my belly. I don't look away. "You didn't give me much of a choice."

He lifts his hand slowly, deliberately, bringing it towards me as I remain pressed against the wall. His other hand hovers near my waist, not touching but close enough that the absence of contact feels like its own kind of torment.

"You don't understand what you bound yourself to," he says, voice roughing.

"Then tell me," I say, "What am I bound to?"

His studies me for a long moment before answering. His hand finally settles on my waist, firm, anchoring. The contact sends a jolt through me, sharp and electric.

"Too the clan," he says, his voice rough, "To its blood, it's fight and to the man who stands in front of you."

My thoughts slip away, leaving only the warmth of him and the heavy pull of his presence. The air between us feels tight, alive with it.

Kallesie goes very, very quiet.

That does it.

He exhales as if something broke loose. His hand comes up, bracing against the wall beside my head, caging me in without touching me anywhere else. The restraint is worse than any claim.

"You're playing with fire," he says.

I meet his gaze, heart racing, voice steady despite it. "So are you."

For a moment, neither of us moves—the torch crackles. The silence stretches thin, trembling.

Then his mouth finds mine, not rushing, nor gentle. Controlled. As if he's holding back something enormous. The kiss deepens slowly, deliberately, every second layered with promise. My hands slide into his cloak, fingers curling into the heavy fabric as if it's the only thing keeping me upright.

When he pulls back, it's barely an inch. His breath ghosts my lips.

CHAPTER 27

PRIVATE CHAMBER

ELARA

That inch disappears the moment I blink. His lips brush mine again, and this time there is no restraint. His eyes search my face, dark and unreadable, like he's gauging how far he can go before something final tips.

I swallow, suddenly aware of every place we're not touching. The night presses close around us, heavy with unsaid things, and I realize this pause is a choice. Whatever he's holding back isn't doubt. It's power. And knowledge of what happens if he lets go.

He exhales, slow and steady, as if anchoring himself. When he lifts his hand, brushing my jaw with the starkest linger, the promise flips into something almost unbearable. This isn't the beginning of a kiss anymore. It's the beginning of whatever comes after we stop pretending; this is an example.

He moves. Slow, deliberate steps, the kind that had my pulse skitter. The crimson cloak clings to me like a second skin; the black beading catches the flicker of candlelight. His gaze trails down, not in a hurry, until it feels like he'd stripped the cloak away without touching me.

"Yup. Stalking mode engaged. We're at 95% pounce probability."

He reaches for me, tracing my shoulder tenderly, before curling into the fabric. His grip tightens. My breath catches.

With one decisive motion, he tears the corset apart, the ripping sound a sharp sound in the silence, threads snapping like brittle twigs.

Before I can react, he guides me backward, step by step, toward the bed. His touch is firm, his focus composed.

The backs of my knees hit the mattress. In the next breath, we are both falling onto it, his mouth finding mine in a fierce, claiming kiss that makes my toes curl.

"Aaand... we have liftoff."

His lips are warm and unyielding, tasting faintly of smoke and the sharp whiff of winter air. The kiss isn't patient; it's a demand, a statement, yet it carries an undertow of heat that pulls me in deeper. His breath mingles with mine, each movement of his mouth sending a shiver spiraling down my spine. His lips detach from mine as he slowly trails kisses down my neck and breasts. He keeps his gentle kiss on my skin until he reaches just below my belly button, before he slides a finger in between my folds. I moan softly as his finger goes deeper. "Helios."

"What, Elara?" he says, looking up at me, smirking.

A long, drawn-out moan escapes as he increases speed, finding my clit with his fingers, sending me almost over the cliff of an orgasm.

"You're not allowed to cum just yet," Helios commands.

"Why? I don't know if I can hold it." I grow more impatient after a wave of pleasure makes my toes curl.

He chuckles, withdrawing his finger and then drawing it over his tongue. He savours the delicious taste, his tongue gliding over his lips as if to relish my arousal. My body sags in relief before another wave of pleasure grips me as his mouth replaces his finger. Sucking and nibbling on my clit. I grab his hair while his tongue moves inside me, my moans grow louder when I feel his finger join his mouth. His finger moves in and out slowly, then faster, curling just right.

Another orgasm rips through me, and I swear the entire clan can hear us. "Helios, I need you now," I say, my voice almost desperate.

He chuckles, meeting my heated gaze. "Do you need me, Elara? Where do you want me?"

My response comes out almost begging. "I need you inside me. Now."

He smirks while he slowly gets off the bed to take his ceremonial cloak off. Slowly unbuttoning as if he has all the time in the world, while I am on the verge of losing myself, the silver shirt slides off just as slowly, revealing his broad shoulders, and his black pants finally come off. And that's it… I'm losing it.

His muscles coil with every motion. I lick my lips because I'm hungry. It’s a specific kind of hunger, a hollow ache that starts low in my belly and pulses outward. It's from looking at the way his chest is like carved granite, his perfect six-pack right down to the V where his underpants dip, the muscles tighten to showcase his body even more.

From the bed, I watch him standing beside me, and my mind drifts. I wonder what he tastes like if I slide closer and let my tongue trace the center of his chest. Would his sweat be sharp and salty, or would it carry the raw, unfiltered essences of him?

“Like what you see?” he says while I am checking him out.

My response falls hot and bothered. “Yes, I do.”

He is finally just in his undergarments. The outline makes my mouth run dry. He slowly removes his garments. He stands in front of me in all his naked glory. His erection springs free while he touches himself. He stalks closer to me like prey hooked in his web. He grabs my legs and moves me to the edge of the bed, standing between my thighs. “You’re mine,” as he lines himself at my entrance and plunges, making me moan in pleasure as I feel his entire length in me. I moan at the fullness of him, and he answers with a deep, echoing grunt, his movement matching mine. I buck my hips upward before he pins me to the mattress with his hips. “Let me claim you like you deserve to be claimed.” He smirks before sinking into me again.

A long cry escapes my throat as his speed picks up, and we move like tides, raw, rough, and unrestrained. Suddenly, the pleasure rises, close to the peak when he rubs my clit, thrusting hungrily inside me. A warm wave lifts from the pit of my stomach as he thrusts deeper, and I wail his name loudly, as I come apart beneath him. The orgasm shatters me while I wrap my legs around his waist tightly, just as he groans and follows with a double thrust, and his release fills me. But he doesn't let go. He peppers kisses all over my neck and chest before pressing his lips onto mine.

The fire roars in the hearth, its glow painting jagged shadows over the walls. My pulse hasn't slowed, not really, though the frantic edge of it has shifted into something deeper, heavier. Heat clings to my skin, part from the flames, part from him.

He doesn't move far. His arm is still draped across my waist, weighty and certain, like he is staking a claim even now. His eyes study me, sharper than the edge of a blade, yet holding something beneath, something he doesn't seem willing to name.

"Still in one piece, little wolf?" His voice is a deep rumble, teasing on the surface, but I catch the faint thread of something.

Kallesie's voice purrs in my mind, equal parts smug and exasperating. "*I told you he'd snap eventually. Honestly, I'm just proud it took him this long.*"

I ignore her, keeping my gaze locked onto him. "I'm not so easy to break."

One corner of his mouth twitches, almost a smile, but he raises a hand to push a stray lock of hair from my cheek. That single touch is far more dangerous than any earlier fury because it doesn't demand; it lingers.

Beyond the chamber walls, the muffled sounds of the clan's night filter in: footsteps on stone, low voices, and the restless howl of a hellhound. But here, time seems to hold its breath.

His palm finds my shoulder, thumb tracing my mark there. "This changes things," he murmurs, more to himself than to me.

I don't ask what things. I am not sure I wanted to know.

Helios

The firelight dances across her skin, catching on the curve of her jaw, the wild strands of her hair that escaped during the storm between us. She looks at me like she isn't sure whether to fight me or stay exactly where she is.

It is maddening.

Part of me wants to pull her back into the chaos we just barely stepped out of, to keep proving she is mine until the sun rises. The other part, the one I don't trust, wants to keep her here, still, so I can memorize every inch of her without the haze of fury in the way.

"This changes things," I say, and I mean it. I don't take what isn't mine. But Elara… Elara is no longer just an initiate under my command; she is part of my clan now.

I feel her pulse beneath my fingers where they rest over her mark on her wrist, steady, insistent, and undeniably strong. She doesn't flinch, doesn't shy away. That is enough to make my control thin again.

I need to pull back. Instead, I stay where I am. Because for the first time in years, the thought of letting go doesn't sit right with me at all. The quiet stretches between us, every second heavy with everything left unsaid, and then it breaks.

CHAPTER 28

THE CHALLENGE

ELARA

The quiet between us doesn't last.

A sharp knock breaks the stillness. Helios doesn't move at first, his gaze still locked on mine, as if daring whoever is on the other side to interrupt.

The knock came a second time. Louder.

With a growl, he pushes off the bed, tugging his pants on but leaving his shirt off. The firelight catches on the planes of his chest before he crosses the chamber in three long strides and unlatches the door.

Alasdair fills the doorway with a grim face. "We have a problem."

Helios' reply is all steel. "Speak."

"Morrigan's envoy arrived early. They're demanding an audience. And…" His eyes flick toward me, hesitation in the glance. "They know she's here."

My stomach tightens. "How?"

"Doesn't matter," Helios says, already moving. "No one touches her."

Alasdair's eyes lock on mine, sharp and unyielding. "Listen, Elara," he warns, his voice low, "being trapped in Morrigan's Sanctum with her envoy and her could be a trap."

Helios squints at me, and I feel the weight of his decision heavy in that moment. I don't need to hear the rest to know what he is thinking because I am thinking it too.

He looks at me and says, "I had your clothes transferred to my room."

I give him the look that we'll be talking about later. My eyes land on the dark pile on the chair. Black leather trousers slide over my legs, tight but flexible, reinforced along the thighs and knees. Straps loop around my calves and hips, faintly clicking as I adjust them. The sleeveless vest comes next, clinched at the waist with more buckles, flattened and braced across my chest. I shrug into the long leather coat borrowed from Solene. It drapes heavily over my shoulders, sleeves swallowing my wrists, and hem brushing my socks. Hidden hands. Silent movements. The boots slide on last, black leather laced and buckled tight. A belt threaded with loops for my hidden weapons rests across my hip, securing throwing blades and an extra bowstring, anchoring me in place. If I go with him, I'm stepping straight into the teeth of whatever game Morrigan is playing. If I stay, I hand them proof that I could be used against him.

Neither choice is safe.

I glance at my reflection. Black on black. Sharp instead of softness. Straps and buckles trace my silhouette like weapons themselves. The girl who stood weaponless at the Pit is gone. What stares back is precise, silent, ready, and terrifying.

Morrigan's sanctum is not a place one stumbles into. It is a place that calls you, and the call isn't something you can ignore.

Travelling silently through the spiraling hallways of the stronghold, the atmosphere is stifling from the heavy weight of stone and shadow. The dimming light from the torches lining the walls provides a jagged light for only a moment, but their brightness cannot chase away the weight of the ceiling pressing down upon me.

The hallway continues to twist and narrow, and finally leads me to the staircase that has been carved out of rock itself. Each step I take on the staircase makes only the slightest echo, yet I allow the darkness of the shadows to mask my presence completely, and I let only instinct guide my actions. At the top of the stairway, I am finally at the doors of Morrigan Sanctum.

As I stand in the doorway, the air is heavy with incense so profuse it clings to my nostrils. Shadows dance across the stone walls where black-feathered talismans sway from hooks, their movements too synchronized to be stirred by mere draft. Candles burn low, the flames guttering as if bowing to their mistress.

Morrigan stands before an altar, her back turned, the sweep of her dark robes pooling like a spill of night. When she turns, her eyes gleam in the candlelight.

"You came," Morrigan says, her voice a velvet blade. "Good. This cannot wait."

I swallow. "What do you want from me?"

A faint smile curves the Crow Queen's lips. "Your blood."

The words ring in the air, simple but heavy.

I stiffen. "Why?"

She steps closer, the click of her talons like shoes against the stone floor far too deliberate. "Because the wraths that plague this land cannot be vanquished with steel alone. They are born from shadow, from the wrongness that seeps between realms. Your blood … is different. It is threaded with the mark of the old fires, the kind that can burn through the Veil itself."

Her fingers sweep over my chin, deliberate yet commanding. "A single drop could anchor a spell strong enough to bind them. Enough of it, willingly given, could end their reign entirely."

The sincerity in her tone pulls at something in my chest; the hope that this endless fear might finally end.

But there is something else there too, a flicker in her eyes that had nothing to do with salvation. Hunger, perhaps? Or ambition.

"And if I refuse?" I ask, my voice steadier than I feel.

She smiles wider. "Then you condemn this land to rot and the wraths to feast. And when they come for those you care for, you will know it was within your power to stop them."

The words are perfectly measured, a mixture of truth and guilt, stitched together so tightly it is hard to see the seam.

My heart pounds. I don't answer. Not yet.

She leans in, her voice almost tender. "You don't have to decide now. But you will. And when you do, I will be waiting." The words cling to me, heavy and impossible to ignore, and I can feel the weight of the choice pressing against my chest as I leave.

CHAPTER 29

WHISPERS IN THE STONE

ELARA

The air outside Morrigan's sanctum feels colder, sharper. As if the shadows are following me out, brushing my skin in a silent reminder of the bargain I haven't yet made. The meeting fades behind me, but her words don't. They follow me down the corridor, the moment of decision creeping closer with each slow beat of my heart.

I descend the narrow spiral of stone steps, each footfall echoing in the hollow dark. My mind replays the Crow Queen's voice, those perfectly measured words, repeatedly until they tangle together in a knot I can't untie.

"It could end the Wraths." "It's within your power." "I'll be waiting."

By the time I reach the lower hall, my breath comes in uneven spurts. I want space, but the air here carries a different kind of weight—an unshakable sense of being watched is heightened.

A figure steps from an alcove, cloaked in dark green, a hood shadows their face. "Elara."

I freeze. The voice is male and threaded with a roughness that suggests too many winters in the Highlands.

The man lifts his head just enough for the torchlight to catch his eyes, ocean blue eyes. "She asked for your blood, didn't she?"

My pulse stumbles. "How did you know?"

He gives a humourless sneer. "Because she has asked it before of others. And those who give it … don't always get the ending they are promised."

Something cold crawls up my spine. "What are you saying?"

"I'm saying Morrigan rarely reveals the deal in its entirety," he says, leaning closer. "Yes, your blood might burn the wraths. But it can also open doors best left closed. And I've never known her to resist the chance to walk through one."

I swallow hard. "Why are you telling me this?"

"Because you're not the first to stand where you are. And the last one? We never saw her again."

The torch near them flickers violently, as if a gust of wind had passed, but no breeze stirs the air. The man steps back into the shadows, his voice a whisper now.

"Think carefully, Elara. A queen's promise is not always made for the good of her kingdom."

And then he is gone, swallowed by the corridor's darkness before I could ask his name.

I stand in the middle of the dancing shadows, heart pounding, trapped between the weight of what Morrigan has promised and the specter of warning I have just received.

HELIOS

Her presence reaches me before she does.

That shift in the air, sharp, cold, and tainted with something I don't like, is always my first warning. Elara is coming back from Morrigan's chambers.

I lean against the stone pillar near the training hall entrance, arms folded, watching her stride toward me. Her steps are too quick, her shoulders too stiff. Something has clearly unsettled her.

"Not a tea party, I'm guessing," Vulcan's voice murmurs in my head, dry as sun-bleached bone.

"Not now," I think back sharply.

"Suit yourself," Vulcan replies. *"But I've been around long enough to know when someone walks like that, they're either running from trouble or toward it."*

I push off the pillar and follow her toward the stairs. "Elara."

No response.

"Elara." My voice deepens.

Still nothing.

I catch up to her at the landing, blocking her path with

one arm propped against the wall. "What. Did. She. Want?"

Her eyes flick up to mine, guarded but not hostile. "She wants my blood."

For a long moment, I stare at her. "What?!"

"Oh, this won't end well." Vulcan drawls. *"An ancient murder-bird queen asks for your blood. Sure, let's just give her the keys to the kingdom while we're at it."*

My jaw tightens. "*Shut up*."

"She says it could destroy the wraths," Elara continues quietly. "End them for good."

"Yeah. Or end you," Vulcan mutters darkly.

"And you believe her?" I murmur. Her hesitation is the answer I need. "Elara." My voice drops, but the steel stays. "Morrigan does nothing without stacking the deck in her favor. She's a vulture in a crown. Your blood might burn the wraths, but it could also give her something she's been waiting centuries for. Something we can't take back."

"I know what I'm doing," she says, stepping past me.

"And here comes the part where she ignores you completely." Vulcan sighs.

I shoot my hand out to catch her wrist. "No, you think you know. There's a difference. And if you go through with this without telling me everything, I'll drag you out of her chamber myself."

She narrows her eyes. "Even if it means letting the wraths keep killing?"

I don't flinch. "If it means saving you from something worse."

We stand there, locked in a silent battle, until Vulcan's voice comes through one last time, softer now. *"Careful, brother. You're fighting her... But you're also fighting fate."*

The hallways of the fortress feel different at night. Quieter, yes, but with a heaviness that presses against the skin. Torchlight paints the stone in shades of gold and shadow as I walk deeper into the wing that houses Morrigan's private sanctum.

"Are you sure about this?" Vulcan's voice slides into my mind, a low rasp like a blade on a whetstone.

"Yes," I answer in my mind.

"Funny. You don't sound that sure when you say it out loud."

"I'm not letting her spill Elara's blood without knowing the whole game."

"Then be ready for the rules to change mid-play," Vulcan mutters. *"She's not the type to show all her cards. Hell, she doesn't even play with a full deck; she hides half of it up her sleeve."*

I round the last corner and find the double obsidian doors. They are carved with ravens in flight, wings overlapping like a wall of black feathers. Two guards stand watch, each armed with curved blades and armour so dark they appear to drink the torchlight.

They cross their spears.

"She's expecting me," I say flatly.

"They don't care if she's expecting you," Vulcan warns.

"These types would sooner die than disobey her orders."

I don't slow. "Move."

The guards hesitate just enough for me to push past, my sheer presence making the air thick with challenge. I push the doors open and step into Morrigan's chamber.

The room is a cathedral of shadows. Velvet drapes bleed into the black stone walls, and the scent of something metallic and ancient lingers in the air. Morrigan sits at the far end on a throne of bone and iron, her eyes glinting like a predator in the half-light.

"You come without invitation," she says, her voice smooth as silk over steel.

"I'm here for answers." I stride forward, the echo of my boots like a drumbeat. "You told Elara her blood could destroy the wraths. What aren't you telling her?"

A faint smile slants her lips. "Straight to the point. I always liked that about you."

"Careful," Vulcan murmurs in his mind. *"That's the smile of someone who's already three moves ahead."*

I stop a few feet from her. "The truth. Now."

Morrigan tilts her head. "Her blood is rare. It is touched by something older than your clan's bloodline. Yes, it could destroy the wraths, but it could also break the Veil between realms. That power doesn't disappear; it transfers."

"To you."

"To anyone who drinks it."

"And there it is," Vulcan says grimly. *"The part she*

didn't tell Elara."

My fists clench. "You'll get her blood over my dead body."

Morrigan's eyes glint with interest. "That can be arranged."

CHAPTER 30

STEEL AND SHADOWS

HELIOS

The promise sits between us, heavy and unyielding. I don't raise my voice. I don't need to. Some vows don't echo when they settle. "You'll get her blood over my dead body."

Morrigan's eyes glint with interest. "That can be arranged."

The words come out low and flat, with no roar, no snarl, just the kind of promise that carves into bone.

Morrigan's smile doesn't falter. If anything, it sharpens, like the edge of a blade that had just found the right neck. Her crimson eyes slide over me as though I am a piece of iron she meant to heat, shape, and break.

"Oh, nice line." Vulcan purrs in my head, his tone far too amused for the situation. "*But you know she's filing that one away in her 'How to Murder Helios' journal."*

I don't answer him. I keep my gaze locked on Morrigan's, unwilling to give her the satisfaction of even a blink.

"You're protective, I'll give you that," she says, her voice a silken threat. "But protection means little when fate demands a price."

"Translation: She's already working on how to pry Elara open like a wine cask and drain her dry," Vulcan adds," voice dripping with mock sympathy. "*And you? You're the first thing she'll have to break to reach Elara."*

My jaw tightens. "If fate demands a price, I'll pay it myself."

Her laughter is soft and dangerous. "Not all debts can be paid in coin or blood of your own. Some debts require a rarer currency." She leans forward just enough for me to feel the weight of her words. "Her blood is the only thing that will bind the wraths and send them screaming back to the void. Without it, they will feast on your land, your people, and eventually… her."

Vulcan hums in my skull. *"Oh, good. She's going the guilt angle. I love this part. Watch next, she's going to make herself sound like the hero of the whole bloody story."*

"You think I'll hand her over because you've dressed it up as salvation?" I ask.

Morrigan's smile turns cold. "No. I think you'll hand her over because you'll realize there's no other way."

"There it is." Vulcan sounds almost proud. "*Right on cue."*

I step back, not in retreat, but to put space between her

and me before I forget diplomacy altogether. My hand twitches toward the hilt of my blade. She notices. Of course she does.

"You're still here because you think you can bargain with me," I say, voice rougher now. "You're wrong."

Her gaze lingers, unbothered by my threat. "And you're still here because part of you wonders if I'm right."

I turn, forcing myself toward the heavy doors. The air behind me feels like it is pressing against my spine, willing me to turn back.

"You know," Vulcan murmurs, almost lazily, *"I could give you a dozen ways to make sure she never speaks that prophecy again. Most of them involve fire."*

"Not now."

"Suit yourself. But when she comes for Elara again, don't say I didn't tell you so."

The door groans as I shove it open, the cold hallway beyond a relief after the heat of Morrigan's gaze. I don't look back.

Because part of me, the part I hate, knows she is right about one thing: she won't stop.

And the next time she comes for Elara's blood, I might not have the luxury of walking away.

HELIOS

The door slams behind me, the echo chases me down the stone corridor like a war drum. My boots hit the floor harder than I mean them to.

"You're stomping," Vulcan observes dryly. *"It's a very angry toddler, except you could crush someone if you tripped."*

"Shut it," I mutter, rounding the corner toward the training grounds.

I find Alasdair leaning against a post, arms folded, watching two recruits try not to gut each other with practice blades. His brows lift the moment he sees my face.

"What did she say?" he asks.

"That she wants Elara's blood." The words land like steel hitting stone, blunt and heavy. "And that it's the only thing that will bind the wraths for good."

Alasdair's jaw works. "And you told her?"

"That she'll get it over my dead body."

"Which, to be fair," Vulcan chimes in, *"she looks quite interested in arranging."*

Alasdair curses under his breath, glancing toward the far end of the yard where Elara isn't, thank the gods. "We tighten her guard. No one gets within arm's reach of her without your say."

"Not enough," I snap. "If Morrigan's desperate enough, she won't come through the front gate. She'll tear her way through the shadows if she has to."

"Now we're talking," Vulcan says, his voice curls with anticipation. *"I say triple the guards, hide her somewhere she hates, and arm her to the teeth. Oh, and maybe teach her to bite."*

Alasdair's eyes narrow. "You think Morrigan will move soon?"

"I think she's already moving," I say. "And if she is, I want her to find every path blocked by stone, steel, or fire."

Alasdair gives a short nod and moves off, already barking orders.

"You know this means you'll have to tell Elara." Vulcan points out that, suddenly, it's quieter. *"And she's not going to take it well."*

I stare toward the far wall where the sky bleeds into night.

No, she won't.

But it is better she be angry with me than bled dry for someone else's war.

Later That Night

Elara's Dream

I stand in a place that feels older than memory itself; black sand under my bare feet and a violet sky heavy with stars that seem too close. The wind smells of snow and iron.

From the shadows, a woman emerges, tall and severe, her hair the colour of midnight waterfalls, her eyes like glacial-blue fire. A circlet of woven silver crowns her head, etched with runes that shimmer when she speaks.

"Elara," the goddess's voice is deep enough to shake the ground, yet soft enough to coil around my name like a promise. "Your blood is not Morrigan's to take. It is forged for more than the binding of wraths."

I swallow. "Then what is it for?"

"Find the man who warned you not to trust her," the goddess said, stepping closer until her shadow swallows the black sand. "He holds an ancient scroll written when the first Hellhound Summoners walked the earth. Only then will you learn the truth of your bloodline."

The wind howls, tugging at the goddess's hair like unseen hands.

"Go to him, child of the Amethyst Inferno," she commands. "And do not delay. Morrigan hunts more than your life. She hunts the future of all who bear the mark."

Before I could ask her name, the stars fracture, the sand dissolves, and I wake up with the echo of the goddess's words ringing in my ears. An unbroken thread tugs sharp and restless, like a warning I can feel before I even see her.

CHAPTER 31

UNSPOKEN STORMS

HELIOS

I feel her wake before she stirs. That same thread pulls, insistent and urgent, as if someone has rattled the cage of her soul. She sits up in bed, the moonlight casting silver bars across her face. Her eyes dart, unfocused, still half in a place she can't shake off.

"She's dreaming of me," Vulcan says cheerfully in my head.

"Doubt it," I mutter under my breath.

Elara's gaze snaps to me. "What?"

"Nothing," I say, leaning back in my chair by the fire. "Bad dream?"

She hesitates. Too long. Her fingers twist in the blanket, her knuckles pale.

"Just… something strange," she says finally, voice even

but tight.

"Liar, Vulcan murmurs, his tone almost amused. "*Oh, she's hiding something shiny. Bet you a horn of mead it's about that raven-eyed goddess you don't want to think about."*

I ignore him. "Strange how?"

Elara's eyes flick away, settling on the flames instead of me. "I'll tell you later. I need… I need to clear my head." She swings her legs off the bed and pads toward the bathtub like the conversation is already over.

Every instinct in me screams to push, to demand, to shake the truth out of her before it slips further away. But I've seen that look in her before—corner her now, and she'd shut down entirely.

"You're going to let her stroll around with a secret that might get her killed?" Vulcan asks, tone dripping with sarcasm and warning.

"I'm going to let her think she has space," I say, low enough that only the fire crackles and the demon in my head can hear me.

"Uh-huh. And in the meantime, Morrigan's playing her own game of fetch-the-blood."

Elara comes back with her hair damp, her movements slower, but that tension is still coiled under her skin. She crawls back into bed without looking at me.

I sit there until her breathing evens out again, my jaw tight.

She thinks she is protecting me from something.

She doesn't understand that whatever storm is coming

for her, she would have to go through me first.

Dawn bleeds over the horizon in pale gold, and Elara is still asleep.

She looks so peaceful, but I know better. Peace doesn't cling to you when the goddess of the night has been whispering in your head.

I stand by the window, hands braced on the cold stone, watching the village stir awake far below.

"You're thinking about that man she mentioned meeting outside of Morrigan sanctum?" Vulcan says lazily in my skull.

"Thinking?" I mutter. "No. Deciding."

"Oh, so you're going to play the overprotective alpha again. How very you."

I ignore him, going over every scrap of rumor, every half-buried name I have about the man I have to warn her about. If the goddess is right, he has an ancient scroll that speaks of the first Hellhound Summoners and the truth of her blood.

And if Morrigan wants that blood … I need to know why before Elara is backed into a corner.

"She's not going to thank you for this," Vulcan warns, but his voice carries a thread of approval.

"She doesn't have to," I say, grabbing my sword and strapping it across my back.

One last glance at her sleeping form. She shifts slightly, like she senses I am leaving.

I force myself to turn away before the urge to wake her and tell her everything gets the better of me.

"So, what's the plan, oh fearless leader?" Vulcan asks.

"Find the man," I say, stepping into the hall. "Find the scroll. And find out why the hell her blood is the key to everything."

Vulcan chuckles. *"And if she catches you?"*

"Then she'll yell," I said, striding toward the stables, "and I'll deserve it."

"But some truths are worth the storm." I think to myself.

The ride north is silent except for the Vulcan drumming of his paws and the low, sarcastic hum of him in my head.

"You know, most people ask directions before heading into cursed forest territory."

"Most people aren't me," I mutter, tightening my grip with my knees.

The further up I go, the thicker the air becomes, damp with a weight that presses against my skin. It isn't just fog, it is magic, old and watching.

After hours, the trees part, revealing a weather-worn cottage tucked into a cliffside, ruins carved deep into the stone around its frame.

"That's him," I say under my breath.

"Or it's the home of a deranged squirrel collector," Vulcan quips. *"Either way, I'm entertained."*

I dismount, my boots sink into the moss, and I knock once.

The door opens before I can knock again, revealing a man with hair the color of frost and eyes so pale they seem almost white.

"You're late," he says.

I frown. "Late?"

"You think the goddess of the night sends people to me every day?" He says, stepping aside, motioning me in. "I know why you're here. It's about her."

I don't bother to deny it. "The scroll. I need it."

He studies me for a long, uncomfortable moment, then shakes his head.

"No. Not until I see her. The truth I have isn't meant for you, it's hers by birthright."

"That's not how this works," I say, stepping closer.

"That's exactly how it works," he replies, voice calm and unshakable. "If she's ready for what the scroll contains, she'll come herself. If she isn't, giving it to you would only hasten her end."

"Well," Vulcan drawls in my skull, *"that went as well as a drunk hellhound at a royal banquet."*

I exhale slowly, forcing down the urge to argue. "Then I'll bring her," I say, my tone leaving no room for debate.

The man nods, as if he knew that would be my answer.

“Good. But tell her Morrigan doesn’t just want her blood for power. She wants it to finish what the first Summoners died trying to stop.”

CHAPTER 32

KEEPER'S SECRET

ELARA

Helios returns at dusk. The light behind him is fading fast, staining the sky in streaks of violet and gold, but I barely see it. My eyes lock on him in the calm, controlled way he dismounts and the way he doesn't meet my gaze.

That tells me everything.

"Oh, this is going to be good." Kallesie's voice slides into my mind, all syrupy sarcasm. "*Your fearless leader waltzes back after a mysterious meeting all broody, and you're just supposed to smile? Please."*

I fold my arms. "Where were you?"

Helios doesn't flinch. "With the Keeper."

The name hit like a slap. I take one step forward. "Keeper? The one you said can't be trusted. You went to him without me?"

His jaw tightens, but he stays silent.

"Ohhh, the guilty look," Kallesie drawls. "*Classic. Next, he'll tell you it is 'for your own good,' bet you five gold coins."*

"You don't get to make those decisions for me," I say, voice low but shaking with the effort to hold steady. "If this is about my blood, I deserve to hear it from him myself."

That got him. His eyes flicker-not guilt, not quite, but the kind of tension that means he is holding something back.

"I have my reasons," he says at last.

"There it is!" Kallesie sang. "*My reasons: Translation, 'I did something, you're going to hate me for when you find out.'"*

I take a breath through my nose, trying to keep my temper from spilling over. "You've been keeping things from me since the moment we met. But this?" I shake my head. "This is different."

His gaze softens, almost imperceptibly. "I have something for you. It was given to me for you."

He reaches into his cloak and pulls out a bundle wrapped in an old hide. My hands don't move to take it right away.

"What is it?"

"Truth," he says. "And danger."

"Could he be more vague?" Kallesie muttered. "*'Truth and danger.' Might as well hand you a box labeled 'Here Be Problems."*

Finally, I take the bundle. Its weight is real, almost alive, and my gut tells me whatever it holds will change everything.

And if the look in his eyes is any warning, it will do so at a price.

I tighten my grip on the bundle. "You're taking me to him."

Helios studies me for a moment, then gives a single nod.

We leave before the moon rises, riding into the tangled wilds where the shadows seemed to stretch longer than they should. The air grew colder with every mile, and somewhere in the distance, a low, keening wail slid across the wind.

Wraths.

Helios's posture shifts, shoulders tense, eyes scanning, but he doesn't slow.

"Oh great," Kallesie says in my head, voice dripping in sarcasm. "*Wraths, a mysterious old man, and you carrying a bundle of truth and danger. Definitely not the start of a horror story."*

"They come this far south?" I ask Helios quietly.

"They do now," he replies, equally low.

The further we venture, the more the forest seems to close in, trees bending like they are listening. I catch him glancing at me now and then, but I don't give him the satisfaction of meeting his eyes.

When Keeper's dwelling finally appears, a ruin half swallowed by ivy and moonlight, I realize my heart is pounding, not from fear, but from the bone-deep sense that something inside will answer questions I hadn't dared to ask.

Helios dismounts before me and offers his hand to help me dismount from Kallesie. I ignore it.

"Ooooh," Kallesie purrs in my mind. *"Someone's still mad."*

Most would have ignored the dwelling without a second glance, assuming it was abandoned. That is the point. Keeper does not invite visitors; he tolerates them.

HELIOS

Elara walks ahead of me, square shoulders, chin high, pretending she isn't furious. Vulcan's voice rattles in my head, relentless and loud.

"She's not walking ahead to scout the path. She's walking ahead so she doesn't have to look at you."

"I noticed," I say.

"Good. Now, see the dagger at her hip? If you keep this up, you might find it in your ribs before the night's out."

We stop beneath the arch of blackened stone. Inside, the light bends into a murky gold as fire flickers low in the hearth. Keeper sits there, as though he's been waiting his entire life for this moment—gaunt, weathered, with eyes like pale ice chips.

"You brought her," he rasps, voice like parchment tearing. "Finally."

Elara stiffens. "I thought Helios was the one who met

you. How do you know me?"

Keeper's gaze becomes unnerving. "Child, I have known who you are since before your first breath. Your blood carries the first spark—the one Morrigan covets. The one that should never be hers."

I step forward, jaw tightening. "What is it about her blood that Morrigan wants?"

Keeper's bony fingers drum against the armchair. "The wraths you face now are shadows of what's to come. Morrigan feeds them and lets them loose upon the land, but they are not her endgame. If she has the girl's blood … she will have the key to command them all and what sleeps beneath the Veil."

Vulcan mutters in my head. "*Oh, great. Because controlling an army of undead nightmares isn't bad enough.*"

ELARA

My voice is sharp. "And what am I supposed to do about it?"

Keeper leans forward, his expression hard. "You must find the truth of your blood. Not from Morrigan. Not from me. There is a scroll, an ancient record from the first Hellhound Summoners, that tells of the bloodlines' blessings and curses by the old gods. But be warned… the one who guards it will demand a price you may not wish to pay."

My gut twists. "Where is it?"

"In the ruins beyond the Frostmark pass."

Keeper's gaze flickers to me, almost pitiful. "But you will not both return from that place unchanged."

The fire crackles. Outside, the wind picks up, carrying the distant, hollow wail of a wrath.

And for the first time since we entered, my anger isn't enough to keep the fear at bay.

CHAPTER 33

THE ROAD FROM THE MARSH

HELIOS

The fog clings to the ground, swallowing the trail ahead in a damp grey hush. Even after leaving Keeper's crumbling ruins, the air feels heavier, like his warning has followed us out and refuses to let go.

Vulcan pads steadily beneath me, his paws splashing through shallow pools. Ahead, Elara sits high on Kallesie's back, her violet eyes glowing like sharp lanterns in the mist.

Neither of them looks back at me.

"You're going to let her stew like that?" Vulcan's voice slid into my mind, deep and amused. *"Or is this one of those silent brooding things you do when you've stepped in something worse than swamp mud?"*

"She's angry."

"And whose fault would that be?"

I don't answer.

Elara sits tall on Kallesie, her gaze fixed forward. Her ears flicker. Although I can't hear her words, I can tell by the way Elara's jaw tightens that the hellhound is filling her head with something sharp and smug.

Vulcan snorts, sending up a faint curl of amethyst flame. "*Kallesie's lying to her, isn't she? I can tell. That little tail flick? That's her, I'm roasting him alive, look.*"

The Keeper's words echo, low and grim: "Morrigan will take her blood, not to kill her, but to command every Wrath in the realm... the scroll at Frostmark Pass .... the truth bound to trial and peril...."

"It's not cursed," I say finally, steering Vulcan around a fallen log. "Your blood—It's rare. Powerful."

Elara doesn't look back. "And dangerous."

"She's not wrong," Vulcan says. *"But dangerous makes her harder to kill. Which is good for you, seeing as you seem allergic to keeping her out of trouble."*

"The Keeper was clear," I continue, ignoring him. "We can't let Morrigan get near you. But that scroll … it might be the only way to know exactly what you are. And if he's right, getting it won't be simple."

She finally turns her head, just enough for me to catch the fire in her eyes. "We're still going." She says, and I feel it land straight on me.

Vulcan rumbles approval in my mind. "*Ah, she's decided. Guess we're heading into something sharp and bloody again. My favorite.*"

For the first time since leaving the ruins, the corner of

her mouth twitches upward, barely, but enough to make me think that despite Keeper's warning, we are not broken. Not yet.

ELARA

The pass narrows until it feels like we are riding through the throat of some great stone beast, spiked rock walls closing in on both sides. Snow swirls around us in restless storms, catching in my lashes and numbing my fingers.

Kallesie slows beneath me, her gaze sweeping the drifts ahead. Her ears flicker twice, then she stops altogether, every muscle beneath my legs going taut.

"Tell the glacier to shut up. I smell something ahead of us," she murmurs, her voice curling warm and smug in my mind.

I straighten, scanning the wind-blown trail. "Helios."

"I see it," he says from behind me.

"No, he doesn't," Kallesie says. "*But his pride won't let him admit that."*

I catch a faint curl of heat in the corner of my vision from behind.

Kallesie's tone sharpens in my head. "*We're being followed. Something smells wrong. Hunger and rot."*

Then I catch it. It's faint, but there. A sickly-sweet, decay scent riding in the cold air. Wraths.

"Tracks?" Helios asks.

I shook my head. "Nothing human."

"Because it's not human," Kallesie said. "*It's hunting us. Hunting you."*

I lean forward; my knees tighten around Kallesie. "We need to move faster."

"Smart girl," Kallesie purrs. "*Though I could outrun them with time to spare and still have enough breath left to make Vulcan eat snow."*

A huff of heat rolls from behind, melting a patch of ice at my side.

I see Vulcan's heavy strides pounding behind us, each step leaving a hiss of steam.

Kallesie growls low enough that only I feel the vibration through her fur.

"Say that again, furnace breath."

I glance back. *"Who are you talking to?"*

Kallesie's hair bristles slightly, and a sneering tone in my mind. *"Oh, just Vulcan, furnace breath, and I are having a little chat. Not like you can hear it."*

A low, guttural hiss ripples through the pass. Then another. Shadows slide along the rocks above us too fast. They are catching us.

Kallesie's eyes flare brightly. "*On the cliffs. Left side.*"

Before I can react, snow explodes from the ridge as the first Wrath launches toward us, a ball of claws, teeth, and rags of skin flapping like rotting parchment.

Helios's voice rumbles through the rising howl. "Ride!"

Kallesie surges forward, snow spraying in our wake. Vulcan's massive body barrels through the snow behind us.

But the Wraths don't scatter; they follow, their shapes weave between cliff shadows, the stench of them chokes the air.

Kallesie says in a snarl. "*They're driving us.*"

"Where?" I mutter, and then the ground cracks, snow slumps inward to reveal a jagged pit—a trap.

Two Wraths drop from the cliff's edge, blocking the path back. Another lunges from the pit, and its claws reach for me.

Kallesie rears, molten eyes blazing, and my hands move before I can think. I raise my bow, no arrow knocked, and pull the bowstring taut.

Something answers, and a deep, velvet-dark hum shivers through my veins, pooling in my chest, my arms, and my fingertips. When I release the string, a streak of black and violet light shoots forward-an arrow made of pure night.

It hits the Wrath mid-lunge. The creature convulses with a shriek that sounds like wind tearing through bones, then crumbles into ash.

I stare at my empty bow. My breath comes fast, frosting the air.

"What is that?" Helios demands, steering Vulcan into a wide circle as the remaining Wraths regroup.

"I…I don't know," I say, even though the word "the night answered me" echoes in my mind like a drumbeat.

Kallesie's voice is sharp, almost reverent. "*Oh… you do know.*"

Another Wrath leaps. I draw again, and the night answers.

The second Wrath is faster. It drops low, claws scrape the snow as it darts to my right, jaws opening wider to attack us.

I try another shot, and the arrow of shadow and violet heat burns through its skull. The thing shrieks once and is gone, dust in the wind.

Vulcan slams into a third, his massive weight sending it tumbling into the pit. Steam hisses off his hide as he snarls, molten eyes daring the rest to try.

"*Focus, steam-for-brains*," Kallesie snaps, surging beneath me as she weaves between two Wraths, their claws slicing through empty air where a heartbeat ago. "*Unless you want them chewing your pretty face off, Vulcan, Opps, wrong chat. My bad.*"

A fourth creature scrambles up the rock wall, hissing.

I pivot, draw…

And I feel something trying to answer. The air around my hand grows cold and heavy, and the shadows seem to curl toward my fingers, as if they know me. I shoot, and the arrow is faster this time, less light, more darkness.

It does not just pierce the wrath. It swallows it whole.

Helios's voice thunders through the chaos. "Elara!"

I turn and see him staring at me. His eyes are steel and shadow, something almost like dread flickers there.

"The Keeper's warning," he mutters under his breath, more to himself than to me.

"What?" I shout over the sound of Kallesie ramming another Wrath aside while I try to hold on and aim my bow.

Vulcan barrels into the melee, his massive head snapping one creature in half with a single bite. Steam rolls from his nostrils as he tosses the limp body away.

"*Your aim is sloppy,*" Kallesie shoots back in my head, "*but I suppose it passes for dramatic effect. Gods, this is getting bad. I'll keep letting you in on just enough to keep us.*"

Three Wraths remain, circling now, their movements jagged and hesitant. They know.

Helios urges Vulcan forward, guiding us ahead. The snow melts in our wake, leaving a trail that leads straight to a cave too small for the creatures to follow with their long limbs, but big enough for us to slip through one at a time. I draw again, but this time Helios raises a hand.

"Elara," he says, voice low, "don't burn yourself out. That power is not just yours."

"I didn't ask for it," I shot back.

"That doesn't mean it won't take something in return," he says, steel eyes locking with mine for just a heartbeat, long enough for the Wraths to move again.

Kallesie dives, and I let the bowstring fly.

The world goes violet and black.

When it clears, nothing remains of the Wraths but drifting snow and ash, spinning away into the mountain wind.

The snow settles slowly, and the only sound left is my breath, sharp in my ears.

Vulcan runs behind us, steam curling off his back, and Helios swings down from Vulcan's back with a grunt. His gaze sweeps the empty expanse where the Wraths have been.

Kallesie's sides rise and fall beneath me, her breath warm and steady. "*Too close? Please. I had it handled. We own this mountain now, sweetheart. Wait, wrong chat again, fuck. This is getting embarrassing.*"

I snort, despite myself, the sound halfway between relief and exhaustion.

Helios mutters something under his breath that sounds suspiciously like, "Gods help me."

And for the first time since the Keeper's warning, I let myself laugh just once before the cold wind sweeps it away.

CHAPTER 34

DOWN THE MOUNTAIN

ELARA

The path snakes down the mountainside, a narrow ribbon of snow and ice, and the wind cuts raw across my cheeks. Kallesie's paws crunch over the snow in a steady rhythm, her body warm and solid beneath me, grounding me even as fear tightens its grip again. Ahead, Helios rides high on Vulcan's back, both framed against the silver-grey sweeps of the valley below, calmly and impossibly still despite the wind whipping around them.

"You're brooding again," Kallesie says in my head, her tone all smug satisfaction. *"It's a terrible look for you. Makes your face do that pinchy thing."*

"I'm thinking," I mutter, keeping my eyes on Helios's broad back.

"Same thing," she replies, utterly unbothered.

Helios doesn't turn, but I can see the way his shoulders

stiffen. “You’re quiet.” I tighten my grip on Kallesie’s sides. He replies. “Then again, so are you.”

Vulcan’s tail sways in almost idle rhythm. I can’t hear him, but Helios’s expression changed. His jaw tightened.

Vulcan must be talking to him. Helios speaks flatly. “Vulcan says you’re furious,” He says, “it's because we left without you.”

Kallesie gives a low, throaty snort and tosses her head. “*Understatement of the year.*”

“I’m not furious,” I say through clenched teeth.

“Liar.” Kallesie sing-songs, her voice rich with amusement. “*You’re so mad you’re practically vibrating. I can feel.*”

The keeper’s warning burns in my mind, no matter how hard I try to push it aside: “*The Wraths will come for it until the seal is broken, or you are.*”

Vulcan gives a low, amused rumble in Helios’s mind, his ears twitched, “*Told you, boss. Should’ve brought her from the start. You’re lucky she hasn’t set you on fire yet.*”

Helios mutters something under his breath that the wind tears away.

Kallesie’s tone softens, the humour slipping. “*You're afraid of what it means.*”

“Yes,” I whisper before I can stop myself.

Helios must have heard, because he half-turns on Vulcan's back. His eyes meet mine. For a heartbeat, neither of us speaks. The only sounds are the crunch of the snow under massive paws and the wind sighing through the pines.

Then Kallesie huffs. "*Well. This is uncomfortable. Somebody say something before I have to start biting people to break the tension.*"

We finally descend the final slope, the frozen forest opening to the wide, frost-dusted clearing at the base of the mountain. The air feels thicker here, heavier with the weight of unspoken words.

Finally, I couldn't hold it any longer. "You went to see him without me. "

Helios exhales slowly. "Because it was safer…"

"Don't." My voice pitches, harsher than I intend, and even Kallesie goes silent in my head. "Don't tell me what's safer for me. I heard the warning, but you and Vulcan left me behind like I didn't deserve to hear it with you."

Vulcan flickers an ear and mutters something to Helios that made his mouth twitch, either in annoyance or guilt, I can't tell.

"I am trying to protect you," he says.

"Then maybe next time," I snap, "protect me by trusting me." The words hang between us, bitter and cold as the winter air.

Kallesie breaks the silence with a satisfied hum in my head. *"Finally. I was getting bored.*"

Helios doesn't answer me right away. The forest between us is thick enough to choke on.

Then Kallesie's ears snap forward, every muscle under me going taut. "*Ohhh… this isn't good.*" I straighten. "What is it?"

Her answer is a low, thrumming growl in my skull.

"Wraths. Three... No four of them. Moving fast."

"They smell you," Kallesie warns. *"That Keeper wasn't exaggerating. They're locked onto you like wolves on a blood trail."*

Kallesie's muscles bunch. *"I hate these things. They taste like regret and old socks."*

I almost choke on a laugh despite the terror. "Really not the time."

"Humour is precisely the time," she replies, her voice buzzing like static. "*You die scared, or you die laughing. I have a preference.*"

I don't have time to process the fear. My bow is already in my hands, an arrow ready to fire instinctively. The trees ahead seem to blur, shadows peel themselves away from the bark and snow.

HELIOS

Vulcan swings his massive head toward the treeline, his molten eyes catch a glint of movement. My jaw tightens. "Vulcan feels them too."

The air around us grows colder, sharper, as if the world has inhaled and refuses to exhale. Snow begins to swirl in strange patterns, twisting against the wind.

I rein Vulcan closer, my voice low. "Stay to my left. Don't let them flank you."

She shoots me a sharp look. "Now you want me beside

you?"

My lips twitch, half grimace, half something else. "Now I need you beside me."

The first Wraith emerges tall and skeletal, its black smoke-wreathed form half-solid, half-nightmare. The others follow, their movements unnerving, as if the world skips a frame every time they shift forward.

Vulcan let out a deep, rumbling snort in Helios's mind. His eyes flicker to me. "*Tell your girl to aim for the core. And if she misses, I'm eating the first one that gets close.*"

The Wraths fan out in the snow, their eyeless faces lock on me. One hisses, the sound like wind dragging over broken glass.

"On my mark," I say, drawing his blade in a smooth, deadly arc.

"Mark," She echoes, raising her bow.

The world narrows to breath, heartbeat, and the dark shapes coming for us.

Elara

"Now!" He yells.

I shoot my arrow. Helios charges. Kallesie and Vulcan hit the snow like thunder.

The Wraths scream.

And the mountain stops being cold.

Snow explodes under Kallesie's paws as we weave

between lunging shadows.

Arrows flow from my string faster than I can think.

Too fast.

Each shot sinks into a wrath's chest, not just piercing but tearing the shadow apart like a stone dropping into black water.

I don't understand how I am moving like this.

It feels… effortless. Too effortless.

"Not to alarm you," Kallesie's voice chimes in my mind, *"but you're glowing. A little. Kinda like moonlight that decided to get mad."*

I barely had time to register before one of the Wraths lunged, its claws grazing my arm. Pain flares, raw and biting, but the cold is bone-deep, dragging at my heartbeat.

Helios and Vulcan tear through the side, his sword burning with strange heat in the frozen air. "Stay with me!" he barks.

"I am!" I snap back, spinning Kallesie to line up another shot.

Wraths aren't just attacking; they are circling me like they know something. Like, I am the reason they have come this far.

One darts low, shadow tendrils whipping out. I yank my bow up to block, and I breathe in.

And the world dims.

Not just from the clouds or the snow.

The light itself bent away from me, shadows curling at

my command like startled birds returning to roost.

The Wrath freezes mid-lunge, shivering in place, as if the darkness had turned against it.

I release the arrow, and the creature shatters into nothing.

Kallesie slows just enough to glance back at me with molten eyes. "*...Okay, so... Are we pretending you didn't just do that? Or are we talking about it now?*"

"Now is not the time!" I hiss, drawing again.

"Suit yourself. But just so you know, that wasn't me."

The fight blurs into flashes of steel, flame, and the strange new power curling in my chest like something ancient and awake.

And somewhere in chaos, I feel a presence not watching from the shadows but from the stars.

Nyx.

CHAPTER 35

AFTER THE SILENCE

ELARA

The snow is quiet.

Not the soft, peaceful kind, this is the silencc after something violent has taken everything it could. The power in my chest still thrums, curling like a living thing, and I can feel Nyx lingering in spaces between the stars and snow.

Helios dismounts in one smooth motion, stalking toward me with that look that says I am about to be interrogated like a criminal.

Kallesie snorts in my mind. *"Oh, here we go. Captain Tall, Dark, and Broody is in full lecture mode. I give it two minutes before he starts pacing."*

I slide off her back, landing harder than I meant to. My legs are still shaky from the fight … and from whatever this is.

Helios doesn't waste time. "What in the hell was that?"

"What was what?" I ask, brushing snow off my arm like it is the most normal post-battle conversation ever.

His eyes narrow into slits. "Don't play dumb with me, Elara. You froze a Wrath mid-lunge and…." He makes a frustrated motion with his hands. "…it looks like the night itself is obeying you."

Kallesie Purrs. *"Obeying you. I like that. It has a nice ring to it. 'Queen of Shadows.' I'll have banners made."*

I keep my face carefully neutral. "It is instinct. Adrenaline. Nothing more."

"Stay out of this," Helios mutters under his breath.

I blink. "Talking to yourself again?"

"Don't change the subject." He steps closer, his height casting me in shadow. "You're hiding something, and after what the Keeper told us, that's dangerous. For all of us."

Kallesie huffs in my head. *"Oh, sure, tell him everything right here in the snow with the corpses of evil smoke in the background. Great timing."*

I turn away, adjusting my bow. "If I know what it is, I'd tell you. But I don't."

That is mostly true.

The memory of that strange stillness, that pulled from the stars, lingers in my bones like frost that won't melt. And though I don't understand it, I know one thing.

It hadn't been the Wrath that froze in fear.

It was the darkness itself, answering me.

The snow crunches under Kallesie's paws as we ride side by side, Helios on Vulcan a few feet away. Neither of us has said a word since leaving the Keeper's hidden grove.

The silence isn't comfortable. It is the kind that presses in, heavy.

Kallesie's voice slips into my head like a smug whisper. "*You could just tell him you're not ready to talk. Or, you know, tell him everything and watch him explode. That could be fun.*"

I tighten my grip with my knees. *"Not helping Kallesie."*

Kallesie perks her ears. "*Oh, I like this game. Let's both talk to our riders at the same time. See who snaps first, shit not this again, my baddies, Elara.*"

"Don't you dare…" I try to say it in my head, but she's closed me out.

Helios lets out a slow breath, his steel gray eyes fix ahead. "The keepers' warning… it isn't just about Morrigan. He thinks there's more to your bloodline than even you know."

Dread slams into my stomach like iron spikes. "And you didn't think to tell me sooner?"

"I was going to," he said evenly, "but you've been … unpredictable lately."

Kallesie growls in my head. "*Translation: 'I'm a control freak, and it scares me when you surprise me.*"

I bite back my retort; my fingers tighten on Kallesie's neck. The keeper's words echo in my memory. Find the truth of my blood. Find the guards that hold the scroll of the first Hellhound Summoners. Be warned, they demand a price I have to pay

Somewhere ahead, Wraths are moving again. I can feel them. And if the keeper is right, my blood is about to become either our greatest weapon or the reason we all burn.

The trees here are wrong. Too still. Too black at the edges, like something had sucked the life from their bark.

Kallesie's paws sink into frost-laced soil as we slow Helios and Vulcan pace a few feet away.

"*They're close,*" Kallesie murmurs in my head, her tone sharp. "*Smell it? That metallic tang? That's Wrath breath.*"

"I smell it," I whisper.

Helios's gaze sweeps the tree line. "We're surrounded."

Kallesie huffs. "*Well, that's one way to say we're all about to have a really bad day.*"

"Quiet," I tell her.

"Don't 'quiet' me when something's about to chew on my tail."

Branches shift ahead, no wind, just movement. My bow feels heavy in my hand, the keeper's warning still gnaws at my mind.

Helios leans toward me, his voice low. "When we engage, stay close. If the Keeper's right and your blood—"

"Don't," I cut him off, more intensely than I meant. "We end them. Then we talk about our plans to deal with our mission."

A Wrath lunges from the left, black teeth gleaming in

the dim light. Kallesie leaps before I can think, her jaws closing around its throat in a violent snap.

The woods erupt. Shadows with claws.

Helios's sword flashes beside me. Vulcan plows through two Wraths like they are kindling, tossing one into a tree with a sickening crack.

Kallesie's mind crawls into mine again. "*See? Teamwork. With extra murder.*"

I don't have time to laugh, but damn if I don't almost smile.

Keeper's warning or not, right now there is only one truth that matters.

We fight.

We survive.

And the rest can wait until the Wraths are ash at our feet.

CHAPTER 36

THE NIGHT'S GIFT

ELARA

The first one lunges from the fog before I can draw a breath, blackened claws snapping toward Kallesie's flank. I grit my teeth and let the power in my chest curl hotter and sharper. We fight. We survive. The mantra steadies me as steel and flame blur together, sparks flying with every clash.

Kallesie leaps, teeth bare, cutting a Wrath down before it even lands. Helios moves like a shadow behind me, Vulcan's paws pound the snow, flames and steel answering each other with deadly precision. Another Wrath crashes into the ground, shrieking, its body already turning into ash. And another.

The last Wrath hits the ground with a dull thud, its blackened body already crumbling to ash. The forest falls silent.

Kallesie's chest heaves beneath me, and steam curls

from her fangs. "*That's all of them. For now.*"

Helios wipes his blade clean, his eyes scanning the trees like the battle hasn't ended. Vulcan stands beside him; his molten gaze fixed on the shadows.

My pulse is still pounding, but something else is humming beneath my skin, deep, steady, and alive.

I look down at my hands, and that's when I see it. A faint shimmer along my fingers, like threads of starlight dancing across my skin.

"What the hell?" I whisper.

A pause, then Kallesie's voice slips back in, edged with sarcasm. *"Second time, Elara. You're not subtle about it anymore. Just a bloody glow stick with legs."*

Helios turns, his brows pulling together. "Glowing?"

Before I can answer, the shimmer shifts, spreading up my arms like liquid night, a soft pull tugging in my chest.

Kallesie's voice in my head is softer now. "*That's not you. That's her.*"

"Her?" I ask, but I already know.

"Nyx."

I think of the dream. The way her gaze pierced through me like moonlight through glass. The way she didn't offer power, at least not with words.

But she didn't have to.

I clench my fists, and the glow dims. My heart is racing now for an entirely different reason.

Kallesie chuckles darkly. *"And if it does, I call dibs on*

the meat."

HELIOS

I step closer, eyes locking on her. "What did she give you?"

"I don't know," she says honestly. "But I think … I'm about to find out."

Vulcan snorts, his voice dries in Helios's mind. *"Of course, she's about to find out. Usually right before something explodes."*

Despite everything, the fight, the keeper's warning, the shadow of what my blood might mean… I almost laugh.

Because deep down, I know this isn't just a gift.

It is a promise.

And promises from goddesses never come without a cost.

The fog rolls in so thick it feels alive, swallowing the path and the horizon in the same breath. The moors were wide and open just minutes ago, but now the air presses in heavy, damp, and cold, like it wants to drown the sound out of the world.

ELARA

Kallesie's paws are almost silent against the wet ground, her heat radiating against my legs.

"This is a bad place, pup." Her voice slides into my mind, sharper than usual. "*Too quiet. I can't smell them through this muck, but I can feel them."*

Them.

I swallow, scanning the shifting gray around us. "Wraths?" I ask under my breath.

"Wraths," she confirms, there is no sass in her tone.

Helios rides just ahead, Vulcan's massive frame a shadow in the mist. His posture is tense, shoulders broader than usual, eyes scouting, conquering against the low visibility.

"Keep close," he says without looking back.

"You think I'd wander off for fun?" I mutter.

"Oh, she's prickly." Kallesie draws. "It's *almost like she knows something awful is about to happen."*

The banter doesn't make the air feel lighter. If anything, it makes the silence between each ripple of the fog more dangerous, like the moors are holding their breath.

It happens fast.

The first Wrath bursts out of the gray like a shadow with teeth and bone. Kallesie swerves, her claws tearing up the wet turf, just as another slams into Vulcan's side. The sound it makes isn't human, and hunger thickens it, drags it into something with weight and shape.

Helios's sword sings as it leaves the sheath, a gleam of steel swallowed almost instantly by the mist. I draw my dagger, the familiar weight grounds me even as my heart thuds against my ribs.

One comes for me low, skimming the ground like it has no bones. Kallesie rears, claws swiping. Wraths form shreds into black smoke under her strike, but more move in the mist shapes too many to count.

"They're closing us in!" I shout.

"Then we don't go!" his voice is a snarl over the chaos. Vulcan barrels into another Wrath, breaking its shadowy form apart with sheer force.

We fight in bursts, slashes, and lunges, and those awful, airless silences in between, when the fog presses in close, and I can't tell if the fight is over or if they are right behind me. My arms ache, lungs burn, until Kallesie lunges forward and we break through a thin Veil of fog into open ground.

The Wraths don't follow. Not yet.

I slide off Kallesie's back, shaking with adrenaline, and see the graze along Helios's forearm, growing maroon against the black of his sleeve. My side throbs where one had caught me, a shallow gash, but it burns like ice.

"You could've gotten yourself killed going at them like that!" I snap, moving to press a strip of cloth against his arm.

His mouth curves into that infuriating half-smile. "Brat."

I freeze, glaring at him. "Excuse me…"

He doesn't let me finish. His hand cups the back of my

neck, pulling me in until his mouth is on mine, rough, unexpected, and disturbingly addictive. My anger tangles with the heat between us, leaving me breathless when he pulls back.

"I'm sorry," he murmurs against my lips.

The fog still clings to the moors behind us, shifting like it is waiting for another chance. But for a moment, I just let myself stand there, his hand warm on my skin, the Wraths a shadow we'll deal with later.

CHAPTER 37

THE MOOR'S PRICE

ELARA

The fog clings to the moor like a living thing, each breath damp and heavy in my lungs. The sting of the last wrath attack still lingers on my side, every step reminding me that even survival comes at a cost. The keeper's words loop in my mind, and I know the shadows we left behind haven't forgotten us.

"Elara of that blood, if you would uncover the first Hellhound Summoners, you must give what is demanded. The price will be yours and yours alone."

My hand strokes Kallesie's fur as she pads at my side.

The warning lingers in my head, quiet but absolute.

"Honestly," Kallesie drawls, her tone dripping with sarcasm, *"if this payment nonsense ends up being a bucket of blood or your left shoe, I'll be the one to negotiate. You're hopeless at bargaining."*

"Not helping," I mutter under my breath.

"Correction: I'm the only one helping. Without me, you'd probably try to pay the fog itself a compliment and call it even."

Despite the ache in my ribs, a fleeting, bitter curl tugs at my lips.

Carved from stone and shadow, Helios looms beside me. His eyes rove over the shifting white void, searching for the keeper's trail. His presence steadies me, a constant, unyielding wall against the strange press of the fog.

HELIOS

At my heels, Vulcan pads with fluid grace, eyes burning steadily through the haze. His low rumble is more like a dry chuckle than a growl.

"Careful," his voice slides into my mind, thick as smoke. "*That... wasn't for you or was it either way you take it."*

I glance at him, narrowing my eyes, unsure if he is mocking me or warning me. Even in this dim haze, his presence presses me against me, steady, watchful, impossible to ignore.

My lips twitch.

"Keep your senses sharp," I say quietly. "The Keeper never sends anyone where the shadows are empty."

She adjusts her bow across her shoulder, wincing at the pull in her injured side. "Simple hasn't exactly been our style."

We trudge onward, boots sinking into the spongy earth, the moor whispering with the weight of unseen things. Every few steps, shadows stir in the fog, hints of shapes that dissolve when I try to focus on them. My instincts scream that the Moor itself is watching.

The Keeper's voice returns, threading through the mist:

The scroll is hidden where the fog remembers blood. Follow the silence and pay what is owed.

ELARA

I swallow hard. "Follow the silence?"

"Fantastic," Kallesie snorts in her head. "*Because in case you haven't noticed, this entire place is the world's largest funeral shroud. Everything is silent. Your bloodline better be worth this."*

Helios stops abruptly, his hand lifts in warning. Ahead, the fog thins just enough to reveal a cairn of ancient stones, stacked high and weathered by centuries. At its base, faint runes pulse like dying embers.

"That's it," he says, his voice low, reverent, and wary. "The scroll will be bound within."

My pulse quickens. I can feel it too: the tug in my veins, the whisper of my grandmother's teachings, and the echo of something older than my clan, older than the hellhounds themselves.

As I step forward, the moor itself shudders. From behind

the stones, a figure emerges, cloaked, faceless, dripping shadows. Its voice rasps like wind through hollow bones.

"Payment," it demands, stretching a hand toward me. "Bloodline seeker, what will you give for truth?"

The fog thickens, pressing against her skin like a second heartbeat. Kallesie hisses inside my mind.

"Oh, this is going to be good. Please tell me you've got something better than your lunch to offer."

Helios shifts closer, protective, but he does not interfere. This is my trial. My bloodline. My price to pay.

My hand trembles as it finds the dagger in my belt. I can give blood, that is the obvious choice, but some instinct deeper than that warns me it won't be enough. The Keeper never dealt in simplicity.

The cloaked figure tilts its head, as if sensing my hesitation. "You carry within you what was severed long ago," it rasps. "The first Summoner's blood calls from your veins. What will you give to know her name, her truth? A piece of yourself must be left in the moor."

My breath hitches. A piece of herself. Not just blood. Something deeper.

"Don't even think about offering me," Kallesie snaps sharply. "*I may be sassy, but I'm useful."*

My fingers tighten on the dagger. My mind races with what I can give that won't break me but will still satisfy the moor's keeper?

Slowly, she lifts the blade, and the fog curls around its edge like hungry fingers.

My voice threatens to break, but I don't let it. "If truth

demands a piece of me…"

I raise the dagger toward my palm and cut with cold precision.

The fog recoils as my blood strikes the stones, hissing like fire on ice. The runes blaze, brighter and brighter, until the entire cairn shudders and splits down the middle.

The figure's voice booms, both warning and promising.

"The payment is accepted. Seek the scroll, but beware the answer you desire may unmake you."

I stagger back, clutching my bleeding hand. Helios catches me with unyielding strength. His eyes lock on the opening stones. Within, faint golden light spills out, ancient, waiting.

The Keeper's prophecy has just begun to unfold.

The opening widens with grinding shrieks, stone dragging against stone as the fissure tears deeper, carving the Moor like a wound, and the air trembles beneath the weight of something older than time.

I press my bleeding palm against my side, the sting burning sharper than the wrath's wound. Helios keeps a firm hold on my arm, steadying me as his gaze locks on the opening.

"Well," Kallesie mutters, her tone only half its usual sarcasm, *"either it's a library door or the world's most ominous oven. Want to guess which?"*

I force a shaky laugh. *"If it bakes bread, I'll be impressed."*

"Oh yes, bread. That's exactly what ancient creepy cairns guarded by fog phantoms usually hold."

Kallesie's voice softens, *"though. Careful, Elara. The Keeper never gives without taking more."*

Helios releases me slowly, as though testing if I can stand on my own. "This is your bloodline's trail," he says, his voice low and solemn. "But you won't face it alone."

The promise in his eyes steadies me more than the grip of his hand ever could. I nod, drawing a slow breath, and step toward the light. The cairn's interior is a chamber of stone, its walls slick with age, marked with runes that seem to breathe with her heartbeat. At the center rests a pedestal of black rock, and atop it, bound in strips of leather and ash-colored sinew, lies the scroll. It pulses faintly, as if alive.

My steps falter. The pull in my veins grows stronger with every breath, a magnetic ache dragging me toward the relic. "*Oh, that thing definitely wants to eat you,"* Kallesie says flatly. "*Just saying. We can always turn around. Pretend none of this ever happened."*

But my hand is already reaching. My blood, still dripping from the wound in my palm, hisses when it strikes the stone floor. The scroll trembles in response, the bindings loosen like a beast stirring from sleep.

The cloaked figure's voice echoes through the chamber walls, no longer contained to a whisper. "The first Summoner's truth will bind you… Or break you. Her name calls through your blood. Do you claim it?"

I freeze; breath catches in my throat. Claim it? That is the choice. To take the scroll is to invite the truth of my bloodline into myself, whatever it is, whatever the cost, it could get rid of the Wraths for good or make it worse.

Helios's voice is a steady anchor beside me. "Elara. Whatever waits in there, you have the strength to endure it."

HELIOS

Vulcan snorts softly in his head. "*Or she dies. But yes, encouraging words, Alpha. Very inspiring.*"

ELARA

My jaw tightens, but his gaze never leaves mine—my heart hammers. The Keeper has warned that the answer can unmake me. Yet my grandmother's words whisper from memory, "*The amethyst inferno is yours to carry, child. Don't fear the fire.*"

I press my bleeding palm onto the scroll. The chamber explodes with light. Runes along the walls blaze, the fog outside screams like a thousand dying voices, and the scroll unfurls itself in her grip. The leather wrapping slithers away like a snake retreating into the dark, and ancient ink bleeds across the parchment.

A single name burns into my mind, searing hot and true.

The first Hellhound Summoner.

My bloodline's beginning.

My breath tears out of me as the chamber shudders, and the scroll pulses with power.

The prophecy has just revealed its first piece, and I realize the truth might be far more dangerous than the Keeper's warning had promised.

The chamber doesn't settle after. *It tightens.*

Like something unseen has drawn closer, listening now that I've heard enough to matter.

The scroll remains warm in my hands, but the pulse has changed. Slower. Heavier. No longer forcing the truth into me, now it waits, like it knows I'll reach for the next piece whether I should or not.

I don't move, but my awareness does. It drifts, pulling towards something I can't see.

Towards the Veil. I don't know how I know that's what it is. There's no line etched in stone, no visible barrier. But I can feel it now in a way I couldn't before. It thins in places. Strained, like a fabric stretched too far, ready to give if something pushes hard enough. Or long enough.

A cold pressure settles behind my ribs, spreading outward, slow and intentional. It doesn't belong to the scroll. It doesn't belong to me.

It lets me feel how it presses back. Not empty. Not silent. Waiting. The words form without permission certainty. Contained.

It comes from the other side. My breath falters. Because the prophecy doesn't show me all that's over there, but only a huge black hand pushing against the veil, the fabric of the Veil showing the ripples across the sky.

My fingers tighten slightly around the scroll, grounding myself in its solid weight. "Contained by what?" I whisper, though the chamber offers nothing in return.

The question lingers, heavy and unresolved—and the answer comes, not as words, but as a shift. A realization that settles in my bones. The first Hellhound Summoner didn't just walk this path; they survived it. They fight a Primordial Wrath itself, not alone, but with the goddess Nyx at their side.

Suddenly, everything tilts.

The Veil isn't just a barrier. It's a restraint, and a restraint doesn't exist unless something needs to be held. A faint tremor runs through the stone beneath my feet, subtle enough I might've missed it before. Now, it feels like a response, not to me, but to that.

To whatever presses against the other side. I swallow hard, my throat suddenly dry. It's not trying to break through. Not yet. It doesn't need to. The understanding unfolds slowly, each piece settling heavier than the last.

The Veil is weakening, and my blood is the key to either releasing it or keeping it locked up.

It shows me the name… Shae.

CHAPTER 38

THE PROPHECY

ELARA

The first Hellhound summoner. I stagger back, breath tearing from my throat. The scroll throbs with power, its black script alive, the words etched in a rhythm that matches my racing heartbeat. Shadows along the chamber walls lengthen, stretching claws toward me, as though even the stone itself bent to listen. The Keeper's voice coils inside her skull, the echo of that warning, *the truth will demand its payment.*

My knees nearly buckle. Payment. What more could the prophecy want than blood?

Kallesie's snarl winds through her mind and edges with mocking smoke.

"You opened it. You touched what should've been left to rot. What did you expect, a bedtime story, Elara?"

I bite down on my panic, forcing my words out through

the bond. *"It's not just a story,"* I tell Kallesie. *"It's her. The first, the one who started all of this. The Veil is thinning and whatever lies behind is waiting."*

"Oh, delightful," Kallesie purrs. "*A ghost with worse manners than me. I can't wait."*

The chamber shakes violently, and dust cascades down like pale rain.

"Elara!" Helios's voice cleaves through the chaos. He reaches me in strides, his presence a shield against the trembling chamber—Vulcan beside him, molten eyes smoldering like coals waiting for breath.

"What did you do?"

"I didn't…" My chest heaves. I point at the parchment, its power continuing to pulse as to match my heartbeat. "It showed me her name. The first Summoner."

Helios goes rigid. The chamber's fire twists across his features; his eyes hold a chill that no flame can warm. Not dread. Not reverence. Something dark, unyielding. Recognition.

The parchment split the silence with words that aren't spoken but feel etched straight into the marrow of our bones.

The first shall rise when the bloodline awakens. The price will be demanded. The hounds will not be chosen freely.

Ash explodes outward, drifting in black spirals that settle against my skin like a funeral Veil.

My heart stutters. "Helios…"

His jaw flexes as though it is a grinding stone.

"The Keeper was right."

And then quieter as his hand tightens on his weapon. "And we are out of time."

HELIOS

I have seen men unravel under the prophecy before. Seen them tear ranks, clinging to the promise of glory or salvation whispers in the dark. Prophecy never gives. It takes.

And this one, this curse truth bound to Elara, is worse than any I have faced. I keep my stance rigid, though my pulse hammers like war drums. Morrigan would feel this ripple. That Crow Queen never missed the scent of blood, and Elara's… Gods help us, Elara's blood is prophecy incarnate now.

If Morrigan gets her hands on Elara, if even a drop spills into that witch's grasp, the balance would break. Her blood scorch Wraths—but it might just as easily tear open doors that were never meant to be touched. With Morrigan pulling the strings, that fire is a chain, not a weapon.

Vulcan lets out a low growl that vibrates through my bones. *"She marked by Morrigan, the one who meant to claim her blood. You know what that unleashes."*

"I know," I growl back. *But I will not let that happen.*

"You swore the same once before," Vulcan reminds me, mercilessly. "You promised to keep her safe … *And you buried her instead. Her blood burned, and you still failed.*"

My grip on my blade tightens until the leather creaks. That's a wound that will never scar. And perhaps that is why the Keeper had dragged him onto this cursed path again, because he had already paid once in failure. I will not fail Elara.

I look at her then, her hair dusted with ash, eyes wide but burning, Kallesie's presence crackling in her gaze. She is trembling, yes, but she hasn't broken. And that frightens him more than if she had.

"Elara," I say, forcing steel into my voice, "we can't stay here, not after this. Morrigan will already be moving. She can't have your blood. Not a drop."

Elara barks back, "I know that. Hell, if she gets my blood, we are screwed. I got that. The Veil must not be open, or the worst kind of wrath we have ever seen will be awakened."

My gaze never leaves Elara's. "We seal this chamber. We bury it. And from this moment forward, no one, not the Keeper, not Morrigan, not even the gods themselves, gets near you without going through me."

A shiver trembles through her breath, but she lifts her chin. Defiance. Strength. Foolish, radiant strength.

And I know at that moment that if prophecy demands payment, it will have to carve it from my bones before it touches hers.

Elara

The chamber has been sealed. Stone presses over stone, mortar binding the doorway until no trace of the prophecy's chamber remains. Yet even as the dust settles, I can still feel it like an ember under my skin, glowing, waiting.

His hand slides across my forearm over the ash that landed earlier. I swear the warmth still lingers there, along with a name burned into my mind—the first Summoner. Kallesie prowls the edges of my mind restlessly. "*You think walls will keep it hidden? Child, prophecy seeps. It leaks like blood through bandages. Those hungry enough will smell it.*"

My breath hitches, though I try to mask it. "It's done. We sealed it. No one can get in."

I glance at him, his face unreadable, but my eyes are sharp. "No one has to. Word carries on the air. And if I'm right, Morrigan is already listening."

The sound of her name makes the air feel colder. Morrigan. Shadow queen. Devourer of fate. A whisper in every darkened corner of the world. Of course, I've heard of her—every Summoner has—but never like this. Never with such immediacy. Such certainty. We ride hard through the Moorlands, the fog curling around us like grasping fingers. The Hellhounds move beneath us in long, fluid strides, their eyes molten, cutting through the mist, their presence both a comfort and a warning.

Every few steps, I feel Morrigan's presence pause… whispers cut through the mist. Too faint to follow, too keen to dismiss.

I hear them too. He knows by the way my shoulders tense, my hand never leaving the hilt of my blade.

"Whispers," Kallesie breathes, her voice all smoke and teeth. "*She has sent her hunters. They're near, though not near enough to show their faces—clever little crows. Waiting for the moment, your pulse slips too fast. Waiting for a drop of blood."*

I swallow. "They're watching us, aren't they?"

Helios doesn't answer at first. Vulcan appears, having scouted ahead to make sure it is safe for us to enter. Finally, he said, "Yes. But whispers are all they dare now. They're testing the air, circling. If Morrigan wanted you taken quickly, we'd already be in chains. She wants to wait. To weaken us first."

HELIOS

"Or she wants to frighten you," Vulcan growls in my mind, his voice a furnace in the dark. "*Fear cracks a shield faster than steel."*

My jaw clenches. I know it is true. Elara's blood is the key. Her bloodline is now tied to the prophecy, too heavy for even a seasonal warrior to bear. If she falters, Morrigan will not need to send blades. She would already be halfway victorious.

I slow our pace, scanning the fog. Every rock looks like a crouching figure, every curl of mist a reaching hand.

"Elara," I say finally, his voice quieter but steel-edged, "listen to me. No matter what whispers you hear, no matter what voice calls you, do not answer. Do not bleed. If you give them so much as a drop, we lose everything."

ELARA

"I hear you, Helios," I murmur, lifting my chin against the ghost light. "They won't touch it—not while I draw breath."

Kallesie purrs and slithers out, amused. "*And I'd like to see them try.*"

But even as she speaks, I hear it again. Softer this time, closer, weaving through the air.

Kallesie's voice… Or a woman's whisper, dreadful and intimate, crawling into my ear. "*Blood sings, little Summoner. And I will have yours.*"

I spin, but the fog only thickens. And far off in the mist, the faint sound of wings beat against the silence.

CHAPTER 39

MORRIGAN'S GAME

MORRIGAN

The chamber thrums with whispers the moment I arrive. The Wraths press close to the walls, their formless bodies writhing like smoke in a storm. They know. They taste the shift in the air when the prophecy whispers into the world again.

I sit upon my throne of bones, the curl of my lips sharp as the edge of a dagger.

Elara's blood, not merely a key to history, not merely a name burned into a dying prophecy, is more. It is the one thing that can tear the Veil completely open. The one thing that can unshackle the prison that holds back the oldest of her kind: the Primordial Wrath. A thing so vast and cruel even the Hellhounds themselves once fled from it.

"Little Summoner," I murmur, my voice silken and dangerous. "You are both the lock and the blade. With you, the Wraths will not be shadows bound to hunger. They will be real and unstoppable. And with you, I will rip the Veil wide enough to let him through."

The Wraths shudder, hissing in ecstasy, their whispers rise.

"Blood. Blood. Blood."

My talons drum against the arm of my throne. I can almost taste it, Elara's veins spilling open, the gate, my power uncoiling into the dark.

But there is another wrinkle in my weave.

He steps into the hall, and all the darkness pulls strangely around him, as if uncertain whether to obey or retreat. Shade. He is not what he appears to be. Wraths know it before anyone else, their hunger faltering in his presence. I say nothing of the power coiled beneath his skin, but I do not underestimate it.

His eyes catch the chamber's dim glow, light blue, sharp as the ocean at dawn. They should not exist here, in a place drowned by shadow. Yet they do, refusing to yield to me.

He tilts his head at my throne, a smirk tugging at his mouth. "Still whispering to your pets about blood? Careful, Morrigan, you sound desperate."

The Wraths hiss, shadows lash at him, but none dares to touch him.

My smile does not waver. "Desperate? No, Shade. Patient. A spider waiting for the fly to tire itself."

He chuckles, low and rough, his smirk devastating. "Sometimes flies bite. And that girl isn't a fly, you know. Her blood can close the Veil, too. She can starve your pets forever."

Wraths recoil at the words; their whispers shriek through the chamber.

My eyes narrow, my talons flexing against the armrest. “Careful what you say here, mortal. Bones break easier than you think.”

Shade’s smirk deepens, eyes gleaming like lightning over water. “Not mine.”

For a heartbeat, even the shadows seem to listen to him.

I study him, an irritating edge mixed with intrigue. He warned Elara. He lingers too close to the path of prophecy, yet he never swore allegiance to anyone. Always walking the edge between sides, laughing at the rules that bind others.

“Tell me, Shade,” I purr, “why do you want to protect her? What is she to you?”

His smile fades, replaced by something colder, sharper. “The only one who can still choose. And you’re not going to take that from her.”

Then, as if bored, he turns and vanishes into shadow, leaving only the echo of his words.

The Wraths seethes. I lean back against my throne, eyes gleaming with the burn of ancient hunger.

Elara’s blood could end my Wraths. But it could also bring me the portal I crave, the storm I have been building for centuries.

The girl will spill.

And when she does, Primordial Wrath will awaken.

SHADE

The chamber is dark, the walls breathing with whispers. Morrigan let them curl around her like serpents, their voices feeding her with promises of power, blood, and the portal that would tear the world apart.

And then footsteps. Bold, careless, echoing against the stone as though the darkness bends back in irritation.

I stroll into her lair with the easy swagger of a man who has no right to be alive in a place like this. My coat is worn, blade half-hidden beneath, and my eyes, light blue, sharp, and unbothered, like the ocean under sunlight, catching on her like a challenge.

Most men bow or at least breathe carefully in her presence. I smirk.

"Morrigan," I say, my voice carries a drawl that mocks respect.

"Still whispering about blood to things that crawl at your feet?" I ask, my voice low and unimpressed.

I tap on the sacred wood of the table, where the map of Elara's movements lay half-unfurled.

The whispers hiss louder, curling like smoke around Morrigan's shoulders. Her lips curve into a smile that never reaches her eyes. "You play a dangerous game, mortal."

I tilt my head, my eyes gleam like I have heard it a hundred times, and I still find it amusing. "Danger's the only game worth playing."

For a moment, the chamber seems to bend toward me, the Wraths lurk in the shadows quivering, confused, as though they can't decide if they want to rip me apart or recoil from me. My presence disrupts them.

Morrigan's smile is thin, and she lets her hand rest against the nearest Wrath's jaw, commanding it with a flicker of thought. "Careful, Shade. Mortal bones are so easy to break."

My grin widens, irreverent. "The only one who can still choose. And you're not going to take that from her."

The whispers surge, restless, their warning clear: This man does not bend. This man does not belong.

Morrigan studies me, her hunger for Elara's blood momentarily dims by something rarer: curiosity. I am dangerous not because of what I am, but because of what I refuse to be. Unclaimed. Uncontrolled. And that makes me unpredictable.

Exactly the kind of chaos she might one day need or regret not destroying when she had the chance.

I step out of Morrigan's chamber and let the heavy doors shut behind me.

The corridor is cold, but not enough to cut through the heat still clinging to my skin. Her magic always lingers. It sinks into stone, into air, into anyone foolish enough to stand too close for long.

The dark moves with me as I walk.

It slips along the walls and curls at my boots, quiet and watchful. The stronghold is never truly silent, but this part of it comes close. Just the crackle of dying torchlight. The faint scrape of my steps against black stone. The feeling that something is waiting before I see it.

I know I'm not alone down the hall. No sound. No warning.

If they're stupid enough to wait for me outside Morrigan's chambers, they can be stupid enough to show themselves first.

The corridor bends toward the west wing, shadows gathering thick between the torches. Moonlight spills in through the tall arched windows, silvering the stone in broken strips. I round the corner and catch the shape of someone leaning near the last window at the end of the hall.

Still.

Unbothered. Like she belongs there. My jaw tightens before I can stop it. Of course. There are very few people in this world reckless enough to seek me out in the dark.

Only one does it like she knows I won't make good on the threat.

I slow as I near her, then stop a few paces away. She doesn't move. Doesn't flinch. Doesn't bow her head or step back or do any of the things smart people do when I'm in a mood like this.

Moonlight catches the edge of her face, the line of her throat, the mouth that has always looked too close to trouble.

My shadows settle at my feet.

Traitors.

"You have terrible timing," I say.

That only makes her smile widen.

I should keep walking. Should leave her standing there

with that look in her eyes and whatever problems she dragged into my night.

Instead, I stay exactly where I am, because I already know if she came all the way here, it's not for nothing. And because some mistakes are easier to make when they're looking back at you.

She pushes off the wall at last, slow and easy, like she has all the time in the world. I hate that I notice the way she moves.

I hate that I remember it.

"You look annoyed," she says.

"I am annoyed."

"Good." Her gaze drags over me, taking in more than I'd like. "I'd be worried if Morrigan's little gathering didn't ruin your mood."

My expression doesn't shift, but something in me sharpens.

She catches it.

She always does. That's the problem.

"Why are you here?" I ask.

Her eyes hold mine for a beat too long. "Straight to business?"

"With you? Always."

A quiet laugh leaves her, low and knowing.

It lands somewhere under my ribs and stays there.

I should hate that too.

Instead, I wait.

And she studies me like she's deciding how much truth I can stomach tonight.

"Ah, Nyreth murmurs through the dark corners of my mind. *"Your favourite bad decision has excellent timing."*

"Shut up," I think.

His amusement curls through the bond like smoke.

CHAPTER 40

THE LAST WHISPER

ELARA

The battlefield is silent at last.

The Wraths have been driven back into the fog, their shrieks fading like dying stars. My bow sags in my grip, my arms numb, and my heartbeat syncs with the thrums of Kallesie at my side.

The quiet doesn't feel earned, just borrowed.

For the first time, I allow myself to breathe. To believe I survived.

But then the Keeper's voice returns low, echoing, as if the moors themselves carry it over the wind.

"Blood of the First... the payment is not yet made."

I stiffen, my gaze snapping upward. The fog is churning, not with Wraths this time, but with something heavier, alive, as though the shadows themselves had learned how to breathe.

Kallesie growls, eyes narrowing. "*Something is listening to you, girl. And it should not be.*"

And then Morrigan's voice drifts across the moor, smooth and cold as glass. "Your blood is the key. And I will have it."

MORRIGAN

The battlefield stinks of blood and ash. I stand on the edge of the moors, my cloak drags through the wreckage as my Wraths slither back into the fog at my command. They are restless and hungry, but I'll let them wait. There is no need to waste them now, not when the game has only just begun.

I watch Elara waiting for the moment her blood falls. Even the smallest cut, a hint of crimson, would make the air heavier, and the ground beneath me shifts. Just as the thought of it stirs the hunger I've been chasing, a thread of power I can almost taste.

My lips curve into a thin smile. The girl doesn't even understand what she carries in her veins. That kind of ignorance is delicious, fragile, and full of cracks waiting to be split open.

Shade's eyes flicker in my memory, too sharp, too knowing. He was right; the whispers were all about Elara. I will carve his throat one day for his insolence, but not yet. He is mortal, gifted, and stubbornly unclaimed by fate. I almost admire the way he burns against the dark.

I raise my hand, fingers dripping shadows like ink, and the fog trembles as my Wraths melt into it.

Their shrieks echo across the moor, fading like dying stars.

Silence follows.

Elara stands in the distance, bow in hand, her Hellhound coils at her side. Bruised, shaking, but still defiant, she stands her ground and has the nerve to smirk in my direction. I let the girl breathe, letting her believe she has won. It is a sweeter cruelty to allow hope.

The whispers around her thicken, a thousand voices thread into one, the Keeper's tone bleeds through:

Blood of the First… the payment is not yet made.

I smile, my teeth glint in the dim light. I step into the fog, letting it devour me until only my voice remains.

The fog surges, swallowing the last scraps of battlefield light. Somewhere in the distance, something older than Wraths stirs awake, something I alone can hear.

And the moor shudders in response.

CHAPTER 41

ASHES IN VEINS

ELARA

The fog never lifts. It clings to the bones of the ruined village, a damp shroud that muffles every breath and turns the smallest sound into a warning. The ground feels unsettled beneath my boots as the moor hasn't finished answering whatever stirs it. Each step I take kicks the blackened earth, and ash rises between my boots as if the ground itself still smolders.

Kallesie walks at my side, molten light bleeding from her eyes and nostrils. She is too big for the lane between the broken cottages, but she makes herself fit, a shadow stitched with fire.

Helios walks a few paces ahead, shoulders rigid beneath his torn leathers. Vulcan stalks beside him, every muscle taut with silent fury. The bond between them pulses sharp and disciplined, where mine with Kallesie is wild, unpredictable, and untamable.

It has been two days since the battle on the moors—two days since the Wraths fled into the fog. I hope silence means peace, even a sliver of it. But the Keeper's words still haunt me, whispering truths about my blood, about the price it will demand. And now, with every step into the ruin, I know the cost has only begun.

A sound breaks the silence, wet, ragged coughing. Helios's hand goes instantly to his blade. Vulcan bares his teeth. Kallesie lowers her head, molten violet eyes narrowing into slits. The coughing turns into choking, then gagging, and then screaming.

We round a shattered wall and find survivors. Twenty villagers huddled around a dying fire. Faces gaunt, eyes red from smoke. For a heartbeat, relief stirs in me. Survivors mean hope. Survivors mean we aren't too late.

Then the smell hit. Rot. My stomach lurches. The same reek that clings to Wraths like a second skin, the stench of decay that has no place with the living.

Some villagers raise their heads, whispers rip through them. One woman clutches her boy, a lanky child no older than twelve, his face pale, sweat slick on his brow. His wide eyes catch mine, desperate. "Please," his mother begs, her voice raw. "Help him. He…he won't stop shaking."

Kallesie's warning snaps sharply in my mind. "*Elara. Don't go closer.*" But my heart pulls anyway.

An old man lurches forward, falling to his knees. His body seizes, every vein bulging black beneath his skin. A howl rips out of his throat, guttural and wrong.

"*Back away,*" Kallesie growls.

His jaw splits with a sickening crack. Teeth blackened.

Eyes dissolved into molten voids. Claws tear through his fingernails.

"Gods," Helios breathes, his sword flashes free. But it isn't just him. Five more villagers convulse. Their families hold onto them, sobbing, begging. Black veins bloom under their skin, bones twist, and voices warp into something that doesn't belong in this world.

"They're turning," I whisper.

Helios's gaze remains on me. "Into Wraths?"

I nod, throat tight. Wraths aren't supposed to be born here. They came through the Veil, but now something spreads through the villagers, silent and relentless, like a disease that doesn't just kill, it devours. I can feel it in the air, in the pulse of the ground, and I know it's a matter of time before it finds the Stronghold.

The first one staggers upright, limbs jerking like a broken puppet. Its head snaps toward me. Hunger burns in its blank face.

And my blood answers. Heat tears through my veins, molten and demanding. My hand presses to my chest as if I can hold it in, but the Wraths smell it. Want it. The creature lunges.

Kallesie crashes into it midair, her massive jaws snap around its torso. She slams it down, ichor spraying. Fire burns where her fangs touch, and the Wrath shrieks and claws at her molten hide.

"Elara!" Helios's roar pierces through my haze. My bow is in my hands before I even realize it, and I notched an arrow. The Wrath rips free of Kallesie's jaws and charges me again.

I fire my arrow.

The arrow strikes shallow, black veins writhing out like roots. My blood sticks to the arrowhead. I'd cut myself stringing it, and the reaction is instant.

The Wrath convulses, shrieks, and then collapses into ash that scatters across the cobblestones.

The square erupts.

The other survivors scream.

They see it happen. My blood strikes, and another falls.

"Elara!" Helios barks. More villagers' collapse, bodies twist, screams break into unholy howls. Vulcan barrels into one, claws raking, ember eyes burning. Kallesie tears another apart, and fire spills from her throat.

I fire repeatedly, every arrow smears with my blood. Wraths turn to ash. But the more I killed, the faster the others turn, as if my blood isn't just ending them but accelerates their corruption.

"They're feeding on you," Kallesie snarled. "*You don't command them, Elara. You drive them mad. You cannot control it. Only the end."*

"I don't want control!" I shout, shooting another arrow through a Wrath's skull.

"Then be ready to burn everything."

Chaos devours the square.

Families scream as loved ones start to transform. Vulcan

rips one half-formed Wrath from the fire, its face still crying out for its wife, before Helios's blade cuts it down.

And then I see him.

The child.

The twelve-year-old boy clutches his mother's arms, his eyes wild. "Mama," he gasps, "it hurts. What's happening to me?"

Her arms crush him to her chest, tears streaking her smoke-stained cheeks. "Stay with me. Please, stay with me."

But I see the black veins crawling beneath his skin, the tremor in his limbs.

"No…" The word breaks from my throat.

"Elara!" Helios shouts, slaying another Wrath, but I can't move.

The boy screams. His spine arches, and teeth crack into jagged points. His hand stretches, fingers split into claws. His wide eyes roll back, then open wide and endlessly.

"Please…" he chokes, then the plea breaks into a snarl.

"Now," Kallesie's voice is sharp as a blade. *"Or he'll take her with him."*

My hands shake violently as I raise my bow. The boy lunges, jaws open, claws swiping for his mother's throat.

I aim and fire.

The arrow strikes deep in his chest. Fire sears through him. He convulses once in his mother's arms, then crumbles into ash that scatters across her lap.

She screams a raw, shattering sound and clutches the dust as if she can hold him together.

And the survivors turn their terror on me.

HELIOS

Elara is shaking, bow half-lowered, blood dripping from her fingers. The light beneath her skin pulses dangerously, and her veins glow like fire. Her face is white with shock.

She just killed a child. And the Wraths know it.

Vulcan slams one into a wall, ember eyes flashing. "*She burns too brightly,"* he rumbled in my mind. *"They will never stop coming for her."*

I see it too. The Wraths aren't just attacking. They are drawn. Every pulse of Elara's blood is a beacon, calling them, driving them into frenzy.

"Elara!" I shout at her again, slashing another Wrath before it can reach her. She doesn't seem to hear me at all.

If I don't get her out soon, the fire inside her will consume her from the inside out.

Survivors cling to the edges, trembling, half turned like ash, burned before they had a chance. The square is a slaughter, and I can't look away. Every step I take, I crutch over the debris of what's left of them.

Wraths lunge and burn. Families wail as their loved ones are lost in the massacre. Ash drifts thick as a blizzard, coating the square.

At last, the final Wrath falls beneath Vulcan's jaws.

Silence drops, broken only by the mother's sobs as she clutches the ashes of her son.

The few survivors recoil away from Elara. Whispers spread like poison; curses, blood witch, not human.

Elara sways, gripping her bow like it is the only thing holding her up. Her eyes meet mine, and in them I see she believes them.

I cross the space and catch her arm, grounding her. Her skin is hot, her pulse, a hammer of heat beneath my fingers.

"You are not alone," I say, low and fierce.

Her jaw trembles. She whispers so softly that only I hear it. "The keeper is right. This is the price."

The ground shudders again beneath me, and my stomach twists as I realize the screaming hasn't stopped.

CHAPTER 42

THE KEEPER'S WARNING

ELARA

The silence after the screaming is worse than the battle.

Ash clings to my skin, stinging my eyes, thick in my throat. The square that once held laughter, gossip, and children running barefoot is now smeared in black ruin. Survivors huddle near the fire pit, but their eyes aren't on the Wraths we burned to nothing. They are on me.

And through the silence, I still hear the Keeper's voice.

"Your blood is the key. The Veil will answer you, or it will destroy you."

The boy's mother crouches in the ash, hands empty where her son had been. Dust streaks her cheeks, her hair tangled with soot. When her gaze finds me, her face twists into something I can't name.

"Blood witch." The words cut sharper than any blade. She spits into the dirt.

They all step back, gathering their children close, as if my shadow alone will infect them. I want to tell her I am sorry, that I didn't want to shoot the arrow, that I didn't want his scream to be the last sound she will ever hear from her boy again. My lips won't move. My hands shake too badly.

Kallesie's gaze burns into me. *"Let them hate you, little flame. You saved them, even if they don't want to see it right now."*

Her voice is sharp, like claws tearing through flesh, but it carries weight. She presses her massive head against me, forcing me to steady myself on my feet. I dig my fingers into the heat of her fur, grounding myself against the tide of stares.

But I can't escape the mother's sobs. I killed her son. Even if I saved the rest, even if his body had already begun to twist into something monstrous, it doesn't matter. His blood is on my hands.

And, gods help me, the Keeper was right. My blood already costs more than I can bear.

HELIOS

I hate the way they look at her.

Their eyes aren't just afraid, they are condemning as though Elara had dragged the Wraths into their homes herself. As though she hadn't stood between them and ruin, spilling her own blood until her veins glowed.

Vulcan prowls at my side, hackles high, ember eyes

hard. "*You can't stand here forever, Helios. They will turn on her if you let them.*"

"I know," I mutter under my breath.

Elara's face is pale, lips bloodless. She doesn't even notice the way she sways until Kallesie presses against her. I want to walk to her, pull her into my arms, but every eye in the square is already carving into her. If I touch her now, I'd only sharpen the target she already is.

Vulcan growls deep, a vibration that rumbles through the ruined square. "*You guard a firestorm and expect the world to love her? You're the fool here, not them.*"

"Shut up," I hiss, though he isn't wrong. Elara's blood terrifies me, too.

The Keeper's words return, bitter in my mind. *"Her fire is no gift. It is a burden. And burdens break those who carry them."*

I clench my jaw. If the Keeper is right, then Elara is breaking already. And I can't let her.

Elara

We leave the village before dawn. No one asks us to stay. No one says thank you. They press tighter around their pitiful fire and watch us disappear into the fog.

The road curves into the forest, where roots twist like bones and mist slicks the branches. The Wraths' corruption is spreading here, too. The trees bleed sap black as ink, and the air hums with something unnatural.

Every step we take is a step toward the Stronghold.

An echo I cannot silence, each pulse begs me to spill some of my blood, to call to the shadows scratching at the edges of the Veil.

"You are not prey," Kallesie growls in my head. *"Stop trembling like you are. You are a flame. Burn, or you will be consumed."*

I clench my jaw and blink hard. "I'm not trembling."

"You are," Helios says softly, glancing at me. His steel-grey eyes, too sharp, score through the mist. He doesn't push, doesn't scold, but the way he watches me feels worse, like he can see every fracture in my armour.

The Keeper's warning twists again in my skull. "The Veil will not be held back forever. When it calls, you will answer."

I drop my gaze and keep walking.

HELIOS

The fog thickens as we press deeper into the forest. The silence isn't natural, not even birds sing here.

Vulcan pads ahead, tail stiff. *"They're near."*

I grip my sword tighter. "Wraths?"

"Not whole ones," he says, ember eyes narrowing. *"Half-turns."*

My stomach twists. I glance at Elara. She has gone still, her hand clutching her bandages, her eyes distant.

Something in her blood is stirring; I can feel it in the way she stands, raw and unpredictable.

"Elara," I say.

She doesn't answer.

The first half-turns lurch out of the mist. Its skin split, black veins running across it, mouth open in a wheezing rasp. But unlike Wraths, its eyes still have a pale, terrifying blue colour.

"Kill me," it begs. "Please, make it stop…"

Then its voice cracks into a growl, jaw snaps wider than bone should allow.

"Elara!" I bark, but she has already raised her bow.

Blood slicks her fingers from her bandaged arm. She shoots the arrow.

The Half turns convulsively, screams, and falls to ash.

The Keeper's warning rattles in my chest. "Every life ended by her blood will draw the Veil closer."

Gods, is that what I am watching?

Elara

The ash scatters, but I can't breathe. Because behind it, staggering out of the fog, is her.

The boy's mother.

Her hands are clawing at her own skin as if she can tear the veins out, her face warps by shadow. Her eyes meet mine; wide, bloodshot, and still human.

"No," I whisper, stumbling back. "Not you…"

She lunges.

Kallesie's roar shakes the trees as she barrels forward, slamming into the woman and snapping her spine with a single brutal crack. The body collapses, twitching once, then stills.

I drop my bow. My stomach twists so violently that I think I'll be sick.

"Do not weep for what is already dead," Kallesie says, though her tone is quieter now. "*She is gone the moment the veins take her."*

But I can't stop the tears burning my eyes. The Keeper warned me that my blood will doom more than it saves. Is this what he meant? I slowly walk to where her body is turning to ash and say a silent prayer that she makes it back to her son on the other side.

HELIOS

I kill three more Half-Turns before Elara moves again.

Vulcan fights like a beast unleashed, fire drips from his jaws, and his claws rake through corrupt flesh.

But it is Elara who terrifies me most.

Her arrows strike true. Each Wrath burns faster and screams louder. And with every kill, her glow flares hotter. She shakes as if she might shatter, but gods help me, she doesn't stop.

When it is over, the clearing is carpeted in ash. Elara stands in the middle of it, bow lowered, chest heaving. Her eyes meet mine, and I see what she won't say; she hates herself more than the Wraths.

And I remember again what the Keeper said, voice like iron through the dark: *"When her fire burns, you will have to choose whether to follow her... or stop her."*

ELARA

We find shelter in a hollow alcove beneath a ruin watchtower. My hands won't stop shaking.

"I can't," I whisper finally, staring at the blood dried across my palm. "I can't keep doing this. They turn faster around me. I make it worse."

Helios crouches in front of me, tilting his head until I have to look at him. His eyes burn like steel lit in a forge.

"You save lives," he says. "You don't make it worse."

"You see them…"

"I see you keeping them from ripping me apart," he snaps, "you're mine to guard, Elara. Until the end. Don't carry this alone, you have me and the clan to lean on."

My breath catches. His hand clutches mine, warm and solid. The word I am afraid of hovers between us—love, but neither of us speaks it.

"Pathetic," Kallesie grumbles in my head. *"Just say it, boy shit, Elara wrong chat."*

Despite everything, my lips twitch, just for a moment.

But the Keeper's warning won't leave me. "The Veil will answer to you, or it will destroy you."

The fog thickens as night falls. I try to sleep, but the air shifts, unnaturally. My veins pulse like they've been snared.

Then I hear it.

A whisper curling against my ear, sweet and poisonous.

"Open the Veil, little key. Or watch the world drown in ash."

I jerk awake, sweat chilling my skin. Shadows slither at the edges of the alcove. Morrigan.

She isn't here. not yet. But I can feel her, closer than it has ever been, like I'm not alone, even though I am.

I wrap my arms around myself, shaking. For the first time since Wraths began to turn, I am certain this isn't by chance. This is her design.

And she wants me.

The Keeper was right.

CHAPTER 43

SHADOWS BETWEEN US

HELIOS

I sense it even before I lay eyes on her, the heaviness of her recent realization, thickening the air around us, clear and undeniable.

The night presses close, heavy and suffocating, like a blanket soaked in ash. Fog creeps across the ground as we leave the village behind, curling around the broken stones while smoke still drifts from the ruins.

Every step toward the Stronghold feels like wading through memory itself. Each ghost of the villagers' last moments lingers between us, silent but accusing. I scan the shadows; every twitch of movement makes my knees tighten around Vulcan's sides. Something isn't right. Elara's silence feels heavy, deliberate, and the air whines with warning.

The silence is the worst.

We leave the village behind the blood in the square, the screams, and the ash blowing in the torchlight. Their faces follow us. The boy's wide, terrified eyes when Elara shot the arrow into his chest. The mother wails as she clutches nothing but dust. The others pulled away from her, their fear sharper than grief.

I keep my jaw tight and my breath even, but each step gnaws at me. I have seen battlefields littered with corpses, villages erased, and even children who didn't escape the slaughter in raids. But never this. Never have I seen a child twist into something not his own. And never have I watched Elara with this kind of dread, waiting to see if what happened finally breaks her.

Elara walks ahead, stiff shoulders, dark hair matted with sweat and streaked with soot. The bandages on her arm glisten dark with blood. She hasn't spoken since we left the ruins. Her silence weighs heavier than the fog.

Kallesie pads at her side, molten eyes narrowing at every sound in the trees. Vulcan stalks beside me, every muscle stiff, molten ember glowing faintly in his throat.

I watch the way Elara moves, the faint stumbling in her step, and the way her hand twitches near her bow, when no threat has shown itself. She is wearing herself down too quickly. Her blood answers to the Veil like a drumbeat, and every time she bleeds into her arrows, it takes more from her than she ever admits.

My chest aches.

"Elara," I call softly.

She doesn't turn. Doesn't slow.

When she falters again, I can't watch it anymore. "Sit."

My voice comes out sharper than I intended.

She hesitates, then obeys, lowering herself onto a fallen log.

I kneel before her.

The bandage is soaked through. When I peel it away, the wound is closing, but the skin around it is pale, fevered, and trembles faintly with each pulse. Her blood shimmers under the surface, alive in a way no human blood should be.

"You're trembling," I murmur.

She forces a smile that never touches her eyes. "I'm fine."

Vulcan's growl rumbles low in my mind. *"Fine" is the word humans use when they are about to fall apart. Do not let it fool you."*

I ignore him, focusing on cleaning the wound. The water stings her skin; she bites back a hiss, fingers twitching. I steady her wrist, my fingers touch hers. She doesn't pull away. For a heartbeat, the world narrows until it is only her and me, fire and exhaustion coil tight between us.

Her gaze lingers on mine, searching. "You're staring," she says softly.

"I am making sure the bleeding stops." The excuse feels brittle, breaking in my mouth.

Her lips tilt in the faintest curve of a smile.

Elara

Kallesie's words fall like thunder into my mind. I can see it in her quivering expression, before I catch the meaning. *"Stone man staring again. You two are ridiculous. Might as well admit it and be done."*

I roll my eyes, a quiet grin slips through despite herself. My chest tightens at the sight. I don't tell him what Kallesie is saying. Some things aren't mine to tell.

I glance down at the fresh bandage around my arm, then away before I can think too hard about the way his hands lingered there.

Helios

I finished wrapping the bandage, but my hands lingered a second too long before I forced myself to pull away. I should have let it go sooner. Should have warned her not to bleed herself dry for every Wrath we come across. I know Elara well enough to know warnings would only make her fight harder.

Her lips part on a soft breath, and for a second, I think she might reach for me. Gods, I want her to. She leans back instead, brushing ash from her sleeve, and the moment breaks apart.

"Rest," I say quietly. "We can't afford you collapsing before the Stronghold.

She nods, her gaze dropping to her bandaged arm, then to the ground. That's when the air shifts. The Veil stirs.

It begins as a ripple in the fog, faint and thin, like a thread pulled too tight. Then the birch trees groan, branches bend, though no wind touches them. The air becomes more concentrated with acrid and metallic.

Vulcan stiffens on the other side of me, molten eyes narrowing.

"It moves," he warns. *"We will not be allowed peace for long."*

A pulse crawls up my spine, gnawing at my chest, alien and hungry.

Elara feels it too. Her hand skims over her bow.

Elara

Kallesie prowls closer, lips back from her fangs.

"Oh, look," she mutters dryly into my mind. *"Your moment of sentiment is interrupted by the Veil. Delightful."*

"Fuck, I mutter, scanning the fog.

The mist thickens. Shapes press close, blurred at first, then sharpening into something wrong—too many limbs. Shadows stretched too long. They don't walk so much as lurch forward.

My hand goes to the bow.

"The Veil," I say.

HELIOS

"Yes," I say, my voice low. "It's thinning."

A crack rips jaggedly through the fog like a wound torn open. Sound spills from it screams layered over screams, rising, and twisting until they curdle into silence.

Elara's eyes snap on mine, fire and fear burning there in equal measure.

"Then we have no time to waste."

The tear hangs open, bleeding shadow like ink in water. Faces flicker inside with half-human, half-Wrath, mouth open in endless screams. Rot pours from it in thick waves.

Fuck.

The thought slams into me so hard it nearly knocks the breath from my lungs.

I know these faces.

Not strangers. Not wraths born in the darkness. These are the same villagers we saved from the half-turned wraths back there—the same hollow-eyed survivors who clung to life with blood on their skin and terror in their eyes. We saved them.

And now they're the ones rushing us.

My stomach turns as steel meets flesh. For one sickening second, all I can see is that village again, smoke choking the sky, children crying, bodies piled in the mud. We fought for them and bled for them.

My grip tightens around my sword until my knuckles ache. They were supposed to live. Instead, they came back wrong.

"We need to find Elara and Kallesie. Vulcan." I say.

"Jump on and let's go. I don't want to fight them as much as you don't." Vulcan responds.

ELARA

I pull back another arrow. Then I see their faces. My breath catches so hard it burns.

No.

The bow nearly slips from my hand.

I know them.

Not just the torn skin or the blood streaking their mouths. Not just the jerking, unnatural way they moved, like their bodies no longer belonged to them.

Their faces. The villagers.

The same people who huddle around that makeshift fire after the attack, wrapped in smoke and ash and silence. The same people who stare at me from across the flames after the Half Wrath fall beneath my blood-streaked arrow.

My stomach turns.

And the whispers.

Blood witch.

The words slam into me so hard that it feels like they're being hissed into my ear all over again.

My pulse stutters. Because I know what this looks like.

I know the signs.

The ruined skin.

The wrongness in the eyes.

The way their bodies move is like something is fighting beneath the surface.

My chest caves in.

They look exactly like the mother, and her son did before I put an arrow through them. The memory hits so fast it nearly knocks the breath from my lungs. The woman was clutching her boy beside the fire. Her hand locked around him as she could still keep him safe. And then the change. The hollow look. The split second where fear becomes something else. My whole body goes cold as the memory starts to fade.

"We need to run Elara!" Kallesie growls in my mind. She comes from behind me and forces me onto her back.

"We need to find Helios and Vulcan," I say to her.

"Damn men can come find us for a damn change."

We take off towards the birch treeline, the last screams and shouts, Half turned Wraths fading behind us. I don't look back.

Leaving them… it feels wrong. The thought claws at me, but there is no time. Not now. Not if we want to make it back to the Stronghold.

The birch trees rise ahead, pale and quiet. Relief hits me at the thought of seeing Helios and Vulcan. We are not alone.

But the memory of the Half Wraths we left behind

lingers, like a shadow I can't shake.

CHAPTER 44

Stronghold's Shadow

Helios

The night doesn't allow us much longer.

Through the fog, the gates of the Stronghold rise like a mountain, heavy with the weight of old grief from us retreating from the army of Half Wraths. Even before we reach them, I feel the eyes of unseen watchers tracking every step, judgment presses into the marrow of the air.

The walls are not just stone. They are memories of every scar of past wars etched into their surface, every victory, every betrayal. And as the fog swirls against them like restless spirits, it is hard not to feel that the fortress remembers.

Elara walks by my side, her steps measured and deliberate, though I can see the strain in the way her shoulders hunch against her exhaustion. Each drop of blood she shed in the village weighs heavier than the iron gates ahead of us.

I want to be able to carry the weight for her. But I can't. I ache for her to take her into my arms, but I'm powerless. Not here. Not with every gaze already picking apart her defenses.

Vulcan's gaze scans the shadows. Kallesie prowls like a storm barely leashed, her glowing purple eyes catching every guard station along the battlements. The flick of her tail and the twitch of her ears betray irritation that seeped through her bond with Elara.

The gates creak open with the groan of ancient hinges, revealing a courtyard crowded with soldiers and petitioners. Conversations are quiet at the sight of us. Some faces hold relief. Others fear.

I block every face, every whisper, and lock my gaze on the high steps climbing to the council chamber, the heart of Hue, where everything that matters waits.

ELARA

Every step toward the chamber feels like walking barefoot across glass. Even fully healed, my arm still aches, each heartbeat recalling the price I paid in that cursed village.

The wrath of a child's face rises in my memory. My arrow had burned him to ash, and still I'm hearing his scream.

Kallesie's voice curls sharply in my mind.

"Bravo, Summoner. Marching into the lion's den while half bled and haunted. Truly inspired strategy."

I smirk faintly, brushing ash from my sleeve. “Quiet,” I mutter, though I don’t mean it. Her sarcasm anchors me in its own way.

Helios’s hand glides over mine for a fleeting moment, as if unintentional, but the heat of it steadies me more than I want to admit. I force myself to look forward, shoulders square, as though I haven’t been unravelling piece by piece since the moors.

HELIOS

The council chambers swallow us whole.

Torchlight flickers against stone walls lined with banners of Summoner houses; their sigils faded with time, but still heavy with meaning. The Elders sit on their raised thrones, shadows pooling at their feet as if the Veil itself lingers here, watching.

Keepers move like restless birds along the edge, robes whispering, hands weaving subtle motions as if stitching the world back together. Their murmurs tangle with the crackle of fire, half prayer, half conspiracy.

All eyes turn to us as we enter—some wide with awe, others narrow with suspicion.

Elder Therian rises, tall and lean, his white robes moving with calculated grace. His gaze pauses on Elara, then me, before returning to her like a hawk circling prey. “You return from the southern villages,” he says, voice even, but heavy enough to crush. “Alive. But not without cost, I see.”

Elara

I meet his stare, jaw clenched. "Yes, Elder. The villages are getting attacked. The Wraths…" My voice catches. I force it steadily. "They are no longer bound to the portals. They are turning here. From flesh."

Whispers ripple through the chamber. The sound of fear, disbelieving, sharp.

Therian's eyes narrow. "Explain."

Before I can, Helios steps forward.

"Her blood burns through them," he says, voice low but steady, carrying to every corner. "The Half-turned turn into ash from the inside out, but the rest—pushes us back. We kill what we can, but it is her blood alone that slows them. Without it, nothing would have survived."

The chamber erupts in murmurs. Awe. Relief. And beneath it, envy.

I can feel their eyes burning into me, weighing me, and measuring whether I am a weapon or a threat.

Kallesie's commentary slips like a blade into my mind.

"Ah, yes. Stare harder, old men. Perhaps your glares will do what the Wraths could not."

I bite back a smile. If only she knew how close I am to laughing in their faces.

HELIOS

Elder Mirath leans forward, his expression engraved with suspicion. "Your blood is dangerous," he says, voice sharp as a drawn blade. "If overused, it may destabilize you—or worse, draw the Wraths to us. We cannot afford another catastrophe."

Elara flinches, almost imperceptibly.

I can't hold back. "She has done more than any of you," I say, each word deliberate. "While you argue in the shadows, she bleeds in the dirt to keep the world standing."

Vulcan's voice rumbles in my mind, warning edged with pride. *"Strong words, master. Be ready to cut with them if they strike back."*

The chamber stills. Dozens of eyes flick between us. Elara squares her shoulders, exhaustion etched into every line of her, but defiance burns still.

"I know the cost," she says, voice clear. "And I will bear it. My blood will not endanger anyone here, not unless I fail to protect everyone first."

Silence falls, heavy, suffocating.

Finally, Therian leans back, and their hands fold. "Very well. But know this: power unchecked is as deadly as Wrath. Misuse will not be tolerated."

ELARA

Their dismissal burns hotter than any Wrath fire. Not gratitude, not even acknowledgment. Only warning and fear.

Kallesie whispers, her dark amusement. *"See? They fear you more than the monsters. Delightful, isn't it?"*

I swallow the laugh that threatens to escape. If I give in, they will call me unstable. Broken. Dangerous. Maybe they already are. Helios's hand touches mine again. Brief. Grounding. My chest tightens at the feeling. I hold onto it like a rope in a storm.

The corridors outside the chamber are colder than the night air. Shadows stretch too long, curling unnaturally as though the Veil seeps through the cracks.

I feel that gnawing pulse at the edges of my chest, that hungry silence in the air. The council might believe in decrees and warnings, but stone walls could not hold back what is already spilling into our world.

The Veil whispers here too, faint and metallic on the tongue, pressing just beyond sight. It unsettles me and makes me want to draw my bow and shoot another arrow. But Kallesie's voice forges in my skull.

"Don't even think about it. You're already cracked, Summoner. One more drop and the shadows will drink you dry."

I exhale slowly, gripping Helios's hand a little tighter.

The warmth anchors me. The fog pressing at the fortress walls feels distant for just that moment.

But the reprieve won't last. Nothing ever does.

HELIOS

We move on, side by side, in defiance of the world.

The council's whispers behind us—suspicion, jealousy, and fear; but none of them matter compared to the quiet fire in her gaze.

The Veil is not done. The night ahead will be long.

I reach for her hand, sliding my fingers over hers. She doesn't pull away. For a heartbeat, it is enough.

Vulcan's voice comes low and grave. *"The shadows gather. The Veil stirs. Soon, it will demand its price."*

But for now, her hand in mine means we are still here. Still fighting. Still together.

And in the shadows, unseen eyes watch.

Morrigan's plans press closer.

CHAPTER 45

When Shadows Breach

Helios

The watching doesn't stop once we are inside.

The council chamber empties in fragments, like a body slowly bleeding out. Elders drift into side corridors, their robes sweeping stones, their whispers dissipating into the air. Their words aren't loud, but I don't need to hear them to know what they say.

Elara. Dangerous. Bloodline. Risk.

The torches sputter, smoke curls low, the flames pale as if starved. Even Vulcan shifts uneasily, ember-bright eyes flickering toward the corners where shadows cling too thickly.

"This fortress thinks itself immune," Vulcan's voice rumbles in my mind, with a growl. "*But stone cracks. And shadows do not respect walls."*

He isn't wrong. I feel the weight of the Veil pressing

against the Stronghold like a tide against a cliff. I steal a glance at Elara, who walks beside me, her bandaged arm hidden beneath her cloak. She is holding herself steady, but I can read the tightness of her jaw and the too-careful cadence of her steps.

The Stronghold has always been heavy with judgment, but tonight it feels heavier with something else expected to come crashing through the walls. The kind that waits with teeth bared.

ELARA

The voices of the council still ring in my skull, overlapping, dismissive, and suspicious. They look at me like I am a weapon shrouded in skin, not a girl who has just cut herself open to stop an entire village from turning.

Kallesie's molten purple gaze flickers at my side. *"Oh, they love you," she* says, her voice a purr edged with acid. *"You bleed yourself hollow, save their world, and what do they do? They plot ways to leash you. Charming lot, these Keepers."*

I ignore her or try to. I want Helios's hand again, the grounding weight of it, but the corridor is full of Summoners. Eyes everywhere. Watching. Waiting.

Then a sound.

A scream tears through the Stronghold, shrill, jagged, and cuts through the air like glass.

Every summoner stills. Every torch bending in the same direction, flame tugged by a sudden draft.

The Veil shudders.

Helios

The scream grows into many, echoing up from the lower halls. Boots trample on stone. Then a Keeper appears at the corridor's far end, face pale as ash, robes spattered with something black.

"They're inside!" His voice cracks, raw with terror. "The Veil, it's torn, the Wraths…"

He doesn't finish.

The wall behind him splits open in a jagged wound of shadow. From it crawls a shape that had once been human. Its flesh hangs loose, twisted by veins of black fire, eyes void and bottomless. Not half-turns. Not salvageable.

Forsaken.

The first to complete the transformation, these Wraths are fully turned monsters, unlike the others, whose bodies and humanity are consumed by whatever cursed force animates them.

Elara

The corridor erupts. Summoners shout spells, and steel rings against stone—the forsaken shrieks, a sound that peels the skin from my bones.

Kallesie's voice strikes sharply in my mind. *"Bleed,*

girl. You know what it takes. Do it now, or you'll be next."

I fumble for my dagger, my fingers slick with sweat. My bandaged arm pulses, screaming at me to stop, but I ignore it.

"Helios!" I shout, even as I slice open my palm. Blood wells hot and bright, dripping onto the stone.

The Forsaken lunges, its claws raking across the floor. The moment my blood touches the ground, the Veil recoils, a shriek of shadow rips backward. Creature staggers, not stopped, but slowed if not broken, its advance trembling under its wait, and my blood smeared onto the arrowhead. Aiming fire.

"Strike!" I yell.

HELIOS

I don't hesitate. Vulcan surges with me, flame bursts from his body in a rush of molten heat. My blade bites deep into the Forsaken's chest, sizzling as Elara's blood weakens the creature's form. The smell is acidic, with notes of rotting and burning iron.

The Forsaken collapses, body convulsing, but already more shadows writhe in the torn wall. Too many.

Vulcan snarls, eyes ablaze. *"They come hungry. And they come knowing."*

I glance at Elara. Her face is pale, lips pressing thin with pain. Blood drips from her hand, already pooling darkly. I wanted to rip the dagger from her grip, to tell her not to give them more, but I know it is pointless. Without her blood, we'd all be dead.

And the council knows it too.

They just don't want to admit it.

Elara

The chamber dissolves into chaos. Wraths pour from the tear, limbs grotesque, eyes hollow. Summoners fight, but their blades pass through smoke and bone that refuses to break.

One younger Summoner, barely old enough, slashes his own palm, desperate to mimic me, desperate to prove he is enough.

His blood falls uselessly.

Wraths tear through him in a single strike. His scream stops halfway, his body crumples, splitting into two.

My stomach lurches. I want to be sick, but there is no time. My bloodline, curses or not, is the only shackle holding the Wraths back.

"More!" Kallesie barks. "*Give more, or they'll drown us in shadow."*

"No," I whisper, voice shaking. "I can't…"

But I did.

The dagger bites deeper into my palm, and the world erupts in scarlet. My blood hisses where it touches stone, burning through shadow like acid.

The wraths shriek.

Helios

She is killing herself in front of them all. And for God's sake, the council watches, their faces white, their bodies frozen in awe and fear.

I slay another Wrath, fury burning hotter than Vulcan's fire. "Do something!" I roar at them. "She's saving your lives!"

Some move sluggishly, their spells weak sparks in the onslaught. Others did nothing at all; their fear anchors them uselessly.

Then, through the chaos, the shadows thicken, drawing together like threads weaving into cloth. A figure emerges, tall and terrible, hair black as oil, eyes burning violet.

Morrigan.

"Elara," she purrs, her voice echoes from everywhere and nowhere at once. "Little sister bleeds so sweetly. You'll open the gate for me yet."

Elara

Her presence nearly breaks me. My blood burns hotter, and my lungs lock. Morrigan's face is cruelly beautiful, her smile sharp as broken glass.

"I am not your sister," I spit, rage shaking me more than

fear could.

Kallesie bristles, molten eyes flaring. "*She reeks of chains and hunger. Hold your ground, Summoner. Or we'll both be dragged through that tear.*"

Morrigan laughs, the sound writhes through the Veil itself. "You've already fallen into my shadow, Elara. She hisses venom in each syllable. "Every step, every heartbeat… They belong to me. And your blood… it will feed the Veil itself. Stand if you dare, but you cannot stop me."

Her form unravels before I can strike. The Wraths fall back into the rift, vanishing with her. Silence crashes over the chamber, heavy and suffocating.

Bodies litter the floor. Smoke curls in every corner. My hand bleeds freely, and the stone beneath me hisses and cracks from the power of it.

Helios

I catch her as she sways, pulling her against me. Her blood soaks through my robe, hot against my chest. She doesn't resist, leaning into me, breath shallow.

The council stands in ruins, their chamber wrecked, their dead strewn across the floor. Yet their eyes still look at her not as a savior, but as a threat.

"She is too dangerous," Elder Mirath hisses. "If Morrigan wants her blood, it must be bound."

"She just saved your lives!" I snarl, tightening my grip

on Elara. "Without her, none of you would be standing."

Vulcan's eyes glow hotter. "*Say the word, and I'll burn them to cinders.*"

I don't answer him. But the thought lodges in my chest.

Because if they turn on her, if they try to cage her, I will burn the world before I let them.

Elara

My vision blurs, but I catch Helios's words. Fierce. Defiant. Like fire in the dark.

The council's fear presses in, thick as the smoke. But I am not afraid of them. Not anymore.

The Veil was breached. Morrigan was here.

And I am the key she wants.

CHAPTER 46

THE BITE OF BINDING

ELARA

I don't have time to think about what that means.

Kallesie's growl isn't her usual mocking rumble. It is warped and jagged, as if her voice has been dragged across glass. Her molten-purple eyes sputter, streaks of black ash swirling through them.

My hand freezes against her fur.

She's changing.

"Don't look at me like that, girl," she snaps in my head, still trying for sarcasm, but her voice shakes. 'I*'m fine. Just... tired. Same as you."*

But she isn't fine. Panic claws through me as the bond frays and burns out, the infection tearing through Kallesie faster than I can breathe. The same black rot that twisted villagers into half-Wrath is sliding along the tether of my soul and hers.

If it takes her, I will lose everything.

"Elara?"

Helios's voice rises above the panic. He stands ahead, torchlight gilding his cheekbones, his steel-grey eyes sharpening with suspicion. Vulcan looms beside him, steady, unreadable.

I open my mouth to answer, and then Kallesie stumbles. Just one paw drags, claws scraping stone. But Kallesie never stumbles.

Not once.

The cold in my spine freezes solid.

That's when the whisper slides into my mind.

Not Kallesie. Not the Keeper.

Nyx.

"The bond breaks when infection takes hold," she purrs, silk wrapped razors. *"But there is one way to anchor her. Burn the rot out before it roots."*

My throat closes. *"How?"*

Helios glances sharply at me, but I barely notice.

"She must bite you," Nyx says.

The world tilts. *"Bite me? Kallesie's fangs can split stone. She can render me in half a heartbeat."*

Nyx's chuckle drips with poison. *"Your blood will kill Wraths. But to the infected, it heals. If she drinks before the infection settles too deep, you may yet save her."*

My knees buckled. I stagger back, shaking my head. *"No. There has to be another way."*

Kallesie's growl rattles through my skull. *"What are you hiding from me, Elara?"*

And for the first time since binding to her, I can't answer her.

HELIOS

Something is wrong. I can feel it leaking off her in waves.

I close the distance and catch her wrist. Her pulse hammers, frantic, under my thumb. "Tell me."

Her eyes meet mine, silver flickering with shadows. Fear. Desperation. Not the sharp defiance she wears like armour; this is breakable.

"It's Kallesie," she whispers. "The bond… It's fraying."

The word strikes like a blade. Infection.

Vulcan shifts beside me, embers glowing hotter. *"If it reaches the hound, the Summoner will follow."*

"Elara," I say carefully, though dread drags claws down my ribs, "if there's a way…"

She interrupts me with a violent shake of her head. "You don't understand. The way to save her … it's not simple."

I somehow keep my voice steady by force. "What did Nyx tell you?"

She doesn't answer. She doesn't have to.

My jaw clenches. "If it's your blood…"

Her eyes widen because I'd struck true.

Damn her. Damn Nyx. Damn the Veil.

My hand closes around hers, useless against what's coming. I can face blades, Wraths, death itself, but not this, not when it comes to her. But this—this asks me to stand still while she walks willingly into pain, and I have never felt more powerless.

"Elara." My voice frays on her name. "If this is the only way, then I'm here. You do not face this alone."

Her lips part like she wants to argue, but her gaze flicks to Kallesie, who sags lower, molten eyes dull with black streaks.

My chest twists. She is going to do it anyway.

ELARA

Helios's words should steady me. Instead, they tear me open because he doesn't understand.

If Kallesie bites me, she'll taste my blood. And once she tastes it, the hunger will be permanent. Irresistible.

I can lose her to infection.

Or lose her to me.

Either way, I lose.

Kallesie lifts her head, eyes dimming, fear flickering through them. Fear. For the first time, my hellhound is afraid.

And I realize with a hollow ache that I am not the only

one I might not save.

"Bite me," I whisper.

Her ears snap back. A strangled growl rattles her throat. Her fangs gleam like ivory scythes.

"Don't ask me that," she hisses in my mind. *"I'll tear you apart."*

"Yes," Nyx purrs inside me. *"Let her taste you. Let her bind tighter than death itself."*

"Elara.. I know you have to do this. I'm scared—scared of everything that could go wrong—but… I trust you. Just make sure she doesn't bite your jugular vein; if she does, you will bleed out like a stuffed pig."

"She already is!" My voice cracked. "If I don't, we both die!"

His grip falters. I see the war in his eyes.

And then Kallesie collapses against me. Her breath comes ragged, her glow going black. The bond seizes, choking, tearing, and burning.

We are dying. Together.

"Do it," I whisper, baring my throat.

Kallesie's muzzle hovers an inch from my skin. Her fangs graze my pulse. She trembles, fighting herself, fighting me, and fighting the bond.

Then the infection surges.

Her howl splits the night.

And she is struck.

Her fangs are buried deep in my shoulder. Fire explodes

through me, liquid lightning tearing every nerve apart. I scream, my body convulsing.

My blood pours into her. The bond ignites white-hot, threads blazing as shadows burned away. Her infection shrieks, ripped from her marrow.

But the fire didn't stop her.

It rages through me too, consuming and relentless.

HELIOS

Madness.

Elara starts shaking in my arms, her wail splits my skull open. Blood soaks her sleeve, running hot down her arm into Kallesie's maw.

I should rip the beast off her. I should draw my blade.

But I can't.

Because I see the shadows boiling out of Kallesie, turning into nothing under Elara's fire. The infection burns away. She is healing her and saving her.

And killing herself.

"Elara!" I roar, while dragging her by her waist and her other arm, desperate to free her. Kallesie's jaw locks tighter, flames of bonfire flickering against my skin.

Vulcan growls low, eyes like molten steel. *"If you break them apart now, both die."*

God damn it.

I grip her like I can hold the world together, but she's slipping through my fingers. The bite just above her right shoulder pulses, dark and hot, and her body convulses around it, jerking and twisting as her scream tears through the air—my name, my soul, everything. Blood coats my hands, my arms, my chest, and I don't care. I hold her. I have to hold her, even as panic claws at me and the fear of losing her nearly crushes me.

And I swear if she slips away, I will tear the Veil apart to drag her back from death's door.

Elara

The fire eats everything. My veins, my breath, my soul.

I try to pull back, but she's already there. Her teeth sink into my shoulder, just above the joint, and fire explodes through me. Sharp, molten, alive. My scream rips free before I can think, raw and desperate.

In the center of it, Kallesie. Her molten eyes blaze, purple unfurling through black, and I can't look away. My stomach twists violently, my chest heaves, and a tremor runs from my spine through my fingers, jerking me against her.

The shock hits like a live wire. My muscles seize and spasm, trembling uncontrollably. I claw at her neck, nails biting deep, and my own blood trickles hot and slick between us. Every pulse of it rattles through my veins like a hammer. My vision fractures, edges of the world flickering, tilting. I can barely stand.

I gag as metallic copper floods my mouth. My arms jerk on their own, twitching with each jagged surge of pain. Every nerve is alive, screaming. My teeth chatter, my lungs burn, my legs threaten to buckle, but my body won't obey me. It convulses, and I am trapped inside of it, every heartbeat a spike of terror, every breath an impossible effort.

Her ragged voice slices through me, broken and raw, scraping along my nerves. *"Elara..."*

I shudder violently under it. My skin prickles, every hair standing up, everything quivering, and I feel utterly dangling above a void I can't see.

Time fractures. Second stretch, collapse, I can't move away. I cannot stop it. I am consumed by the bite, by the shock, by her. Every pulse of pain, every shuddering gasp belongs to this moment. I am powerless, undone, and terrified beyond reason.

Her jaws tremble against me, but she doesn't let go.

And beneath the fire, I feel Nyx again. Her voice slithers soft and sure.

"Yes. Burn together. One cannot live without the other now."

The bond roars, alive and wild. Unbreakable.

I am not sure if it is salvation.

Or damnation. That's the last thought before darkness takes me.

CHAPTER 47

KISSED BY FIRELIGHT

ELARA

The darkness loosens, clawing away from me, and I jerk awake, every nerve aflame. Helios's arms hold me solid, unyielding, impossible, and I cling to him like a lifeline, though pain rips through my shoulder, jagged and relentless, like molten claws dragging through flesh and blood.

I scream, raw and ragged, body convulsing with aftershocks that make me shiver uncontrollably.

Fire. That's what it feels like; fire set loose inside my veins, scalding every nerve, tunnelling straight into my heart.

"Kallesie!" I cry, not a command, but a plea.

She's there, looming, molten eyes wild and wrong, black lacing through violet eyes. The moment my blood touches her tongue, something snaps, the corruption recoils, shrieking as if it burns. For a heartbeat, the tether between us steadies.

But at a cost.

Agony surges back into me, white-hot and merciless. I stagger, clutching my shoulder as the fire races outward. My cursed blood doesn't know which way to turn. It is Wrath-killer, life-binder, and poison all at once. It can't decide where the infection ends and where I begin.

"Elara!"

Helios tightens his hold, pulling me closer, strong and desperate. Vulcan prowls behind him, with a mix of growling low, the sound vibrating like thunder, and a whine of restless fear, can't voice.

I can't breathe. The tether with Kallesie pulls taut, and both of us writhe in mirroring agony. My pulse stutters, tangled with hers. If she dies, I will follow. If I fall, she will collapse into shadow.

The thought carves itself into me with brutal clarity.

We are one. We have always been one.

Kallesie lets out a sound half-howl, half-sob, and presses her massive head against my side, trembling. She is fighting it.

"Stay with me," Helios says, his voice rougher than I've ever heard it. He lowers me to the stone floor of the hallway, cradling me close while Kallesie presses tight against my other side. His hand hovers uselessly over the wound, slick with too much blood.

"Elara, look at me. Don't you dare close your eyes."

I force them open, though black is already edging the

corners of my vision. His face swims above me, firelight paints him in gold, shadowing the hard line of his jaw, the stern chisel of his cheekbones, and the storm in his steel-grey eyes.

"You're burning up." His thumb brushes my temple, tender in a way that aches worse than the wound. "What the hell did she do to you?"

"She… has to." My breath catches. Each word slices through me. "My blood burns, Wraths, but it can heal her too. Nyx said."

He presses a hand to his mouth, jaw tight, not surprised, just furious and desperate. Later. Not now.

"Don't you dare let go," he growls, voice low and raw. "Not now. Not ever. Stay with me, Elara."

Another convulsion tears through me, pain arching like lightning. Kallesie yelps, her claws rake the stone beneath us. The tether screams with fire.

"Gods," I gasp. "It's in both of us."

"No." Helios's palm presses harder to stem the bleeding, though we both know it's not from the blood loss that will kill me. "Don't talk like that. You're not going anywhere."

Shadows leap in the firelight, stretching like grasping fingers across the arches of the hallway. For a terrifying moment, I think they belong to the Wraths, that Morrigan's leash has already tightened, but the night hangs heavy and still and waiting.

Only us. Only this torment.

I bury my face against his shoulder, sweat soaks my hairline, and the metallic tang of blood fills my mouth. He holds me tighter, arms trembling. He sets his lips on the crown of my head, not a kiss, just raw, desperate contact, as if he can't stop himself.

"You fight everything," he whispers hoarsely, voice nearly lost to the crackle of fire. "But don't you dare fight me. Don't fight this."

Another wave of agony rips through me, and I claw at him, at Kallesie, at anything to stay grounded. The bite blazes brighter, and through it, I feel Kallesie shifting. The infection is ebbing from her, but it drags me with it.

"Helios," I croak, my chest tight, "I can't lose her."

His whole body goes rigid. His grip tightens until I think he might break me, but it's his voice that cracks instead.

"No. No, Elara." His forehead presses to mine, his breath uneven. "You don't get to tell me that like it's already written."

The firelight pulses, then steadies. The wild corruption in Kallesie's gaze dims, smothered. Her chest rises and falls in a steadier rhythm. My blood takes root and scorches the infection back into silence.

But it leaves me hollow.

My body sags, a rag doll in his arms. His voice still calls to me, but it sounds far away, muffled by the roaring in my skull.

"Elara! Stay awake. Stay with me."

I will try. God, I try.

He presses his lips on the crown of my head again, then grazes my cheek, desperately and unrestrained. "You don't get to leave me," he breathes against my skin. "Ever."

My hand, shaking and blood-slick, rises blindly to find his face. My fingers curl against the hard line of his jaw, dragging his eyes to mine. He is breaking open before me, cracks of fear and something else that has always burned beneath.

I pull him down.

The kiss isn't soft. It is fire on fire, a clash of desperation and fury at the world that keeps trying to tear us apart. His mouth devours mine, stealing the air I can't find on my own, pouring something fierce and grounding into me when the darkness claws too close.

The tether thrums. Kallesie presses closer, her heat wraps me in a cocoon of bond and fierce loyalty. Helios's hands shake as he holds me, one hand buried in my hair, the other clamping over the wound.

I am not sure if I am dying or being dragged back to life.

When the kiss breaks, he stays close, his breath ragged, our foreheads pressed together. The firelight guides him in gold and shadow; his eyes stripped bare with desperation.

"Promise me," he says, voice raw. "Promise me you won't ever let go of that bond. No matter the cost."

My throat burns, but I manage the word. "Promise."

Kallesie's low rumble fills the clearing, weary but alive. For now.

The fire cracks, sparks spiraling into the night like tiny stars. My body aches, every nerve raw, but I cling to him, to her, to the fragile tether that has not yet broken.

Kisses by firelight. Burn, but not consumed.

Not yet.

CHAPTER 48

THE COUNCIL'S VERDICT

HELIOS

The chamber still smells of smoke and blood. Firelight licks the stone walls, painting them in restless gold. For once, I dislike its warmth. It reminds me of her skin, of her pulse hammering beneath my hands when she collapses, of the bite that should never have been asked of her, of the terrible intimacy of her blood on Kallesie's tongue.

Now she sleeps in my bed, tangled in sheets that bear too much crimson. Her dark hair stuck to her temples, dry with sweat and streaked with blood, she doesn't have the strength to wash it away.

Kallesie curls tight against her, molten-purple eyes restless. Every so often, her chest rumbles low, a sound that vibrates the floor, as if daring the world to try touching Elara again.

Vulcan paces along the far wall, massive paws silent as smoke. In the firelight, Vulcan's outline shifts, all shadow, muscle, and furnace heat. His presence presses into my skull, iron-edged and unyielding.

"You should not let her rest so close to danger. If the infection lingers in the bond."

Enough, I say. *She saves Kallesie. She survives the cost. Both of them deserve this rest.*

Vulcan's replies are a snort of hot iron. "*And what if the bond drags her under anyway? You'll burn with her. You know it as well as I.*"

My jaw aches with the force I use to hold my silence. I press a palm against the window frame, staring down into the torchlit courtyards below. Stronghold's silence has teeth, the quiet before Wraths tear through villages.

"Elara," I whisper before I can stop myself.

She stirs, lips part, her breath uneven. My hand itches to reach for her, to pull her into my chest, but I stay still. Wanting her is reckless enough. Wanting her when her veins burn with power that I don't fully understand is madness.

The air shifts.

A heatless flame flickers into being in the corner. It coils upward, weaving into shape. Vulcan bristles, teeth bare, but even his presence dims under the weight of what takes form.

"Nyx," I hiss.

Her smile is ash and blade. *"You are slower than I thought, Helios."*

I step between her and the bed. Vulcan's hulking shadow looms beside me. "If you've come to feed on her dreams, you'll find both of us between you and her throat."

She laughs, and the sound unfurls through the shadows like a secret the night has kept for centuries. "You mistake me for Carrion. I am no Wrath. I am the voice of the Veil itself."

"Elara needs rest," I said, jaw tight. "If you've come to torment her—"

"Not her. You."

Her eyes burn through me, stripping me raw. "The blood she carries unravels the Veil with every drop she spills. You've seen how it sears heatless, how it forces open rifts. That fire burns both ways. One more breach, and the Primordial Wrath will step through."

My grip whitens on Vulcan's tether in my mind. *"The Primordial?"*

"The first Wrath. The one even I dare not name." Nyx's voice is sharp like a drawn blade. "Do you think fog-moors and broken villages are the worst of it? No, Helios. She carries the tinder of apocalypse. And you…" Her gaze pins me in place. "…you stoke the fire every time you let her bleed for you."

"She saves lives when she fights," I ground out.

"She destroys herself," Nyx answers flatly. "Each cut thins the Veil. Each wound makes the oldest stir. Do you not feel it? The crawling air, the whispering shadows? Even your Council senses it. That is why they move against her."

The flame of her body gutters, unravelling into smoke, but her voice lingers like coal dust in my lungs.

"Choose wisely, Helios. Do not let love blind you, or

you will both burn when the oldest rises."

And she is gone.

I stand frozen, knuckles aching, staring at the charred corner of the chamber. Love. The word clangs against my ribs, undeniable now.

I turn back. Elara has shifted in her sleep, one arm curls protectively over her stomach, and Kallesie presses closer, rumbling softly. My chest tightens so steeply I have to sit down. I sweep a lock of hair from her cheek. She doesn't wake, in a whisper soft as breath, she calls out my name.

"Helios…"

God help me. I lean in, touching my forehead to her, just that bare, desperate contact. I want to tell her everything, but words stuck like splinters. If Nyx is right, if the Council already suspects, what right did I have to claim her at all?

Vulcan's voice rumbles in my skull. "*You already have.*"

The knock comes like a hammer.

"Helios," a guard calls from beyond the door. "The Council summons you."

Of course they do.

The Council chamber smells of stone and fear.

Seven seats curve in a crescent, lit by braziers that spit sparks into the vaulted dark. Their faces shift with the firelight-stern, uncertain, hostile. I know them all by name, but tonight they look like judges at an execution.

“Helios,” High Councilor Varrek intoned, his beard silver as the steel at his hip. “You stand not only as Alpha of Vulcan, but also as protector to the Summoner. There are grave concerns.”

“Speak to them,” I say, keeping my stance iron straight.

Councilor Serathe leans forward, eyes glitter like knives. “Reports reach us of villages turning entire households into Half-Wrath. The infection spreads unchecked. And who is there at the center of it?”

“Elara has fought to contain the Half-turns,” I snap.

“Contain?” she spat. “Or provoke? Her blood opens rifts, Helios. Do not pretend to be ignorant. You’ve seen it. And you expect us to believe she is salvation, not catastrophe?”

Murmurs ripple through the chamber. Some nodding. Some fear.

“She is young,” another councilor says, voice soft. “Unstable, yes. But her power turns Wraths into ash. Without her, we’d already be overrun.”

“Without her,” Serathe jumps in, “the Veil might still be whole.”

My teeth grind together. “She is the only reason we stand at all.”

Varrek’s eyes pin me. “Is that the commander speaking… or your heart?”

The words cut sharper than steel. Silence sufficed.

“You endanger us all,” Serathe presses. “Your bond blinds you. You let her bleed when any sane commander forbids it. Will you risk unleashing something older than the Wraths … for the sake of your attachment?"

The chamber is still.

Vulcan's voice coils cold in my chest. "*Say it. Stop lying to yourself.*"

Yes. My heart is hers.

But not here. Not before them.

Another councilor, younger, clears his throat. "Then bind her power. Forbid her blood's use except in direst need."

Varrek nods. "So, it shall be. You will see it done, Helios."

I bow stiffly. "If it keeps her alive, I already intend it."

Dismissed, I leave with their whispers gnawing at my back. Nyx's words twist with theirs until I can't tell where one ends and the other begins. Do not let love blind you. She has a fracture.

My chamber welcomes me with firelight.

Elara is still sleeping, shifting faintly. Kallesie's growl stirs, then quiets as she presses tighter to her. Vulcan pads past me, settling at the threshold like a sentinel.

I sit at Elara's side and finally let myself take her hand. Warm. Fragile. Alive.

"I don't care what they say," I murmur into the quiet. "You're not their weapon. You're not their fracture. You're mine."

Her fingers twitch in her sleep, curling weakly around mine.

And just like that, the firelight isn't mockery anymore. It is an oath.

I will not let her burn.

Not while I still draw breath.

But I can feel shadows gathering, watching, waiting. Every pulse of her body, every fragile tether between us, calls to something older, something patient. And I know she is already here.

CHAPTER 49

MORRIGAN'S HAND

MORRIGAN

They cling to one another, thinking their oaths can protect them, but I feel every tremor of her pulse, every desperate breath he swears to guard. Every heartbeat, every flicker of defiance, sharpens my hunger and reminds me how fragile their hope truly is.

The torches gutter in their sconces, throwing the chamber into spasms of shadow. Light belongs to others; their temples, their sanctuaries, their fragile dreams. The darkness is mine. My cloak. My inheritance. My children.

The circle crouches at my feet, Half-born Wrath twists into something both less and more than flesh. Smoke clings to their bodies, Veils of ash that refuse to decide whether to form bone or shadow. Faces split and close like wounds that can't heal. Their eyes burn with jagged points of hunger.

The infection has taken root.

I feel satisfaction coil low in my chest, sweet and cruel. So many failures have littered the path where villages turn to cinder, captives waste in endless attempts. I had flayed them, bled them, and carved rites into their very marrow, and most had dissolved to nothing. But not these. These still knelt. They are still hungry. They still obey.

"My children," I purr, letting the word ripple into the chamber, smooth and coaxing. "You crawl in the shadows because of my will. You hunger because I feed you. Do you remember what you were before me?"

They hiss as one. The air thins, cold like knives. One stretches its neck until the vertebrae crack, its jaw splits wide into teeth that are not teeth, its maw opening too far.

"Yes," I whisper, leaning into the hiss. "You were nothing. Fragile scraps clinging to names no one remembers. But I…" My lips curl. "I have made you eternal."

Their forms convulse, rippling like smoke torn by wind. Hunger sings back to me, a vibration thrums in my bones. I understand it. Better than priests understand prayer, better than lovers understand vows. Hunger is the truest language.

"Do you feel it?" I ask, stepping into their circle. My robes drag over stone carved in black sigils, each line deep and raw as an old wound. "That pulse beneath your skin, the heat that is not heat? That is the Wrath's breath inside you. The Primordial dreams beyond the Veil, and through you, its dreams already seep into this world."

One creature arches back, shadows peeling away from bone in ecstasy. Others crawl forward on all fours, claws raking stone in grotesque rhythm—the circle shivers, alive with want.

I kneel. My hand touches the deep carvings cut in the floor, sigils that had cost me hours, lives, and sanity. They throb faintly, drinking in the wavering light, pulsing like veins.

"You wonder why I starve you," I murmur as a lullaby. "Why do I give you scraps instead of drowning you in its voice? You think it is cruel? No…" My smile widens. "It is a necessity. You are a chorus, not a song. The Wrath itself waits. I will call it. I will wake it up. You are only heralds."

They screech, forms collapse forward in unholy reverence. The chamber shakes with it, but with one flick of my wrist, the shadows recoil as if struck.

"Patience," I croon. "Patience, and you will feast."

I rise and move between them, their hunger reaching for me like hands through smoke. My shadow stretches across the floor, long and sharp, a blade drawn in darkness.

"The Veil resists me still," I confess, low and intimate. "I have burned through every rite. Bled with every offering. Still, it holds."

They twitch violently, bodies spasming in their need for answers.

"And do you know why?"

I let silence stretch, my steps circle them like a predator.

"Because the Veil is bound to her."

Their eyes flare in unison, fire in hollow sockets.

"Elara."

The name slices the chamber open. My Forsaken's ripple in agitation, shadows shuddering like waves across their skin. The Veil trembles at the sound, shrouding me like a lover's sigh.

"Yes," I breathe. "She carries the resonance. The cursed bloodline that anchors the Veil. She is the key. Not me. Not you. Her."

Their hisses grow frenzied. They want her. I am hungry for her.

"And I will give her to you," I promise, stepping into the circle's heart. "But not yet. Not while she resists. If she fights, the Veil holds. If she suspects, the door stays closed. So, what must we do?"

I crouch low, staring into the nearest burning sockets.

"We will break her without breaking her. We grind her with fear, corner her with loss, and strip her until the only path left is the one I place before her. She will open the Veil herself, believing it salvation, believing it victory."

I laugh, the sound sharp and sweet. "And she will deliver the world into my hands."

The chamber erupts. Silent shrieks. Claws gouging stone. The air pulses with frenzy. They can see it now, the Veil tearing, the feast rushing in.

I raise my hands. Darkness gathers, pressing down on the chamber. The sigils ignite in crimson, bleeding up the walls, scrawling over my skin like living tattoos. My voice falls into the old tongue, syllables jagged like broken bones, words that taste like iron.

"Primordial Wrath, dreamer beyond the Veil … hear your daughter's call. Hear the hunger of your children. The gate shudders. The world trembles. Soon."

The air bows underweight. Something vast presses against the chamber, bending my knees, crushing my breath. A half-born screams in agony that is ecstasy, shadows burning into marrow.

For an instant, I feel it. The heartbeat is beyond the Veil. Slow. Ancient. Stirring.

A whisper slithers through the chamber, not a sound but a sensation. Hunger presses against my mind, cold and endless. My lips tremble.

"Yes," I whisper back. "I hear you."

Visions bleed into me, villages split open, the sky tears to ash, and oceans boil black. Shadows coil around the bones of kings. I sway, clutching the sigils, shuddering with exhilaration.

"Elara will bring you forth," I vow, voice trembling with joy. "Through her blood, I will awaken you. Through me, the world will burn."

The Half-Borns writhe in worship. Shadows howl without sound.

And for the first time, I think I hear the Wrath answer.

A soundless hunger.

A promise.

So very close.

CHAPTER 50

THE FORSAKEN

ELARA

Something answers. Not a voice, not yet, but hunger that presses at the edge of the air. A promise threaded through the damp, heavy night. The smell hits me next, iron and rot cling to the damp air like a second skin, thick and choking. Even the shadows seem afraid of this place, recoiling from whatever waits in the corners, and I know I am not meant to be here untested.

Kallesie pads at my side, molten purple eyes gleaming. "*You're stalling,*" she murmurs, her voice curls in my skull like smoke. "*The longer you wait, the more they become what Morrigan made them.*"

"I know," I whisper. My shoulder throbs where her teeth had sunk into me, the flesh still sore from her desperate attempt to purge the Wrath's infection. A reminder of how close I had come to being one of them.

Helios walks ahead, steel-grey eyes sharp, every step

coiled with that barely contained violence I've come to rely on. Vulcan stalks at his heels, embers flickering in his gaze.

The sound comes next, scraping, dragging. At first, I thought it was the groan of old timbers in the ruined villages we had entered, but no, it was claws on stone. Human voices twisted into something too hollow, too sharp.

"Stay behind me," Helios says, his tone flat, but I hear the tension beneath.

I shake my head. "If they're half-Wrath…."

"They're not," Kallesie rasps, through the bond, grim amusement curling around the words. "*Unless your standards for alive have dropped dramatically."*

Kallesie's snarls ripple out as she stands beside me. The infection has ripened. They're gone.

Gone.

The first figure lurches into view. My stomach twists.

He had once been a man, a farmer, perhaps, judging by the tattered remnants of work clothes clinging to his frame. But his skin is stretching too thin, black veins crawl like roots beneath the surface. His mouth gapes wide, too wide, teeth lengthened into jagged shards. And his eyes…

Not eyes. Malice burning where life should have been.

More shapes follow. Ten. Fifteen. Twenty.

The Forsaken.

I want to retch. Not just because of what they are, but because I recognize one of them. A boy, twelve years old. His small frame hunches, mouth slathered with shadow. I remember his face from the night we tried to save the village. His mother had begged me to protect him.

And now…

"Elara," Helios warns, seeing my hand tremble on the hilt of my blade.

Kallesie's molten eyes flare. *"Don't falter. Not now. If you hesitate, you die. And if you die, the rest of us follow."*

I tighten my grip. "I won't."

But the words feel like they fall on death's door.

HELIOS

Elara's face has gone pale, her jaw set in that way I have come to know too well; the look of someone breaking but refusing to show it. I want to reach for her, to anchor her, but the Forsaken are closing in.

"Hold the line," I say, my voice harsher than I mean. Vulcan turns his eyes toward me.

"You're snapping because you're afraid she'll fall apart," Vulcan rumbles. *"Afraid you'll lose her. Again."*

I ignore him, drawing my blade. Steel gleams dully in the flickering shadows—the Forsaken move with jerks, like puppets pulled by strings.

"Elara."

Her eyes meet mine. Wide. Haunted. Gods, I want to tell her I love her. That the word burning in my throat every night isn't a weakness, but I can't. Not out loud. In a world like ours, words carry too much power, and I will not risk it turning love into a curse.

"Stay with me," is all I say.

And then they come.

The first Forsaken lunges. Vulcan is faster. His massive jaws clamp around its throat, embers searing flesh, tearing shadows apart in a spray of ash.

Another barrels into me. Too strong. Its claws rake sparks off my armour as I drive my blade up through its chest, feeling the unnatural heat pulse before it disintegrates into smoke.

Behind me, Kallesie's roars shake the ground. She advances with determination, and her purple eyes focus as she engages the Forsaken with forceful efficiency. "*Pathetic,*" Vulcan rumbles in my mind. "*These are Morrigan's gifts? They taste like rot and ass. Don't give me that look, Helios.*"

Elara fights. God help me, she fights. Her blade trembles, but each strike lands true. When the child lunges at her, her hesitation freezes in midair.

"Elara!" I shout.

Elara

Her eyes met mine, wide and pleading, and my stomach twists. Gods, not again. Not a child, not this.

Kallesie's voice snaps through my mind. "*He's not a boy anymore. He's a grave wearing skin. Finish him.*"

And with a sob catches in my throat because for one terrible heartbeat, all I see is the boy he used to be —but I do it anyway, praying to the gods for forgiveness as I swing my blade.

The blade sinks into the child's chest, and for a moment, I think I hear his voice. Not the hiss of Wrath. Not hunger. Just a boy's cry. And then he dissolves into shadow, scattering across my boots. Even as he falls, a part of me recoils, screaming that this should not be happening. Yet Kallesie is right. He is no longer a boy. And I am the one left standing to bear it.

Something breaks in me with him.

Kallesie's molten gaze locks on mine. "*Better you than him. If you hadn't, he would have torn your throat out. Remember that when you mourn.*"

I hate her for being right.

The Forsaken press closer. A swarm. My shoulder burns where the old wound throbs, weakness gnawing at me. Helios's blade flashes beside me, steady, unyielding, his every movement a promise of protection.

I want to lean into that promise. Gods, I want to say the word we haven't said yet, the one sitting on my tongue like fire. But the Veil pulses in the back of my mind, Morrigan's shadow whispering even here.

She is coming for me.

And the Forsaken are only the beginning.

Helios

When the last Forsaken falls, the silence digs into my chest, crueler than any screams.

Elara stands with her blade limp at her side, and ash clings to her lashes. Her shoulders shake, but she hasn't broken.

Vulcan pads back to me, muzzle black with soot. His eyes glow faintly. "*She won't survive this path if you keep pretending. Say the word.*"

I tighten my jaw. Elara's gaze meets mine, full of grief and steel. And for one fragile heartbeat, I almost did.

Instead, I reach for her hand.

She lets me.

The ashes of the Forsaken swirl around us, carried on a wind that isn't a wind at all. The Veil pulses faintly against my senses. Morrigan is nearby.

And Elara is the key she wants.

I tighten my grip. Morrigan will not have her. Not while I'm still drawing breath.

CHAPTER 51

ASHES IN THE STRONGHOLD

ELARA

I feel him before I see him, the presence that drags my heartbeat in jagged rhythm. Morrigan is near, and the Veil hums within my hunger. Every nerve in my body tightens. I am the key they want.

The gates of the Stronghold rise before me, black stone towers, claws into the dark sky. Their torches bleed smoke into the wind, and for the first time, the sight of home fills me with dread.

My legs barely carry me. Every step jolts the wound in my shoulder, the memory of Kallesie's bite still burning under torn flesh. Only Helios's arm keeps me upright. His steel-grey eyes don't leave me, even as the guards at the gate level their spears, treating me like a threat.

"Open," Helios barks, his voice iron.

The guards obey, but the whispers carry. Wrath is

crawling through the air. Contagion. Forsaken. Their eyes burn into me like I am already claimed for death.

Kallesie limps at my side, molten purple eyes flashing with irritation. "*Let them stare. I can still swallow them whole, broken or not.*"

I might've smiled at her stubbornness if I didn't feel so empty. Every whisper pierces deeper than steel. They don't see the Forsaken child's face when my blade went through him. They only see me now as a summoner marked by blood and shadow.

We cross into the courtyard, where braziers throw their light across stone scars from old battles. I thought I might collapse there and let the stone swallow me, but fate has sharper plans.

The council is waiting.

Seven figures in cloaks and armour stand beneath the arch of the doors, their expressions carved from suspicion. High Councilor Varrek speaks first.

"Elara," he says, and my name feels like a sentence. "You and your Hellhound are summoned before us."

Helios bristles, Vulcan looming behind him with eyes narrowed. "She needs rest. She nearly bled herself dry to stop the Forsaken."

"Forsaken?" Councilor Serathe spits the word like it is poison. Her keen eyes linger across me, glittering like knives. "That is what you call them now? Whole villages twist because of what? Because her blood thins the Veil?"

A ripple of murmurs stirs among the others. My stomach turns to lead.

“I don’t…” The words break in my throat. My hands still tremble, bloodstains dark under my nails. “I don’t mean for it to happen.”

Kallesie presses nearer, snarling. *“They’d blame you for the moon falling if they could. Hold your ground.”*

But I can’t. Not here, under their stares.

Varrek’s gaze bores into me. “Your presence spreads the infection. Your blood opens doors better left closed. Tell us, Summoner, when you slew the Forsaken boy, did you feel the Veil shudder?”

My lungs seize. How did he know? My chest tightens as a panic attack is closer than I would like to admit. The air feels impossibly thin, like a quiver under the weight of his words. My blade feels heavier in my grip, as if it has carved not of flesh but the sky itself. The world tilts, trembling at the edges, and a shiver runs down my spine. Gods… everything I thought I understood snaps, and I’m left raw, exposed, staring into the truth I can barely bear.

Helios steps forward before I can answer, fury sparking him off like steel on stone. “She saved that village from annihilation. Without her, the Forsaken would have broken through and spread farther. Without her, you’d already be dead.”

“She provokes them!” Serathe snaps, eyes blazing. “Can’t you see? Wherever she goes, the Wrath follows. She and her cursed bloodline pull at the Veil, and she bleeds at your command like a weapon. Helios... this isn’t savable. It’s a storm that will consume everything.”

Her words strike harder than the bite ever did. I glance at Helios, afraid he might side with them.

But his jaw is set, his voice iron. "You see a tool. I see the only thing keeping us from extinction. Without her power… all of this—gone, reduced to ash."

Murmurs swell. Some nodding, others scowling.

Varrek lifts a hand, silencing them. "Helios. Is that the leader in you speaking… or your heart?"

The silence that follows crushes the air from the chamber.

Helios's eyes flick to me. The answer is clear to them, though he says nothing. And that silence is louder than any declaration.

"Enough." Varrek's voice cracks like thunder. "We will not decide tonight. But hear this, her blood is forbidden. She may not cut herself for battle again unless directed by this council. One more breach, and we may not contain what comes through."

My chest tightens, shame and fury warring in me. Forbid me? As if my blood isn't my own?

Helios inclines his head, stiff, his hand a fist at his side. "If it keeps her alive, then so be it."

They dismiss us.

By the time we reach our chamber, my legs give out. Helios catches me before I hit the stone, carrying me the last few steps and lowering me onto the. Kallesie curls against me at once, a mountain of heat and shadow.

Her gaze warms, but her words are cutting. "*You should have bitten them back, Elara. I'd have helped.*"

"Not helping," I mutter weakly, pressing my forehead against her rough hide.

Helios lingers by the fire, Vulcan at his side, the weight of the council's words thick on his shoulders. His silhouette in the firelight is broad and unshakable, but his eyes are storm-tossed when they meet mine.

"You don't believe them," I whisper. It isn't a question. It is a plea.

He crosses the room to me, kneeling at the bedside—his hand hovers just above mine, not quite touching. "I believe in you. That's the difference."

The words tear me open. My throat aches with the things I want to say: how his steadiness anchors me when my blood betrays me, how every time the darkness reaches for me, his voice drags me back, keeping me from falling apart.

Kallesie gives a low rumble, almost chuckling. "*Say it, or I will.*"

Vulcan's glare narrows. "*Stay out of it,*" he muttered, though only Helios hears.

Helios pushes a lock of hair from my cheek, his touch unbearably tender. "Rest now. We'll fight them tomorrow. The Council. The Wrath. Whatever comes. But you…" His voice cracks. "You don't fight alone."

My eyes burn. I want to tell him he is wrong, that in the end, it will always come down to my cursed blood. But when his hand finally takes mine, warm and grounding, the lie of comfort is the only thing I cling to.

Sleep pulls at me, heavy and dark, but as I drift, I feel it.

Shadows lurking at the edges of the room.

Morrigan's laughter, fainting as smoke, seeping through

the walls.

The Stronghold isn't safe anymore.

CHAPTER 52

HUNGER'S CONFESSION

HELIOS

The Stronghold never sleeps.

Even at this hour, the torches bleed smoke through their stone arteries, and the murmurs of guards drift beneath doors like drafts. Inside our chamber, only firelight and my heartbeat remain.

Sleep should come easily here. It usually does.

But the air carries a weight I can't name, pressing gently against my ribs, like a warning whisper too soft to hear. The stone walls hold the warmth of the day, yet a chill settles anyway, slow and patient.

I listen to the distant shifts of boots, the sigh of flame, the old sounds of a place that has outlived every threat thrown at it. Tonight, those sounds don't soothe. Something changes. Not enough to see. Not enough to touch.

Elara lies on our bed, dark hair spilling across the

pillow, her face caught between exhaustion and something far more dangerous: trust. It is a fragile thing, easily shattering. And gods, I had no right to it.

I have not disclosed the information discussed by the Council. I haven't mentioned Nyx's warning that her blood is the reason for the Veil's fracture. I haven't told her because I can't. Every time I look at her, every time she whispers my name with that soul-stripping rawness, the truth lodges in my throat and refuses to move.

And now here she is, mine to guard. Mine to lose.

Vulcan sprawls near the door, embers glowing in his eyes like twin furnaces. Kallesie presses tight to Elara's side, a molten-purple gaze fixed on me with suspicion I can't even resent. She knows. She always knows what I don't tell her.

Not just her blood, not just her strength in battle, but Elara, the woman who fought when she should have run, who kissed me once as if dying and living are the same.

My hands curl against the bed frame.

Her lashes flicker. Her lips part. She stirs in the sheets, and for an instant, the fire cracks loud enough to drown the silence between us. Then her voice comes soft and hoarse.

"Helios."

It strips me bare.

I lean closer, my breath ragged. "I'm here."

She blinks up at me, eyes glassy with fever and fire. The bandage on her shoulder is dark with blood, and the scent of it coils through the chamber like smoke. My control frays. My need sharpens.

"Stay," she whispers.

God damn me, I did more than just stay.

I bent and pressed my mouth against her temple, then lower, breaths mingling. The kiss she gives back isn't the desperate, half-dead thing from the clearing. This one is alive, burning, urgent. She drags me down into her hunger, into the truth I try to deny.

Steel-grey eyes. That's what she once said about me, as if they could never soften. But now they are hers.

I kiss her like a confession, like damnation.

ELARA

The world narrows to his weight, his heat, and the fire running beneath his skin.

Helios kisses me like I am the only tether left to him, like letting me go means falling into the same abyss we fight every day. His hands, gods, his hands are careful and desperate, cradling my jaw, sliding into my hair, pressing into the curve of my waist like he can't decide whether to worship or claim.

And I want both.

It isn't pain that consumes me now, it's the ache of wanting him, needing him, of knowing letting go would mean falling into everything we fight to survive.

"Helios…" I breathe his name into his mouth, and it breaks him. I feel it. The shudder, the restraint snapping like a bowstring. His body presses harder against mine, pinning me into the mattress, firelight striping his bare arms in gold and shadow.

For so long, we fought it: the bond, the pull, the way our Hellhounds circle one another as if they knew before we did. But there is no battlefield here, no Council, no gods, or Wraths—just us.

And I am done denying it.

I lean toward him, gripping his shirt until the fabric rips. His skin is hot, ridged with scars that map every war he has survived. I trace them with my mouth, dragging teeth across the line of his throat until his groan rumbles through me like thunder.

"Elara," he warns, voice low, frayed.

"Don't stop."

I mean it. Every syllable. If this is another form of fire that will burn me hollow, then let it. I already have marks. Already cursed. But this? This is mine to choose.

His mouth descends again, hungry, devouring. His tongue tangles with mine, rough, wet, and perfect. The sheets tangle around my hips as his hands slide lower, gripping my thigh, hauling it around his waist. My pulse stutters, heat pooling low and relentless.

I gasp. "I want you."

The words ignite him.

HELIOS

I freeze for only a second. Just long enough to feel the weight of it.

Gods, I'd tear the world apart before denying her again.

My hands, trembling with hunger, trace every curve and scar on her. The bandage slips from her shoulder, exposing the bite mark, still angry, still red. For an instant, I hesitate, but then she tugs me down, teeth sinking into my lip, eyes blazing with challenge.

"Don't you dare treat me like I'm broken," she growls.

A low, hoarse laugh escapes me. She doesn't know what that does to me, how it splits me open.

I obey.

I tear the last of the cloth from her body, letting the firelight bathe her skin. She is every kind of blasphemy: scars, strong, trembling, and beautiful. My mouth works down her throat, and her chest, my tongue circling her perfect nipple until her back arches, her cry muffles against my hair.

"Helios…"

Her nails rake my shoulders, demanding, guiding, and claiming to me as much as I claim her. And when I slide lower, when I taste her, her entire body goes taut, then breaks open with sound.

God, she is a wildfire.

I devour her like prayer, holding her thighs apart as she rides the waves of her orgasm across my tongue, gasping my name repeatedly as she teeters on the edge.

When she shatters, trembling beneath my mouth, I rise over her, shaking with restraint. My lips are slick, my chest heaving.

"I love you," I rasp before I can stop myself.

The words. The ones I swore I wouldn't speak. They tear free like a confession to the gods I don't believe in.

She kisses me urgently and whispers against my lips.

"Then show me."

Elara

The moment he thrusts into me, the world vanishes.

Every wall of the Stronghold, every whisper of Council, or shadow of Morrigan-it all dissolves into fire and flesh. Helios fills me, and stretches me, holds me firm when the world wants me to break me. I cry out, clutching him, dragging him deeper until our bodies lock, until his groan tears through the chamber like thunder.

There is no gentleness left—only hunger.

He drives into me with a relentless rhythm, each thrust a confession, a vow, a breaking. His hand tangles in my hair, dragging my mouth to his, swallowing every gasp. My nails carve lines down his back, blood slicking my fingertips, and he only groans harder, faster.

"Know it," I gasp, biting his jaw. "Know you are mine."

"Always," he growls, the word breaks on a thrust that sends me spiraling again.

We move like battle and worship, like ruin and salvation, every sound echoing off the stone walls, a symphony of need. Firelight flickers, shadows bend, and for an instant, I swear the Veil trembles around us.

When my release tears through me, I cling to him, dragging him with me. He buries himself deep, spilling into me with a broken cry, his body shaking against mine. His forehead presses to mine, his breath ragged, his voice hoarse with truth.

"Elara. Gods. Elara."

And I know. He is mine. I am his.

No Wrath. No Veil. No curse can change that.

HELIOS

Afterward, we lie tangled in sweat and firelight, the hounds standing silent guard. Her heartbeat echoes against my chest, steady, alive. For the first time in years, I let myself breathe.

But Nyx's words return like smoke. *Do not let love blind you.*

Too late.

I kiss Elara's temple, my arm tightening around her. "Whatever comes," I whisper, "we face it together."

She tries not to smile as we press against each other. "Promise?"

I close my eyes. "Promise."

And for that fragile moment, I almost believe we can survive it.

The fire died down to embers, but the heat between us lingers.

Elara lay half draped across me, her skin damp, her breath steady against my chest. My hand moves of its own will, stroking her back in slow, reverent lines, memorizing the dip of her spine, the way her body softened against mine once the storm had passed.

For a long while, neither of us speaks. Words would have shattered the quiet, and for once, silence doesn't feel like something to fear.

Her fingers trace absent circles over the scars on my ribs. Each touch is light, but it goes deeper through me than any blade.

"You never let anyone this close," she murmurs at last. Not a question. A knowing.

I exhale, threading my fingers through her hair. "No one but you."

Her lips caress my chest softly. "You're bleeding."

I feel the faint sting of the scratches prickling down my spine. Blood smears faintly across her nails, but I only smile, catching her wrist and kissing her fingertips. "I don't mind. They're yours, carved into me, lingering as you do, impossible to forget."

She looks at me then, really looking at her wet, raw, wide-open eyes. And gods, I almost wish she'd look away, because the weight of it is too much.

Her voice drops. "I thought I'd never… belong to

anyone. Not really. But with you…"

Her throat catches. My chest broke.

I tilt her chin up and kiss the tears before they can fall. "You don't belong to me," I whisper. "We belong to each other."

Her breath hitches. Her hand fists in my hair, pulling me down into a kiss that isn't hungry and isn't desperate. It is something far rarer, gentle. Steady.

When we break apart, she tucks herself tighter against me, her ear pressed to my heartbeat. "Then don't leave me," she whispers, insecurity showing its ugly head.

"I can't. Not even if I try."

The words are soft, but they are true. For the first time in years, maybe ever, I don't feel hollow. I feel the tether. Anchored. Hers.

Around us, Vulcan and Kallesie shift, the bond between them mirroring our own. The hounds have known before we did. They always have.

Elara's breath slows; her body finally gives in to exhaustion. I hold her, smoothing her hair, staring at the ceiling as the fire gutters low.

But in the back of my mind, Nyx's warning still coils like smoke.

Do not let love blind you.

I kiss the crown of Elara's head, my chest tight with dread and devotion in equal measure. She is asleep now, trusting me to keep her safe. And gods help me, I will no matter what I have to become.

For the first time in the Stronghold, I pray. Not to the Council, not to the Wraths. To her.

Her breathing steadies, her lashes feather against my chest as sleep claims her. She clings to me even in dreams, her body curls tight as if she fears I'll evaporate if she lets go.

I smooth her hair back and set a kiss on her temple. "Rest," I whisper. "I've got you."

Vulcan and Kallesie settle at the foot of the bed. Their great shadows sprawl protectively across the chamber stones. The bond between them hums faintly, echoing the tether in my chest. It is the same rhythm—the same vow.

For a moment, I let myself believe in peace.

But then....

The torches gutter. A flicker too sharp, too deliberate.

My gaze snaps to the far wall. A sliver of darkness peels away from the stone, a shape too slender, too knowing to be a trick of flame, a shadow where there should be none.

My hand tightens instinctively around Elara's waist. She turns onto her side and, murmuring to herself, drifts back into sleep, oblivious to everything around her.

The presence lingers, watching. Listening.

Nyx. Or worse, Morrigan, bleeding through the veil.

I bare my teeth into the dark, a silent promise: You will not touch her.

The shadow shivers, then withdraws, leaving only smoke curling in the corners and the faint stench of cold iron.

The chamber is quiet again, save for Elara's soft breaths.

But I know better.

The Wrath is stirring.

The hunt is not over.

And the woman in my arms, whom I can no longer deny I love, is the key they all want.

I hold her tighter, vowing into the dark, "You'll have to go through me first."

And I mean every word.

TO BE CONTINUED

Sneak Peek

Book Two coming Soon...

CHAPTER 1

ASH IN THE VEIL

HELIOS

The walls of the Stronghold still retain her scent.

Not incense or steel polish, but Elara's sweat, shadow, and the sharp-sweet tang of her blood that clings to my skin even after I have scrubbed my hands raw. The chambers are too small to contain what has happened, and I can still feel it humming in my bones.

Her mouth. Her nails raking down my back. The moment her body arches into mine like she is claiming me as much as I claimed her. Gods, the fire is only destruction, but she made me believe it can be a kind of worship.

Now, in the aftermath, Stronghold feels unsteady. My steps echo down the corridor as though the stones resent carrying my weight. Vulcan stalking at my side, molten eyes bright, his voice grating in my skull.

"You're bleeding into her."

"I know," I mutter, and my voice is rough.

"No. Not that way." Vulcan's tail lashes like an ember-scorched chain. "*Your mind. Your judgment. You are already hers more than you are the Council's. That is how she will destroy you."*

I clench my jaw, swallowing words I don't want to hear. He isn't wrong. For the first time since binding with

Vulcan, my loyalty is no longer toward my duties, but toward him.

The Council has warned me. Nyx has hissed it into my ear like prophecy. And Morrigan's shadow still stalks every breath of this place.

Nevertheless, as I recall Elara quietly speaking my name and the moments we have shared, I feel no regret.

That is when the sound tears through Stronghold.

A scream. Not fear, rage.

It echoes down the stone halls, sharp enough to steal every conversation, to send warriors reaching for their weapons. My hand goes to my sword, but Vulcan growls low.

"Not Wraths. Not yet. Something worse."

The floor shivers. Dust drifts from the high arches. The torches along the walls gutter as though a hand has closed around their flames.

"Elara," I whisper. My chest constricts like the air wants to strangle me. I turn on my heel, sprinting for my chambers.

Elara

The sheets cling to my skin, damp with sweat. My body still thrums from him, from us, from the fire we make between us. I feel it even now, lying against the pillows, Kallesie presses close like molten armour at my side.

For a heartbeat, I have let myself forget. Forget the

Wraths. Forget the Council. Forget that my blood is anything more than his taste.

But peace never lasts.

The air snaps cold.

Kallesie's head jerks up, molten-purple eyes glowing like a furnace. *"Elara,"* she growls in my mind, *"get up."*

"What—"

Then I hear it. A chorus of screams cut short, replaced by snarls that have no place in this world. Half-born Wraths. I know the sound now like I know the thrum of my pulse.

I leap from the bed, pulling on my leathers with shaking hands. Pain flares at my shoulder where Kallesie's bite still marks me, but I don't pause. Her body brushes mine, restless, and coils the way she always does when danger approaches.

The door flies open.

Helios.

His steel-grey eyes lock on me, wide with the same fear he never let anyone else see. "They're inside," he says, voice harsh. "The Wrath-born. They're in the Stronghold."

Kallesie bares her teeth. The stones underfoot quake like something vast moves through them.

"How?" I breathe.

Helios doesn't answer, but I see it on his face: Nyx. Morrigan. One of them has found a way to breach the walls without fire or siege.

And then the first one comes.

Out of the shadow behind Helios, half its body made of smoke, half bone. Its eyes are pits of broken light. It screams, and the walls themselves bend toward the sound.

Kallesie launches before I can think. Purple fire explodes from her jaws, slamming into the creature and throwing it into the hall. But behind it, there are more shapes. Dozens.

Helios draws his blade, Vulcan materializes beside him, eyes burning like coal ripped from the earth.

"Elara!" he barks. "Stay behind me!"

I almost laugh. "You know I won't."

And then the corridor dissolves into war.

HELIOS

The Stronghold halls have always been my sanctuary. Now they are a slaughterhouse.

The Wrath-born pour from every shadow, their forms flicker between skeletal flesh and black fog. Vulcan rips into them like a starved beast, jaws snap, claws spark against stone. But every time one falls, two more slither into being.

"Elara…" I turn just in time to see her blade carve through one's neck, her face streaked with sweat and fury. Kallesie fights at her side, a wall of snarling muscle and purple fire.

She shouldn't have been this beautiful. Blood in her hair, eyes fever-bright, veins burning with the curse of her bloodline. But I can't look away.

That is when I hear the whisper.

"Heliosss."

The voice slithers through the stones, through my skull, familiar as poison. Nyx.

"You feel it, don't you?" she breathes, though her form has yet to appear. *"Every drop of her blood spills the veil thinner. Every slay of her blade is an offering. She is not your salvation. She is the herald, and what follows will change everything."*

I swing my sword into a Wrath-born, but my grip falters.

"Elara!" I shout, my voice breaks like a weapon against stone. "Stay close!"

But she is already moving deeper into the corridor, hacking through them, her power spiraling out of control. Each strike lights the hall with a strange shimmer, as if the veil trembles.

I knew then what Nyx meant. She isn't lying. Not this time.

Still, God help me, I can't stop her.

ELARA

Blood sprays across my cheek, hot and slick. My lungs burn, but Kallesie is endless beside me, ripping, tearing, her molten eyes wild with the joy of killing.

"More," she howls. *"Let me tear them all apart!"*

I don't answer. Because at the edge of my vision, I see something far worse.

The walls themselves are bleeding.

Thin cracks had opened in the stone, spilling shadow. It is leaking like smoke, whispering as it spreads. And from within it, I feel it—the slow, pulsing heartbeat of something older than Wraths.

Morrigan's promise. The Primordial Wrath.

"No," I whisper, staggering back.

Helios is suddenly at my side, his hand grips my arm hard enough to bruise. "You feel it too." His eyes blaze silver in the firelight. "Elara, if you keep fighting…"

"What am I supposed to do?!" I scream, my voice raw. "Let them take us?"

A Wrath-born charges. Helios chops it down, his blade sings, and Vulcan snaps its spine with angry teeth. But the hallway is filling faster than we can clear it.

Kallesie roars, her voice fills my mind. *"Elara! The veil is breaking!"*

I gasp; the truth strikes me like a blade through the ribs. It isn't just a battle. It isn't just survival. Each instance of bloodshed and every response to distress contributed to weakening the barrier between worlds.

And I can't stop.

Not without letting them win.

The Stronghold shakes violently, dust raining from the ceiling. And in the trembling, I hear it too: the slow, ancient heartbeat, closer now. Hungry.

Helios turns toward me, eyes wide with fear that has nothing to do with the Wrath-born. He opens his mouth to speak…

The far wall splits open.

And through the crack, a single vast eye stares back at us.

Not human. Not Wrath-born. Something older. Something endless.

The Stronghold screams around us.

And I know that Primordial Wrath has awoken.

AUTHOR'S NOTE

Welcome to Hellhound Summoners.

This story is born from two very different things: watching my husband play *Death Stranding* and my long-standing love for *The Hunger Games.*

My love of the atmosphere, the tension, the survival, but I know one thing immediately: I did not want my characters carrying babies around. So began a wonderful (and slightly unhinged) quest through the realm of mythical creatures in search of an alternative. That's when I stumbled across hellhounds and thought, *yeah. That'll work.*

From there came the next question: how do you get a hellhound?

You summon them.

And just like that, hellhound Summoners came to be.

What started as a mix of inspiration and avoidance turned into a world of fire, loyalty, sarcasm, and bonds that are anything but simple. I hope you enjoy walking this path as much as I've enjoyed building it: Hellhounds, chaos, and all.

Thank you for being here. Until the next time the Veil reopens, and the wraths return to cause more chaos.

The Turning. I want to thank the RawRiot Publishing team of amazing editors. I also want to include my TikTok Family of amazing authors who have taken me under their wing to show me how to fly. I want to say thank you to each of them.

About the Authors

K.D. Lovelace was born in Rimbey, Alberta, Canada. She is married to her high school sweetheart and is the proud parent of three beautiful children. When she isn't writing, K.D can usually be found with a book and coffee in hand, wandering quiet paths on long walks, or spending time with her family. Drawn to stories of survival, loyalty, and otherworldly bonds, she weaves imagination and heart into every world she creates, often blurring the line between the ordinary and the fantastical.

Fun fact: Loki is my actual cat, and he makes a cameo in Chapter 1.

www.ingramcontent.com/pod-product-compliance
Lightning Source LLC
LaVergne TN
LVHW020652110826
845149LV00012B/1965

9781067531003